A CURSE OF LOVE AND WAR

DELANEY NICOLE

CARNATION LIBRARY

This is for all of the people that have been hurt because they care about those that don't want to be cared for. Never stop caring.

PROLOGUE

APHRODITE

*L*ove and lust are tricky. Both are riddled with underlying desire, so it can be hard for some to distinguish the difference.

The air of Cyprus is electric. Something molten lurks in it and makes my skin tingle. The phatnai is bustling. Men shout and laugh over the crowd the more the spirits infiltrate their systems.

I smirk when some of the listeners of conversationalists devote their attention to my passing, rather than their companions. Despite their inner desires, which I feel thrumming through me, I don't stop until I make it to the bartender.

"A glass of red, please."

"Absolutely, miss."

The glass he hands me is a perfect balance of sweet and dry. It goes down like water, which only encourages me to drink faster. By the time I'm halfway through my third glass, the crowd has grown louder with life.

"You look ravishing. May I buy you a drink?" A man with short-unkempt brown hair leans against the bar. The desire that oozes from him clings to my skin like a scratchy piece of fabric.

I swirl my glass in my hand. "I'm afraid you're a bit late for that." I scan the bar, zeroing in on a woman with dark brown hair tied loosely in a braid. She laughs with her friends. A jolt rushes through me and I beam with satisfaction, "But you can buy her a drink."

His eyes settle on her and I feel his desire release me. He bids me goodbye. I watch him approach the woman. She smiles at his swagger and I turn back towards the bar, content with my efforts. I do the same for three more men before I'm able to finish my third glass of wine.

"May I buy you a drink?"

A man with bright red—almost fire-like—hair and sculpted jaw dusted with a darker, auburn stubble stands beside me. Our eyes lock and I feel desire engulf me like a warm hug. I take a sip of wine, but I never stop looking at him. "Seems you're a bit late for that."

He mirrors my smirk, and I swear my body grows hot. Gods, I don't think I've ever been this drawn to a mortal. "Not your next one."

"Who says I'm getting another?"

He leans closer. I feel the desire and lust radiating from him. "Tonight is the last night of freedom for most men in

Cyprus before we go off to war. I think everyone is trying to make the most of it."

"So, you're a soldier." I lean toward him, our elbows almost brushing on the bar. I feel my powers thrum and vibrate against my skin. My eyes grow heavier. "How do you suppose you're going to make the most of it?"

His light brown eyes rake over me, pausing on my lips and breasts. I cross my legs, needing some sort of relief. Gods, it's been too long since I've had a man tend to my needs.

"Let me buy you a drink and perhaps I'll show you."

I don't break eye contact as I extend my hand, waiting for him to shake it. "You've got yourself a deal, soldier."

* * *

I LOST count of the glasses of wine. All I know is my body feels hot, and it only grows hotter the longer the soldier touches me. He holds my hand while he leads me through the streets of Cyprus.

"Where are you taking me?" Something about the mystery of it sends a thrill through me.

"Some place quite special to me," he says.

"Which is?" I ask as he leads us up grand limestone stairs into an even grander building. Pillars surround a large pool of water, torches cast a dim but romantic glow around us.

"The newest temple for Ares." He takes a step into the water, then extends a hand to me. His eyes are molten with desire.

"Do you think it is not crass to partake in such liberties in a temple? Would Ares not be displeased?"

He smirks and it only makes heat pool between my legs.

"On the contrary, I think Ares would approve greatly. Besides, a dip in the water of Ares's temple the night before war is supposed to bring good luck."

My brows raise, but I find his persuasiveness attractive. "And you know this because?"

His smirk grows and it almost looks like he wants to laugh. "I've become quite close to Ares with these recent wars. So, what do you say? Shall we continue the evening?"

The air grows thicker, and I swear it feels like my powers pull me closer to him. "If it will bring you good luck."

He pulls me flush against his skin, hands claiming my back. "Only the best."

CHAPTER 1

APHRODITE

Dear Journal,

Every day that I feel alone, I have this fear that claims a little piece of me day by day. I thought I'd feel closer to Hephaestus ten months into our marriage. And yet, the more time goes on, it feels stagnant, drifting even. I have to find a way to fix this for both of us.

Even as the goddess of love, I sometimes doubt love even exists.

The white tablecloth beneath my elbow scratches my skin as I swirl the wine in my chalice, wondering how much longer I will be alone. Hephaestus said he'd be here an hour ago. Yet, the chair across from me is barren.

"Is there anything else I can get for you while you wait for your partner?" I look up at the server. Her hair is in a tight midnight black braid that falls down her back. Her skin is smooth and dark. Her eyes, however, are bright green like a clover.

"More wine, please." I smile tightly. I shall wait a little longer before ordering dinner. I'd rather not have Hephaestus mad at me for being impatient.

The woman brings my new glass of wine, giving me a kind smile before checking on her other tables. I sip my wine and look around the restaurant. The walls are tan with pillars separating the booths against the wall from the circular tables in the middle. The lighting is dim. A string quartet creates a soothing ambiance. Scents of various meats and other foods fill my nose.

Various men ogle me with hungry stares. The women at their sides glare at me with envy.

I avert my eyes, trying not to draw attention. It's like this everywhere I go. I tamp down the sinking feeling in my gut, worrying that this hollow emptiness that has become me will last forever.

Once upon a time, I reveled in that attention from others. Now, all it has done is cause me problems.

Hephaestus emerges from the crowd. His hair is disheveled but thankfully in a clean chiton. "Sorry I'm late, Aphrodite. I lost track of time welding."

I smile but it's as fast as the kiss he places on my cheek. "It is fine. You are here now."

CHAPTER 2

ARES

If I slept last night, it was only for a few minutes. I was late getting into Olympus after I got a message that my mother needed me urgently. I cleaned my horses and made sure their stables were spotless before practically throwing myself in bed.

I hope this visit is short. Greece grows closer and closer to war everyday since they've decided they want to conquer Mesopotamia. I need to be there the moment it finally does.

"You look like you've been visiting Hades too long," a teasing feminine voice fills the empty hallway of the court.

I turn to find my sister grinning at me. "Well not all of us can get the good looks. I'm afraid you and Eileithyia took them all."

"Come now, Ares, the women think you're quite fetching." She grins, not denying my assessment.

"Hello, Hebe." I take my sister into my arms. It feels like ages since I've seen either of my sisters.

"Hello, brother."

"Only you? Where's Eileithyia?" I ask, looking over my sister's head with ease. I tower over both my sisters. I even have a good head on my brother.

"I'm doing fine, thank you." She narrows her eyes jokingly. "She's aiding a mortal with a particularly hard labor. Seems the two of you can't seem to stay away from the mortal realm. Even Hephaestus has been spending more time there."

I can't fight the grin that pulls my lips. Heat sparks in my veins, turning molten when flashbacks of my last free night in Cyprus two years ago captures my mind. I've been chasing the memory of that woman—*that seductress*—ever since. "If you went there more, you'd realize why we enjoy it so much."

Hebe enjoyed her comfortable life in Olympus. She is the only one out of the four of us that has not cared to regularly visit the mortal realm. Granted, Eileithyia and I have duties that tie us to the mortals. But Hephaestus seems to enjoy it more since my leave of absence. Prior to that, he would pester me to stay and "leave the silly little mortals alone."

"If Hephaestus can change his mind about it, then surely you can," I add with a pointed look.

"Hephaestus is an imbecile, and now thinks he has reasons to go there," Hebe retorts, her eyes growing large.

My brows knit. "What do you mean he has reasons *now*?"

"Forget I said anything," Hebe says quickly, then turns

away from me. "Oh, look at the time. I must be going, and you must be meeting with Mother and Father."

"Hebe!" I call after her, but she is out of my grasp before I can stop her.

Olympus only knows what that meant.

Before I could dwell on my sister's behavior, the sound of someone clearing their throat grabs my attention.

A young man that barely looks old enough to begin warrior training stands with his hands folded behind his back. His white chiton contrasts my red one. I lower my brows at his winged shoes.

"Yes?" I ask.

"His majesty would like to see you now," he says, then turns to leave the way he came.

"His majesty?"

"Zeus," he says, fixing me with a pointed stare as if I should already know this.

What is happening? Since when has my father made people call him that? Does he truly need the ego boost?

"Right," I say. "Lead the way."

I follow the scrawny boy through the corridors of the acropolis until we reach the gathering hall. "You may enter when you are ready."

The boy departs, and I'm left standing in front of the vast limestone doors. I let out a breath before opening the doors.

I finally step in, and the gathering hall is nothing like I remembered. The tables that used to sit in the center are gone, replaced by large limestone chairs that form a semi-circle at the other end of the room. The two chairs in the center are larger than the others, and in them sit my parents.

"Mother," I nod and offer a kind smile.

Hera smiles at me in return.

"Father."

"Ares, how lovely to see you again," Zeus quips, but he does not smile like my mother had.

"Care to tell me what all this is?" I ask, gesturing to the remodeled room. "That boy outside called you 'His Majesty' for gods' sakes."

My father shrugs, but it is my mother who answers, "Much has changed in your absence, dear."

"I see that."

"Enough about the changes. We need to talk," my father insists.

I nod, not ready to hear whatever he has to say. They wouldn't have called me up from the mortal realm if it wasn't something serious, and I have a feeling I am not going to like whatever it is.

My mother nervously looks at my father. He gives her a reassuring nod before she turns her warm honey gaze on me. Of course he's making her tell me, he knows I'll listen to her over him. I always have.

"Darling, we need you in Olympus."

I must have heard her wrong. There is positively no way they're asking me to leave the mortal realm.

"It is time you start doing your duties from here. The mortal realm is easy enough to watch. Of course, you can go there during wars but—"

"No," I bite out through clenched teeth.

"It was not a request," my father says, a storm brewing behind his eyes. "You will stay in Olympus, and you will do your duties as a member of the Olympians. We let you run around with the mortals long enough. It is time to step up and be the man—the god—you are supposed to be."

I narrow my eyes at Zeus. Anger boils in my veins. How dare he accuse me of not being the god I was born to be.

"I am the god of war. I am supposed to be in the mortal realm when they launch attacks on each other. Besides, Eileithyia is always in the mortal realm as well."

Thunder rolls distantly. The sky gets darker as storm clouds fill Olympus's sky.

"If you hadn't interrupted your mother, you would have heard her say when a war is large enough, you may go down to aid the mortals for it. However, war is not constantly going on. Your sister has already agreed to spend more time up here unless there are circumstances that deem otherwise. Therefore, you will follow in her footsteps and live here between wars. Do I make myself clear?"

"And if I don't?" My voice would be lethal to anyone else besides my father.

A deadly chuckle leaves my father's throat, "I don't think you want to find out, boy."

I take a half step forward, but my mother's soft voice stops me, "Ares."

Hera's kind, motherly eyes gleam when they meet mine. She gives me that stare only mothers can achieve, and I want to curse myself. I release a heavy breath, "As you wish."

The storm clouds clear the air and a smile gleams on my father's face. That bastard. I fell into his trap, and I hate myself for it. "Excellent. I trust you remember where your estate is?"

My eyes narrow at my father again, this time annoyingly, "May I go now?"

"If that is what you wish."

I turn, walking as fast as I can out of my father's 'throne room' without breaking out into a run. His voice makes me stop for a fraction of a second. "We are so glad to have you back, Ares. Your mother will be in touch soon for a grand family dinner."

I curse myself as I leave the Mount. I very well just signed my freedom away.

CHAPTER 3

APHRODITE

Dear Journal,
Sometimes, all you need is a nice long talk
with a friend or a really big glass of wine. Or,
if things are really bad, both.

"Aphrodite," Hephaestus's voice fills my ears as I water my wilted roses on the balcony.

The roses were supposed to add to the nature-filled landscape Hephaestus chose for our estate to look over. Green grass and patches of wildflowers stretch to the mountains north of our estate. A stream dissects the hills, flowing steadily until it reaches the oceans somewhere on the south side of Olympus.

"Yes, Hephaestus?"

The wind sweeps his auburn hair over his dark blue eyes. He tucks it behind his ear. "I will be returning to the mortal realm. I wanted to alert you before I depart."

I face him, crossing my arms. "What?"

"I am leaving. Now." He levels me with a stare that says he doesn't know any new way to say it.

"I heard you. You promised last night—after you were hours late to dinner—that you would make it up to me. I am your wife." I huff, annoyed I have to even explain this.

"Aphrodite, I can't deal with your fits. There is a new material I need for welding in the mortal realm. If I do not get it now, I may never have the opportunity to get it again. So, I am leaving."

Hephaestus turns to leave the balcony and I do not stop him.

I have been nothing but cordial and kind to him. Our marriage may have been arranged, but that has not stopped me from trying to make it work.

* * *

"Your dress will be ready in no time, goddess." The modiste smiles, sitting on a chair at my feet as she alters the hem of my gown. "You are going to look beautiful. I am sure your husband will appreciate it."

Even after three days, my stomach still sinks the same way it has anytime I think of Hephaestus being gone. Something has changed between us. While we were never in love to start, Hephaestus at least acted like he cared for me. Now, he's rarely at our estate.

I force myself to smile, "One can only hope."

"With a wife that looks like you, I can't imagine he is anything but happy," the modiste's apprentice adds, bringing another bundle of fabric in.

"He would be a fool not to be," Theodora, the modiste, agrees.

I chew on the inside of my lip until it bleeds.

They're right, a husband should be in love with his wife. He should want to stay by his wife's side. A loving husband would be eager to come home to his wife every day.

The goddess of love is supposed to be in love. Yet the closest I've gotten to that feeling was one night in Cyprus nearly two years ago and that wasn't exactly a faithful feeling.

With shaky hands, I smooth the fabric along my hips, needing the texture to keep me grounded. "Yes, well, only time will tell."

A breath of relief fills my lungs when I step back into the streets of Olympus. I close my eyes and find myself praying to anyone who will listen to keep my negative thoughts at bay.

I struggled finding my place in Olympus. Now, I'm afraid if I allow those thoughts to consume me, they will take me under like a ship in a raging sea. Only, I realize there isn't anyone to listen because I am the one the mortals pray to about love and strife.

So who do I pray to when I find myself falling short?

"You look like hell," a man says near my ear.

"Says the one that smells like the bar. It's midday for gods' sakes," I say, turning with a grin.

"Well, I am the god of wine and pleasure. What do you expect?"

"Hello, Dionysus."

"Hello, Aphrodite." He smiles, then urges me to walk with him.

Children laugh as they chase each other down the cobbled roads. Their mother's call after them, urging them to slow down or be home before dark. Men and women walk together, smiling and laughing like they've never laughed before.

I feel calmer than at the modiste, but I can't seem to shake the last remnants of those doomed feelings. I'm afraid once those start, it can take days to shake them.

"Are you going to tell me what's pestering you or shall I ask until I annoy it out of you?" Dionysus grins. His tan skin looks like it's glowing in the setting sun. His eyes warm.

A scoff leaves my lips before I fight a laugh. "Do not tell me you tried to use your parlor trick on me. Does that really work?"

He snickers as we walk again. "Relax, I wasn't using it to seduce you. I knew it would make you laugh. And yes, it works wonders on men and women."

"Don't tell me you have to use it often," I tease. I know Dionysus rarely uses his power to seduce people. I've watched him do it naturally a number of times.

"I'll have you know—" his brown eyes narrow, "you're deflecting."

"No," I lie through my teeth.

"Aphrodite." He stops and places his hand on my arm gently. "What has been bothering you?"

A sigh passes my lips, I look around the busy streets. "I cannot tell you here. There are too many listening ears."

Dionysus's eyes trace the cobbled road. "Very well, we shall go to my estate."

* * *

A SHORT WALK LATER, we pass the beige limestone columns that lead to Dionysus's party room.

The room smells of sex and wine. I half believe the grape vines that hang from the ceiling trap the scent in.

I sit on one of the burgundy couches, which match the red and purple fabrics that drape the windows.

"I asked the chef to bring up a cheese plate," he says while handing me a glass of wine.

I hum at its satisfying taste. Dionysus's wine always has the perfect balance of sweet and bitter.

"So, are you going to tell me what has been bothering you? I've noticed it for quite a while. You've seemed worse recently."

"What do you mean 'quite a while'?"

"Anytime I see you, you look miserable. You're constantly on edge, you flinch anytime Hephaestus touches you, and you look like you want to vomit anytime a man approaches you. The Aphrodite I knew loved any and all attention she got. She rivaled me for number of lovers taken—"

"I did not!"

He gives me a look as if I'm not fooling anyone and I sink a little more into my chair.

"Don't lie to me, Aphrodite. We're friends. What's going on that's making you so…not you?"

"I—um…" I bring my glass to my lips and take two large gulps.

In truth, Dionysus's honesty shocked me. I've only just started feeling the anxieties about my marriage. Has my body been betraying me?

"Something has shifted in my marriage. I don't know what it is, but I can't help but feel knots in my stomach anytime I think of Hephaestus. He cares more about welding than spending time with me. What if…what if our marriage remains loveless?"

"Ah," he says, taking a few large gulps of wine. "I thought your marriage was working. You said you could see yourself growing happy with him."

I lift my chalice, waiting to meet the sweet taste of something to soften the blow for what I suspect is the early days of a failing marriage.

"That was when Hephaestus was trying to make our marriage work.

"Something has changed. He breaks his promises, never shows up for dinner, and only touches me to have sex but even that lacks intimacy. He's always in the mortal realm."

"Have you tried talking to him?" Dionysus asks, then brings his chalice to his lips.

I nod, feeling that sinking feeling return to my gut. "He doesn't listen. He never does."

He's silent for a few moments. His eyes narrow as he falls deeper in thought. "Perhaps you should find someone who will."

"I will not step out on my marriage," I insist with finality.

"Natrually." He smirks and finishes his chalice with one gulp.

I finish my chalice slowly, numbing that sinking feeling.

"If you wish to be a faithful wife, all I can tell you to do is keep trying. He may come around."

"You really think so?" I hate how the small bubble of hope I feel lifts my mood. I shouldn't rely on the whims of my husband to control how my life progresses.

Dionysus shrugs and the bubble deflates a little bit. "I'll tell you what I do know. You need a proper drink in a proper place. Somewhere that reminds you of how much power and magnetism you have."

* * *

DIONYSUS AND I were greeted like royalty at the Muses. Spirits were handed to us left and right. It'd only taken about four for me to forget why I'd been in such a foul mood.

"You really know what you're talking about sometimes." I giggle through the fuzzy feeling that grows behind my eyes.

The same loopy grins spreads on Dionysus's lips. "Sometimes? Gods, you are not very generous are you? I like to think I'm right most of the time."

"That is to be discovered." I giggle again and raise my glass.

We down the remainders of our glasses. Before I can set mine down, the bartender hands me another. "Orion, you are great at your job. I didn't even have to ask."

He flashes his green eyes and proud smile. "I'm afraid I

can't take credit for this one. The gentleman on the other side of the bar requested I give it to you."

I follow Orion's finger to find a man with pale skin and very short, dark hair. His eyes are hungry when they meet mine. Dionysus leans closer to me. He attempts to whisper but his drunken speech is much closer to normal volume. "I told you men still desire you."

I hold the man's gaze, then raise my glass to him.

CHAPTER 4

APHRODITE

A dull ache fills my head. I expect to feel the sun warming my cheeks through the window, but they feel normal. I sit up, groaning because the pounding in my head intensifies. I open my eyes to find the curtains drawn.

That's odd, I almost never draw the curtains.

I turn to find Hephaestus sleeping in my bed, softly snoring. *Yet again odd.* He hardly ever sleeps in here, unless he falls asleep after sex. But my robes are still intact, so we couldn't have.

Perhaps he waited for me last night—last night.

I scramble out of bed as a bubble of guilt fills me. I let another man buy my drinks. I practically let everyone know I'm okay with advances from men other than my husband— the same thing that got me into all of this mess.

Another surge of guilt filters through me. No one will be surprised if they hear of my endeavors last night. I can almost see and hear Hera telling me it was only a matter of time before I stepped out on her son. I proved to everyone that I am what they say; that I could never be a faithful part-ner, and I am not capable of such things.

My breathing is erratic.

I need to get out of this room. I need to be anywhere but here.

I hurry to change into a clean peplos before I walk as fast as I can toward the only person who would understand.

Dionysus was a perfect distraction from my thoughts. We went to the modiste to pick up my dresses, but not before he offered his opinion on them, of course. All of which were good. We ate lunch at a local restaurant. We even went around to the various shops in the city, trying to find anything that caught our attention.

I bound up the steps to Hephaestus's and my foyer sometime after sundown. The foyer is empathy, as is the rest of the ground level.

Our whole home is suspiciously quiet.

When I open the door, Hephaestus is sitting atop my made bed, glaring.

"Hello, dear," I say, offering the kindest smile I can despite my nerves.

"Where were you?" he asks.

"Shopping with Dionysus," I say, handing him a bag with a new chiton I purchased for him.

He pushes the bag in front of him, deepening his glare, "Last night. Where were you?"

Panic lines my gut. *Does he know?* "I was at the Muses. Dionysus took me there. We hadn't seen each other in ages so we used the time to catch up."

"You were out all night?" Hephaestus stands and walks toward me with the calculation of a predator. "I waited for you. I wanted to apologize for my abrupt leave of absence. But you were out all night.

"You know how much I despise The Muses. It is not fit for a wife's leisure time, unless she is there for more nefarious activities. So tell me, Aphrodite, why did you spend *all night* there?"

He seizes my upper arm, squeezing tightly until I'm sure the ichor is cut off. My face twists in pain and fear coats my throat at the sadistic look in his eyes.

"Hephaestus, you're hurting me."

"Why were you there?" He squeezes tighter until I'm sure the bone will snap.

I try to wiggle free from his grasps but he holds tighter, drawing a pained gasp from my lips. *What has gotten into him?*

"They have my favorite wine. That's all. It's the only place in Olympus that carries it. Even Dionysus doesn't have it. It's why we went."

His eyes stay unmoving. For the first time in my life, I fear my husband. Panic sinks its talons into me. My eyes are stinging. I plead, whispering, "Hephaestus, please."

He releases my arm by flinging it away from him.

I stumble putting distance between us. He could close the distance in no more than two strides, but—no matter how small—it allows my fear to weaken a fraction.

Hephaestus's jaw clenches so hard I half expect his teeth to crack. "Hephaestus, what is pestering you?"

His sharp glare makes me recoil. I fear he'll leave a twin to the already bruising mark on my arm.

"We are having dinner with my parents tomorrow."

Confusion knits my brows. "I do not understand."

"My brother will be there."

Brother? I'd completely forgotten Hephaestus's brother given that he, too, is apparently in the mortal realm most of the time. He hardly ever talks about him.

"Well, it will be nice to finally meet the last of your siblings," I offer, hoping to calm him for my sake.

His deadly glare stays on me until he turns toward my door. He stops with his hand on the door handle.

"Sleep. You'll need it for dinner tomorrow. The last thing you need is another night out."

The lock clicks.

When I look in the mirror, my cheeks are reddened from

the few tears that had escaped my eyes. My eyes shine with alarm and panic. But what catches my eyes the most is my upper arm.

A solid hand print—four fingers on the outer part of my arm and a thumb on the inner part is branded on my smooth skin. Each finger a bright shade of purple already. The tainting of my skin is the tainting of our marriage. While my skin may fade, my memory won't.

I can't help the wail that leaves my lips.

CHAPTER 5

ARES

The sun burns my eyes and my head aches when I finally stand from my bed. *Gods, I need curtains.* I drank way too much at The Muses last night. I've been drowning my sorrows at the bar every night since I signed my freedom away to my parents.

Pulling my arms over my head, I stretch my torso before slipping on a clean chiton. I look back to the blonde woman asleep in my bed. I don't really remember much of our time together. But looking at her now, her blonde isn't the right shade. Her skin isn't as silky as it's supposed to be.

No matter how hard I've tried in the past two years, I've yet to find anyone that compares to that women I met in Cyprus. I'm beginning to think she was a witch that put some sort of curse on my mind.

I sigh, then walk down the stairs towards my kitchen for some much needed water.

"I see you still haven't finished furnishing the estate yet."

I find my mother's blue eyes when I turn. Her loud, chipper voice makes my head pound.

"Mother, to what do I owe the pleasure?"

"Good to see you too, Son," she teases. "I came to invite you to dinner tonight at your father's and my estate. Your siblings will be there. All of them."

I chuckle. Don't get me wrong, I enjoy spending time with my sisters, even my mother when she is not in a mood. But the line is drawn at my father and brother.

"I think I'll pass. If you'd like, we could get together somewhere in the city."

My mother laughs. "Dear boy, it was not a request. You are coming to dinner at sunset whether you like it or not. Besides, I know you miss your sisters. And you can finally meet your brother's wife."

I stop in my tracks. "Since when does Hephaestus have a wife?"

I don't miss my mother's mischievous grin. I fell right into her trap, and she knows it. "Not very long. It's barely shy of a year since the union. Although, she has yet to announce she is with child."

"Mother, what poor woman have you forced to marry Hephaestus? I seriously doubt he found the woman on his own," I ask, lifting my brows.

"Watch how you talk about your brother," my mother says through clenched teeth. She's always been overprotective of my brother, especially since my father barely wanted to claim him. "And anyway, she's new to Olympus. She showed up not long after you left on your last expedition to the mortal realm."

My interest peaks. But that still doesn't answer my question though. "I'm having trouble connecting her arrival in Olympus to her arranged union with Hephaestus."

"Who says their union was arranged?" My mother's brows knit almost as if she is offended.

I raise my brows suggestively and offer her the same pointed stare.

She lets out a puff of air. "Yes, alright. She was causing trouble in the city, so I arranged for her to marry your brother. Gods know he needed a wife."

"What kind of trouble?" I ask.

"That does not matter. What matters is, I need you at dinner tonight. Can you agree to that?" She asks, crossing her arms over her chest and fixing me with her glare.

I let out a sigh. "Fine."

"Good." My mother smiles. "Be a doll and stop at the bakery on your way."

I cork my brow. "Mother, are you to tell me that your renowned chef is incapable of making dessert?"

"Don't mock me," she warns. "My chef is capable, but the blackberry pie and tarts from the local bakery are Hephaestus's favorite."

"So you're insisting on getting his favorite dessert instead of one all of your children like?" I ask, trying to hide my distaste for the blackberry pastries. They are much too sour. Raspberries, on the other hand, are perfect. "Wait a second, that was the only way you could get him to agree to have dinner with me wasn't it?"

My mother's eyes narrow, "Just get the dessert. I must be off. I have to go tell Eileithyia about dinner. I will see you later."

I WALK UP the steps to my mother's and father's estate, dessert in hand, not long after the sun set. The air is crisp and the moon and stars are exquisite—Who am I? Waxing on about stars? Gods, I need to find a nightly companion.

When I enter my parent's not-so-humbling dwelling, I can hear voices coming from the formal sitting room. When I round the corner, I see my brother's red hair peeking above my sisters as they talk to my mother and, who I cannot see but can only assume is Hephaestus's wife.

"Ares!" Eileithyia runs and jumps into my arms.

I oblige in her hug, realizing how long it has been since I have seen her. Though we both spend most of our time in the mortal realm, we hardly ran into each other. Our duties are too different to have any overlap. "It's been ages since I've seen you. We must catch up now that we're both back in Olympus."

"Alright you two, enough with the heart to heart," Hebe groans.

"Jealous?" Eileithyia teases, removing her arms from my frame. Out of the corner of my eye, I see my brother scowling at our interaction. I force myself to still the grin that threatened to escape. Our sisters always preferred me over him.

"Not in the slightest." Hebe scrunches her face to match her mockery. "I simply thought it was time to introduce him to the newest member of the family."

My sisters bound toward my mother who had positioned herself to block the unlucky woman.

"Ares." My mother steps to the side, revealing my brother's mystery bride. "I'd like you to meet Hephaestus's wife, Aphrodite."

My stomach drops and fills with lead at the same time. Is that even possible? I have no idea. My mouth tastes like ash. I'm not sure anything can describe the level of shock coursing through my veins when I see the woman I half expected to look inhuman.

My seductress.

Aphrodite.

I've thought about her nearly every night since we met in Cyprus. I fisted my cock to her memory, but I thought she was mortal. Yet she is not only a goddess, but an Olympian. What cruel joke is this?

I school my features, not letting anyone in the room get the chance to think I know her. I can see the shock and panic in her eyes. Her eyes tell all. Just like I remember.

"Aphrodite, it is lovely to finally meet the woman that has housebroken my brother," I say, offering a hand.

My brother's eyes roll so hard I almost believe they'll get stuck.

"You as well, Ares," she says timidly. Her gentle hand

grasps mine, and I instantly feel that shock of electricity I felt the night we met.

I've been trying to replicate the feeling ever since then but have only come up empty-handed. I know she feels it too when her eyes widen for a fraction of a second.

My father barrels into the room in his white chiton he had fitted to show off his biceps.

"Ah, lovely, everyone is here. Hera, shall we begin dinner," Zeus prompts.

"Of course, dear." My mother nods, ushering everyone into the formal dining room.

I find my marked place at the table, only to learn I have been placed directly across from Aphrodite. Hephaestus glares when he makes the same discovery moments later.

This is going to be a long dinner.

I have to admit my mother's chef is quite skilled, the food was delicious. But that didn't take away from the fact that my brother shot daggers at me the entire dinner. What feels like ages later, we move on to the dessert course.

"Ares," my father says between bites of dessert. Aphrodite tenses at the sound of my name. "I think it is time to reveal why we called this dinner."

"So it wasn't for the family to come together?" I ask, fixing my mother with a pointed stare. She gives me her version of the same look, but I'm not stupid enough to believe this wasn't the plan all along.

"Of course, not," My father says while wiping his beard free of any crumbs. "We did this so the two of you would be here when we broke the news."

"The two?" I ask, praying to whatever old god would listen that this isn't going where I think it is.

"You and Hephaestus."

"May I be excused? I need to go to the restroom," Aphrodite asks my mother quietly, not wasting any time when my mother nods. Her eyes quickly roam the room on her way out. I swear I saw the dark bruising of fingers on her arm.

A flame of anger ignites within me, and I have to keep myself calm. I cannot make a scene at dinner, especially over Aphrodite who I supposedly just met.

"What business do we have with each other?" Hephaestus asks with a bite behind each of his words—well, as much bite as a puppy.

"I'm glad you asked." My father smirks. "Now that Ares is back. It is time we strengthen our ranks. To do that, you will be making weapons for trainees."

"The hell I will," he grumbles.

My father's eyes turn icy. "You will. It is part of your duties to the Olympians."

I would laugh at the look on Hephaestus's face if I weren't also angered at the prospect of working with him.

"My duty is to be a blacksmith, not make weapons so pretty boy over here can parade around with an army of imbeciles."

That flame of anger ignites further. No one insults my men. They lay down their lives every time we go into battle. If anyone is an imbecile, it's him for thinking it's okay to lay a hand on his wife.

I stand, my hands slamming on the furnished wood. My

eyes zero in on my brother with a deadly glare. "May I be excused? Before I wring his damn neck."

My mother doesn't say a word, but she offers a silent nod. Meanwhile, my father's voice raises as I exit. Seems I am not the only one my brother ticked off with his comment.

I wander the halls to figure out where Aphrodite went. I take my time, not eager to get back to the madness. However, when I'm about to give up, I run right into her.

"Oh, I'm sorry—Ares," she says, eyes wide and shock filling her voice. She quickly schools her features, but I do not miss the increase of her breathing. She's nervous.

"Aphrodite, is it?" I ask. I love the way her real name rolls off my tongue. "It is lovely to learn your real name. It seems you weren't so honest during our first meeting."

A huff leaves her lips. She crosses her arms, only pulling my attention to her breasts, which push up higher. My mouth waters remembering how they felt as I fisted them. "That makes two of us. Ares, is it? Seems we both lied about some things."

"Seems we did." I smirk.

Aphrodite's demeanour slips when her himation does the same. I see a glimpse of those bruises again and the same flame from earlier grows. She pulls the wrap-like fabric back over her arms as quickly as it fell. "Ares, if I had known who you were I—"

"Don't finish that sentence. I know how that night went. We were both pleased by the end of it…several times." Rather than the blush I wanted from her, Aphrodite grows more timid, uneasy even. I brush the arm I'd seen the bruise on.

She tenses before relaxing into my touch.

"Relax, seductress. Your secret is safe with me."

Confusion mars her face. "Why would you—I don't understand."

"Because, luckily for you, I dislike my brother. My sisters do as well."

"But if you dislike him so much, wouldn't you want to be the one to tell him you've fucked his wife, timeline be damned?" Her brash words almost make me laugh.

"Certainly not." I shake my head, finding delight in the way the gears are turning in her head.

"Why?" Aphrodite whispers when I caress her cheek.

Gods, this woman is maddening. Brother's wife or not, I'm still drawn to her the same way I was that night in Cyprus.

"I want to see you again."

This seems to snap Aphrodite from the comfort of my touch. She pushes away from me then steps away.

"I am your brother's wife, and you want to see me again? Let me tell you something, I am not a pawn you can use to get back at your brother—"

"That is not why." I tut. "I know you felt it that night too. You felt that raw electricity."

Her eyes darken. I folded and twisted her body, fucking her at every angle imaginable. That night has drawn me from my sleep on the brink of cumming more times than I want to admit.

She clears her throat. "That does not matter."

"And why not?" I taunt.

"Because I am married. I wish to honor my marriage," she mutters through a clenched jaw.

"I'm aware." I smirk. I see her about to give up, about to walk back into the dining room where we will be forced to remain strangers before I decide to throw her a bone. "We do not have to do anything you do not wish to. I merely want to see you."

Aphrodite remains silent, her eyes finding mine with a weighted stare. I cannot help the smile that pulls at my lips as I take in her beauty. The heart shape of her face, the plumpness of her lips, the icy oceans of her eyes. Everything.

I bend, lowering my head for a second before turning to head back toward the dining room. "Think about it, seductress."

CHAPTER 6

APHRODITE

Dear Journal,
I am so totally fucked.

Think about it, seductress.

Ares's flirtatious voice echoed in my ears constantly since the family dinner three days ago. And I have been debating what to do about it endlessly. He lied to me when we first met.

So did you.

I groan internally at the voice in my head because it's right. We both lied about the same things. Besides, my duty as the goddess of love is to be a suitable wife to my husband.

Regardless of who lied, it does not change the fact that I

am a married woman. I must be faithful to my husband. Marriage means something. I would know.

"I need to tell you something," I say, bursting into Dionysus's party room where he's drinking from a wine bottle.

"Well, hello to you too, Aphrodite." He takes another swig of wine. "It must be something exciting given that crazy look in your eye."

"If I tell you, you must swear that you will not tell anyone or so help me, I will end you," I say, fixing him with a fierce stare.

Dionysus may be one of the only people in Olympus that knows the true danger of my temper, but he doesn't let it show. Instead, his smirk turns curious. "I swear. Now, tell me your secret."

"I slept with Ares," I say, then cover my mouth as if it was never meant to fall from my lips.

His eyes grow wide, and my body heats. My stomach churns and I feel sweat bead on my lower back.

"Hephaestus's brother, Ares?"

I nod.

"When?"

"A few years ago. We met in the mortal realm. We lied to each other and claimed we were mortal. It was before I moved to Olympus. What should I do? Hephaestus can't find out. He'll kill me," I ramble, finding the more I word vomit the less hot I feel and the less I feel like I might actually vomit.

Dionysus's lips quirk, "Was it good?"

My head snaps up. "What?"

"Was the sex good?"

"I heard you. Why does it matter?"

His smirk grows to a mischievous, feline smile. "So it was…"

"I hardly think it matters," I say, trying to fight the blush that is climbing up my body at the memory of the best sex I've had in my life.

"And why's that?" Dionyus asks, lifting a curious brow.

My jaw clenches before my stomach turns again. "Because I am married to his brother."

"You should know by now, I am not in agreement with Hephaestus. I've seen what you've been through since the union, so I am quite pleased with this new information. Perhaps you'll act on it again."

Disbelief fills me. "Di, this is not something to celebrate."

He shrugs. "Well, you can continue with the guilt trip if you'd like. However, I will be celebrating. Your love life just got a lot more interesting."

✳ ✳ ✳

I FEEL THOROUGHLY BUZZED by the time I leave Dionysus's estate for the Acropolis on the Mount. This is the last place I want to be, but it's also the only way I can get the tugging I feel in my chest out. I hold my breath as I enter the throne room, hoping it's empty. But my lungs tighten even more when I see Hera talking very tensely with Demeter. *Gods, I hope she doesn't turn that anger on me.*

As if she could hear my thoughts, Hera looks at me with narrowed eyes. "What are you doing here?"

I continue walking towards the back of my chair. "Just doing my duty. You restricted me from doing it any other way, remember?"

It's a shallow dig but it comes straight from the wound she cut herself. Not long before Hephaestus and I were married, I'd held an event for the Olympian Goddesses. A mortal prince in Troy was to pick a goddess of his choosing based on beauty and desire. I hadn't expected to win, and apparently Hera hadn't either. In a rampage, she cut off all of my access to the mortal realm. I was no longer allowed to move between the realms as I pleased since everyone was forbidden to take me. She told others it was so I wouldn't run away from Hephaestus. But I always knew it was because Paris chose me.

Now I'm stuck using a basin enchanted by the Fates to aid the mortals. Anytime I feel that someone needs me, I have to come here.

Hera sizes me up. "Very well."

I fight the urge to roll my eyes even though I really want to. Hera turns her aggression back to Demeter and I release a breath. With that out of the way, I finally make my way to the back of my seat in the throne room. I open the heavy limestone door to reveal the basin. The hollowed room beneath my chair mimics the temples the mortals dedicate to me. Roses cover the upper portion of the small room, just big enough for me to step in. A gold basin sits in the middle of a marble table, shining like the sun's rays.

I trace the enchanted water within the basin, letting it ripple beneath my fingers. The water grows murky as I circle my fingers around the bowl. Clarity comes back to the liquid when it takes on the scene of a couple somewhere in the middle of their lifespan. Tears brim each of their eyes. They look weathered by the trials of life.

"What are we going to do?" The woman whispers through her tears. "Do you even want to be my husband anymore?"

I can feel her husband's heart break just a little bit. His stunned silence makes his wife's heart do the same. My hand warms before I circle the basin again, letting my power flow from me and into the couple.

He grabs her shoulders, lifting her chin to his equally wet eyes. "Of course I do, agapi mou. *I would do anything for you. Don't forget that it is us against the world, not us against each other. Do you still want to be my wife?"*

The woman's heart rebuilds the pieces cracked from the strife they've faced. "Of course I do."

I smile when I feel the husband's heart mirror hers. Circling the basin once more, I leave the couple in peace, satisfied when that pull in my chest is relieved. All I needed to do was remind them of the love they still carry for one another.

I decide to celebrate my success with the mortal couple by working on my own marriage. The mortal couple was worn down and hardened by their circumstances, I'm afraid Hephaestus and I might have done the same thing. Sometimes all we need to do is take a step back and admire why we love our partner. It's easy to lose track of all of their great qualities if all we do is focus on their wrongdoings.

"Aphrodite, it's so good to see you," Kyra, the bakery's owner, greets from behind the counter.

There are a few other villagers looking over the shelves of

pre-made jams and preserves, but they don't bat an eye. They've grown used to my presence, and I have to admit, it makes me feel more relaxed.

"Hello, Kyra," I say.

"What will it be today, Aphrodite? We only have a few of the raspberry and apricot tarts left."

"That's alright. I came to see if you had any of your black-berry tarts left. They're Hephaestus's favorite," I say, searching her display for the familiar pastries.

"We do. I'll go ahead and package them for you."

Kyra delicately places each pastry into one of her signature lilac boxes. Hephaestus left Olympus after our dinner with his family. He said he couldn't be in the same city as his idiot brother. But he came home early this morning, so I thought I'd be nice and bring him his favorite pastries.

"I threw in the last two raspberry ones for you. I know those are your favorite." Kyra grins, sliding the box across the counter.

"Thank you," I say as I hand her my coins. "How are you feeling?"

Kyra runs a hand over her swollen belly. I feel a tug in my chest, beckoning me towards the mother and her babe. I smile knowing it's the love they already share. "Quite well, today at least."

"Do you have any names in mind?" I ask, smiling at the way Kyra rubs her belly absentmindedly with a grin.

"Adrian, if it's a boy. Stella, if it's a girl."

"Both are lovely." I then offer Kyra a goodbye before leaving the shop, meeting the cooling temperature of the night.

The scent of roast meat hits my nose when I enter our home. Our chef's lamb roast is one of my favorite dishes. Did Hephaestus remember?

Hephaestus and one of his apprentices are in our grand dining room, which is similar to the one in Hera's and Zeus's estate but far less regal. He has a series of swords and other weapons atop the wooden table. Annoyance floods me, but I quickly tamp it down. He knows how I feel about sharp objects on the wood.

"Hello, darling," I chime as I set the box of pastries atop the wooden table.

Hephaestus mutters something in return.

I purse my lips. The least he could do is say hello. "I brought you some blackberry tarts from Kyra's."

Hephaestus's eyes fix on the box. They shift to me for a second and I find it hard to see the same Hephaestus from the early days of our marriage in them. "Thank you."

I don't have time to respond before his attention is back on the weapons. He carefully inspects the shine of a sword in the light before ushering his apprentice over.

The apprentice takes the sword and stores it safely in a large wooden box against the wall. I should have known when I saw his apprentices that he would be preoccupied. He never brings them if it is not for work.

The sound of metal scraping against wood draws me from my train of thought.

"Darling, I've asked you not to inspect your weapons on the dining room table," I say, worrying about the number of scratches that will be on the gifted wood. The table was a wedding present from his mother.

Hephaestus doesn't look from the short sword he is wiping, "Yes, but I couldn't wait. These need to be taken to the training facility tomorrow morning. Athena asked me to rush the order. The small supply of weapons they had was rusted."

"Of course but, we have so many other rooms that you could do this in. I would hate for the table your mother gifted us to be ruined—"

"I am doing my job, Aphrodite." His eyes find mine in a heartbeat but they're cold. "I wouldn't expect you to understand."

I can tell he's biting back more. Yet he refrains. Instead, he continues his inspection of the weapons as if I am not here.

"Have you eaten? I noticed the smell of roast when I walked in."

"I told the chef to make a roast. I did not know when you'd be back, so I told him not to make you any," he says without missing a beat.

It feels like someone punched me in the gut. He hadn't remembered my favorite meal.

"I'm sure you can ask him to make you something."

"No," I say, smoothing out my gown with clammy hands. "That is quite alright. I will simply return to town and grab something there."

"Are you sure?" Hephaestus looks up for a second as I make my way out of our dining room.

I put the best fake smile I could to remain the appearance of the agreeable wife I am supposed to be. But even I know it looks quite sad. "Yes, quite. You may return to your work. I know it is important."

Without another beat, I eagerly exit the estate, waiting until the door closes behind me to release the shaky breath that had been plaguing me. My eyes sting, threatening to spill the tears that brims them. *Does he truly think I do nothing all day? That I do not have my own duties?*

I downed my first two glasses of wine at the Muses in less than five minutes. I swirl my third as I rest my head on my other hand. Each sip I take seems to drown the sting of Hephaestus's lack of consideration for our marriage.

I drink the last remnants of my third glass in a single gulp. Setting the glass on the bar top, I wait for the alcohol to make me feel warm and fuzzy. "Orion."

"Yes, Aphrodite?" Orion asks, slinging the cloth he uses to dry glasses over his shoulder.

"I need another glass, please."

Worry flashes across his eyes, which sends another wave of self-loathing through me. I hate people worrying about me. I am not a damsel in distress.

"Are you sure? You don't usually drink more than three unless you're with Dionysus."

"Give me another glass," I say, cutting him a cold stare.

He knocks his knuckles on the bar top. "Coming right up."

The hairs on my neck stand and another rush of warmth filters through me. It must be that third glass of wine.

Orion's eyes bounce between me and someone behind me. His mouth pulls up to the slightest degree as he makes his way to me and places my wine in front of me. "Seems you have a new admirer, and this one would sure stir things up." He leaves me with a wink.

I immediately know who it is. "You've been staring at me every day since you found out I live in Olympus. Are we going to keep this staring contest going or are you going to buy me a drink?"

CHAPTER 7

ARES

*I*t takes me a moment before I realize she's speaking to me. The woman that has haunted my mind ever since that night two years ago takes a sip of her fresh glass. "Seems you've already done that yourself."

I sit next to her as she says, "That doesn't mean you can't buy the next one."

I let out a chuckle, having déjà vu. "Touche."

Orion walks over. "What can I get you tonight? The usual?"

I nod and he walks off to make my drink.

"How often do you come here that Orion knows your order," Aphrodite asks before taking another sip of wine. Her skin looks buttery soft in the dim light. Her silky blonde hair makes me want to run my fingers through it before wrapping my hand around it and—no.

A playful smirk draws on my lips. "I've lived in Olympus far longer than you have."

"Right. You were the one that lied about being from the mortal realm," she says, but I know it's a challenge.

"That didn't stop you from riding my cock all night." I almost laugh when she chokes on her wine.

She narrows her eyes. "What do you want? I'm married to your brother. You will not get any sexual pleasure from me again. So what do you want?"

Her icy eyes catch mine, and I find them glazed over from wine, through something darker lurks in them. Her lips part in the slightest, drawing my attention to them. They're lush and pink, plump enough to make me want to taste. "I'll make you a deal."

She scoffs. "What makes you think I'd want to make a deal with you?"

My finger grazes her thigh under the bar. Her breath sputters and goosebumps erupt beneath my touch. "Because you still react to my touch the same way you did that night."

She glares at me. I half expect that she might walk out of here but then she gives me something. "What's the deal?"

"Allow me to prove to you that I can offer you pleasant conversation tonight without anything to threaten your marriage. If I succeed, we can continue to meet for drinks. If I fail, then we may return to being in-laws."

"That's it? Just conversation? No tricks." Aphrodite pulls her bottom lip between her teeth, and it takes more restraint than I'm willing to admit to not stare.

"No tricks. So what do you say? Do we have a deal, seductress?" I hold my whiskey glass up, ready for the challenge.

She clinks her glass with wine. "As you wish."

* * *

AFTER SEVERAL MORE DRINKS AND a move to a circular booth near the back of the bar, I say, "Why is it that every time I see you, it looks as though a storm cloud is stuck over you? That's not the woman I met in the mortal realm."

"What do you mean?" she asks before taking a leisurely sip. Others may not notice, but her mask slips for the smallest second before the glass touches her lips.

"Ever since our family dinner, you're either drowning your sorrows or moping around."

"Oh, and I suppose a god like yourself is always happy." She tuts, this time taking a long pull from her glass.

"Happier than you, apparently," I say, trying to chip away at the shell she shows everyone else. I've met the woman beneath it, and I want to see her again.

Her head snaps in my direction, and her eyes turn to ice. "You don't know me. You know nothing of my duties."

There she is, the woman beneath that timid melancholy shell. A beat of electricity passes between us while I hold her stare. Her lips part, hardly noticeable to anyone else, but I notice because like that night, I'm hyper-aware of everything she does.

I lean closer, noting the catch in her breath and the subtle way she wets her lips. "I think I know you a lot more than you think."

"Then what do you want?" It's a loaded question, and I know it by the way it rolls off her tongue. Another wave of electricity floods me. Gods, this woman is full of raw magnetism, and I almost believe she isn't aware of it.

"I want a lot of things," I say, leaning even closer to her. Her eyes darken at the suggestive sentence. I'm so close I can feel her breasts against my chest as she breathes faster and faster. She licks her lips.

I smirk and look back up at her. She wants me the same way I want her. "Goodnight, seductress."

I leave without another word, but I have the satisfaction of knowing that one day, she'll be mine again. She just doesn't know it yet.

CHAPTER 8

APHRODITE

Dear Journal,

I've been trying to strengthen my marriage with Hephaestus ever since I met Ares. I do not want to be what Hera and everyone has already decided that I am. I meant my vows when I said them, but he makes it so damn hard sometimes.

"Goddess?" The modiste catches my gaze in the mirror, holding the back of my new gown together.

"Apologies."

"It is all good and well. I asked your opinion on the dress. If it is not to your liking, we still have time to make changes before the big day, or we can create a new one."

"No, do not worry, Theodora. It is lovely, as are all of your creations." I look over the pink gown once more. Theodora always challenges the standard peplos, teetering on the edge of propriety. It is another reason I love her designs.

"Thank you, Goddess. We should get you changed. I must finish this gown before the party. I'm sure Hephaestus will love it." Theodora grins, not knowing her words send a ping straight through me. I consider myself fortunate that the new gown drapes across the part of my arm that is still bruised. No longer an angry purple, my skin has become splotches of faded yellow and blue.

I offer a polite goodbye after I change, finding it hard to breathe when the memory of Hephaestus's hateful eyes flash toward my mind. The sinister look on his face when he nearly broke my arm is enough to make me pause as soon as I leave the shop and take a deep breath.

Seeing Hephaestus in our dining room last night ripped the bandage off of the emotional wound he created that night.

I try to remind myself that no one—besides Ares—knows what happened behind closed doors.

It's impossible.

And yet I still cannot shake the horrible feeling that everyone can see right through me to how much of a fraud I am. Because how could the goddess of love find herself in a marriage so terrible that her husband resorted to harming her? That thought takes me to the cusp of a breakdown.

I hurry from the modiste's shop, hoping to arrive at my estate before my tears start flowing. I offer city dwellers that recognize me the kindest grin I can muster before I practically break out in a run the moment I reach the long drive.

I walk through every room on the first floor before I reach the balcony, the only place I seem to feel any peace. I try to calm myself by picturing my worries flowing from me like the water in the stream near our estate. It takes a while, but eventually, I am calm.

The occasional breeze that sweeps through the air reminds me to take a deep breath, calming me further.

"Ma'am, would you like a cup of tea? I couldn't help but notice your heightened nerves earlier," my maid, Alexandra, asks.

"Yes. I would very much appreciate a cup of your tea, Alexandra."

She bids me her temporary goodbye, and I'm left to my own devices. Alexandra isn't here every day, but the days she is here seem a little better than the rest.

It seems like no time before she returns with a tray of tea in hand with cream and sugar along with it. Alexandra sets the tray on the small table next to me and takes a seat in the neighboring chair. She fixes me a cup, knowing I am completely capable.

We sit in silence for quite some time, simply enjoying the friendly presence of one another. Aside from Dionysus, Alexandra is the only true friend I have in Olympus.

"I do not wish to upset you..." Alexandra says.

My stomach clenches when I catch the look in her eyes.

"I know you have a party in a few days. There is a special cream my mother used to make. It's a healing aid really. It can heal just any minor injury and cover up bruises."

My eyes widen. "Alexandra, it is not what you think. I—"

"Regardless," she begins, "I will not mention it. It is your business. Though most in Olympus enjoy indulging in gossip, I am not one of them. I am your friend first and your maid second. Your secret—whatever it may be—is safe with me."

I grab her hand, squeezing gently as a grin graces my lips. My eyes sting slightly. "Thank you."

I WALK OUT of my bathing chamber after sun down with a cloth wrapped loosely around my body. I halt when I find an unwelcome visitor in my bed chamber.

"Hephaestus," I whisper. The look from a few nights ago flashes in my mind and fear creeps within me. He stands from a pale pink chair that sits in the far corner of my room. "What are you doing here?"

He takes a step forward, timid in his approach. "I wanted to see you, dear."

Dear? That word draws an almost-silent sigh from me. I stalk forward toward my wardrobe, grabbing one of my sleeping gowns from it and wrap the fabric carefully around me. I fasten the front of the gown before turning back to him. "I think it would be best if you left my bed chamber, dear."

Hephaestus takes a few more steps toward me, and I take one step back when he gets too close. Something flashes across his face, something I try to tell myself isn't regret because it's much easier to keep him the villain.

"Aphrodite, please..." His voice is pained. "Let me apologize."

"Apologize?" I whisper. "Hephaestus, you laid a hand on me. You harmed me. You—you left a bruise that I've had to hide so people wouldn't ask questions. Do you know how humiliated I've felt?" My throat hurts and tears stream down my cheeks.

Finding out who Ares truly was and running into him at the Muses aided in distracting me from Hephaestus's abuse but seeing him now forces me to reckon with it. "I never—I never thought I would be put in that situation. Especially by you. Who are you?"

He lets out a shaky breath, and I see a tear fall down his cheek. "I'm so sorry. So, so sorry."

Hephaestus sinks to his knees and wraps his arms around my lower back, pulling me against him. I flinch. More tears fall down his cheeks, and I know that he noticed. "Oh gods, Aphrodite. I am so sorry. I never thought I'd sink so low. Please, forgive me."

"Forgive you? Hephaestus, how do I know that you mean what you say? How do I know that you—that you love me?" Those last words come out as nothing but a croak. He lifts his head, meeting my eyes as he kneels before me.

"I will spend my days proving it to you. Please, Aphrodite. I am not the monster you think I am." Another tear coasts down his cheek. The sheer conviction in his eyes leads me to ponder giving him the olive branch he so desperately wants.

Am I naive enough to believe his words? Maybe. But I want this marriage to work. It must because there is no other way I will be able to live happily.

I lift his chin, signaling for him to stand. "Hephaestus," I plead, hoping the tears that stream down my cheeks tonight are the last he will cause. "You cannot lay another hand on me."

His arms tighten around me before he pulls back, looking in my eyes with a face I'm sure is supposed to look endearing. "I promise."

I nod, not knowing what else to do. There is so much I still need to process. "I think you should go. At least for tonight." He nods slowly and gathers himself to leave.

He leans forward, takes hold of the back of my head, and places his lips on mine. They feel foreign. Whether that is because of his actions or because of the memory of what Ares's felt like, it doesn't feel like it used to. The guilt for almost kissing Ares last night is the main reason I allow my lips to sync with my husband's. I am supposed to love him unconditionally, arranged marriage or not.

Hephaestus's hands start to roam. The tenderness of his lips tells me this is how he plans to show how sorry he is.

Some may think me foolish to allow this, but if this is what Hephaestus needs to prove himself, then I will let him. For the sake of my marriage and duty to the Olympians.

"Aphrodite," Hephaestus whispers against my lips. I grasp his worn chiton and offer a nod. A bubble of nervousness fills my gut, but I attempt to extinguish it. We need this. I saunter to my bed, pulling Hephaestus's hand to follow.

I stop when the backs of my legs meet the soft mattress. Hephaestus finds my hip, and he pulls at the string holding my sleeping gown together. The chill in the air hits my chest and stomach, causing the peaks of my breasts to tighten.

Hephasetus pushes the fabric from my arms, letting the pale fabric pool on the floor.

We separate with the same knowing looks. I lie in the center of my bed as Hephaestus removes his burgundy chiton. Only when he is completely bare does he meet me in the center of the mattress.

His lips find mine with a new urgency, and only then do I taste the alcohol on his breath. I act as though I do not notice it when he continues his frenzy on my lips. I force myself to stifle the pain at his abrupt entrance into me. I let it come out in what I can only hope sounds like a moan.

Hephaestus rarely gives me enough time to become ready for him. Not that he is particularly big, but it is still an unwelcome intrusion when the body is not ready; no matter how much the mind tries to convince it that it is.

Hephaestus's lips trail to my neck. I force myself to let out feigned moans of encouragement. I feel guilt for my body not wanting his. But if this is what will save this marriage, then I'll do it.

His hips begin to stutter, only able to draw themselves in and out three more times before he spills inside of me. His sweaty frame collapses on me, draping slightly to the side so as to not crush me. I finally relax when he is done.

I trail my fingers down his back, stroking leisurely at his hair. I will any negative thoughts about the man at my side away.

We could make this work. He promised.

A sleepy groan leaves him, and he nudges his head closer to me, nestling it next to my breast. "You are a suitable wife."

Suitable

That single word sends everything crashing.

Not a loving wife.

Not a wife he could be happy with.

Not a wife that he loves.

A suitable wife. A wife he plans to use to fulfill his duty and his duty alone. Never his heart.

I am nothing more than a suitable wife.

CHAPTER 9

APHRODITE

In front of the mirror, I smooth the pink fabric of my gown. Theodora delivered it in time for our event tonight. The sleeves of the gown cover my shoulders like a normal peplos, but instead of cinching into thin straps, the fabric flows loosely down my shoulders, stopping below where the ghost of the bruise used to be. Alexandra's healing cream worked like a dream.

It's been two weeks since Hephaestus apologized and yet a pang of hurt catches me off guard. I quickly bury it before it has a chance to overtake me. Tonight, I must present myself as a happy wife. The party may not be for us, but it is the first party we are attending together where we are not in the spotlight. That means eyes will be on us to see if we act the same in the sidelines as we do as the centers of attention. I must be perfect.

"Thank you for the cream, Alexandra. Your mother must have been very talented in healing."

Alexandra fixes the train of my dress before making sure every clip is clipped and every layer is smooth. "It is my pleasure. And, yes, she was quite talented. She always stressed that while we may not get sick as immortals, knowing how to heal the wounds that may kill us is ever more important."

A knock sounds on my door. "Dearest?"

Usually Hephaestus just says my name. Another way to show his expectation to keep up the charade of our happy marriage around everyone. Or perhaps, he believes the other night was sufficient in fixing our problems. I turn, meeting my husband's eye with a timid grin. Alexandra bids her goodbye and slips from the room.

I clasp my hands together at my hips. "Hephaestus."

"Are you ready? I expect guests are arriving on the Mount," he informs, extending his hand for me to take.

My eyes fix on his large hand, the same hand that has attempted to love me and harm me. My mouth dries at the memory of the dark look in his eyes. It was not that of a husband's and yet he is my husband for eternity.

"Aphrodite?"

"Yes, dearest?" I clasp the necklace Hephaestus gifted me at our engagement. His eyes flick to the necklace, which stops right above my breasts. I don't miss the hint of a grin he shows at the sight of it, but his eyes show a different emotion. Something I cannot quite put my finger on.

I take his hand, following him out of our estate and into the chariot Hera and Zeus had arranged. Our ride to the Mount is silent and I can't help but feel a pit grow in my stomach the closer we get. I try to think of any sort of small conversation yet come up blank.

Our chariot stops at the entrance. Hephaestus steps out and offers me a hand. I take it graciously, then let my arm hook around his as we ascend the stairs with the other guests.

This party is to welcome Ares back to Olympus. No matter how much huffing and puffing Hephaestus made toward his mother, she'd said his presence was mandatory to present a united front for not only the family, but the Olympians as well. I half-wished Hephaestus would have won his debate with his mother, but alas, here we are.

"There you two are," Hera says and I stifle my nerves. She would be able to spot them. She is much more observant than most give her credit for.

"Hello, Mother," Hephaestus answers with a smile.

"Hephaestus, Aphrodite," Hera says to each of us with a nod. "You two must take to the dance floor. This is, after all, the first official Olympian event you're attending as a married couple."

Hephaestus tightens his grip slightly, seemingly trying to gain my attention. I rip my gaze from the crowd of people dancing and sipping spirits, meeting his blue eyes with my own.

"We'd be delighted." He slips into the role of an obedient son and adoring husband as through there is no difference between that man and his true self. "Isn't that right, dearest."

You are a suitable wife.

I force myself to match his smile and play the role of his obedient wife. "I'd love nothing more."

And with that, we enter the party as the happy newlyweds we are supposed to be.

* * *

SEVERAL DANCES LATER, I find myself against one of the limestone pillars in Hera's makeshift ballroom. Really, it is supposed to be the Olympians throne room as Zeus likes to call it. Usually, city dwellers only see this room if they're being convicted of a crime or bestowed a great honor. Tonight though, everyone is welcome to celebrate Ares's return.

I scan the crowd to find Hephaestus in conversation with who I can only assume are other blacksmiths from the city. He rarely talks about anything else. I rip my gaze from my husband and focus on the innate details that decorate the throne room.

All of the Olympian's chairs were bare, save Hera's and Zeus's, which were decorated with bright fabrics to symbolize their importance, and Ares's whose limestone chair is across from mine and is draped with a deep crimson fabric. I allow myself to stare at it only for a moment before moving on.

The limestone looks as though it's shining with the amount of gold Hera decorated with. This room usually looks as cold as the stone that makes it. But tonight, it looks warm, inviting even.

A hush falls over the crowd. Zeus and Hera stand together, arms linked, at the entrance of the throne room. Dancers cease for a moment while the floor is cleared. Zeus clears his throat, signaling the beginning of a speech.

"Good evening." He offers a grin. "It is an honor to host this gathering to celebrate my son's return to Olympus. I have no doubt he will excel in his role with the Olympians and bring wonderful improvements to the training facility."

My breath hitches when I take in Ares.

He is clad in a new chiton that makes his fiery red hair stand out more than usual. His arm muscles bulge more than I remember. My mouth runs dry when his gaze catches mine. Did he know I was looking at him? Could he feel it? Or had he already been sparing glances at me?

"To Ares," Zeus's loud voice booms.

"To Ares!" The crowd repeats, lifting their glasses as the music resumes. I lift my glass to toast but find myself unable to speak or do much of anything. Instead, I down the contents of my champagne glass in one sip before leaving the throne room to find some much needed air in an empty corridor.

I examine a mural on the wall, slowly trying to regain composure. The picture is of my sister in-laws. I haven't spent much time with Hebe or Eileithyia, partly because I don't think they enjoy Hephaestus's company all that much.

"My sisters' favorite portrait of themselves." I jump, not expecting anyone to be this far from the party.

"Ares," I say, still somewhat startled by his unexpected presence.

He offers a nod. "You look exquisite tonight, Aphrodite."

I force myself to extinguish the warmth that spreads through me at the compliment. "Thank you."

Silence drapes us while our eyes hold the only conversation we seem to need. It feels like we're playing a game, seeing who the first will be to break. I feel a morsel of heat that I seem to always feel when I'm around him.

I rip my gaze away from him, clearing my throat and casting my eyes back upon the portrait. "You said this is their favorite?"

"Yes." Ares smiles at the picture of his sisters. "Eileithyia says the artist managed to capture the angles of her face correctly. Hebe, on the other hand, has a simpler view of the portrait. She says it makes her feel like a mortal princess. Though she's never been to the mortal realm for longer than a day, she holds a liking to their royals. Something she seems to have in common with our father I'm afraid."

"It's an exquisite piece of art," I say, analyzing it to look at the details he pointed out. Even in the dimly lit candlelight of the corridor, both women look ethereal. Hebe, with her pale features, and Eileithyia with her contrasting dark ones. "Was it done by a local artist?"

He nods. "I believe they also have a collection at the Muses."

His fingers brush mine ever so lightly. But I don't pull away. I revel in the electricity it sparks. It may be wrong but, a touch of fingers in an abandoned corridor is not as scandalous as some make it out to be, I try to convince myself.

The tips of his fingers trace mine. I tell myself the electricity that spreads through my body is a figment of my imagination. Deep down I know it's not. I felt it in the mortal realm too.

I flutter my fingers, feeling more of the calluses that mark his hands. Hephaestus's hands are calloused from the work he does as a blacksmith, but his felt foreign compared to that of his brother's. "I've been thinking…"

"Have you?" he asks, acting as though he is analyzing the portrait with me.

"About your offer."

"And?"

You are a suitable wife.

That same defeated feeling fills me. "I will agree to see you, but we shall only talk."

I turn to find Ares gazing at me with bright, puzzled eyes. "Is that what you wish?"

I nod. "I wish to honor my marriage."

The way he stares at me almost feels as though he's delving into my very soul. Finally, a small grin pulls on his lips, almost mischievous. "Very well, seductress."

Ares bends at his hips, lowering his head in a stiff nod

before slipping something into my hand. He departs without another word.

MEET me at the Muses in three days after sundown.

Ares

FOR THE FIRST time in a long time, I let the small bubble of hope fill me.

CHAPTER 10

phrodite

MY SKIN FEELS hot as I bask in the bright sun. The grass feels soft yet unnatural while I run my hand idly over it from the edge of the fabric I'm resting on. I've always preferred the sea to land but alas, this is yet another way I'm deprived of the things I cherish. A ladybug crawls along my finger, finding a resting place on top of my right hand. Such gentle creatures.

"Alexandra?"

"Yes, miss?"

My eyes meet Alexandra with a half-chastising stare. "You know not to use such formalities when Hephaestus or his parents are not present. I'd like to think we're friends."

Her brown eyes brighten. "Of course we are friends."

"Good," I say. "Now, I have a question that might sound rather strange."

"I'm sure it will not come close to some of the things I witness around Olympus." Alexandra giggles.

I fight my smirk but ultimately fail. I've seen some rather strange things in Olympus, and I haven't been here as long as most. "Have you ever been in love?"

"I thought I was once." Her eyes look off in the distance. "A few years before you arrived, I was engaged. He was a boy I'd grown up with. We were each other's first for everything. But he volunteered to take part in a rather violent war the mortals had started. In his absence, I continued the plans for our wedding. We had a small house in the heart of the city.

"When he came home, he said he'd be returning to the mortal realm for good. He wouldn't say why, but I knew there was someone else. I was heartbroken, but as time goes on I realize more that it wasn't love. It was complacency. We were comfortable with each other's company, but there was never passion." She shakes her head and her eyes hone back in. "Forgive me, it appears I've let myself ramble."

My left hand reaches out to her. "Nonsense. I am thankful for your story. I only wish it had a better ending."

She smiles a smile that doesn't reach her eyes. "As do I."

A calm breeze sweeps through the warm air. The ladybug on my hand crawls around and stops once it finds my palm.

"Aphrodite!" Hephaestus's voice booms from the entrance of my garden. The ladybug flies away as he draws closer.

"Yes, dear."

He stops a few paces away, not bothering to face me fully. "I wanted to let you know I will be gone for a few days. I need more material if I am to work with my brother at our new training facilities."

I feel guilty for the small flutter of relief that fills me at his prospective absence. But it only makes meeting Ares tomorrow that much easier. "Very well."

Hephaestus waits only a moment longer before walking back toward our home.

"Pardon me if I am intruding, Alexandra, but do you ever think you'll try your hand at love again?"

A blush dawns her face. "I believe I should like to try again. After all, I have not experienced genuine love or passion. I believe everyone should experience both at least once in their lives no matter if it stays for a lifetime or not."

"Yes, however fleeting it may be..." I whisper.

* * *

OLYMPUS BUZZES WITH LIFE. I offer smiles to those who recognize me. I'm supposed to meet Ares at the Muses in a few hours, but I decided to stroll around the streets before meeting him.

"Aphrodite." A man beams at me.

I return the gesture. "Orion, how are you?"

"Doing well. I came out to get a few garnishes for our drinks. We ran out." He lifts his hands, showing a small bag. "Will you and Hephaestus be joining us tonight?"

"Hephaestus and I?"

A confused look dawns on his face as he takes in my confusion.

"Yes. When I left his two apprentices walked in. I know Hephaestus does not usually patron the Muses, but they said something about celebrating. I assumed it was about the deal Hephaestus and Ares struck."

"Oh." A strange feeling fills my gut. Hephaestus nearly always brings one apprentice when he gathers materials. So why did he not this time? I shake the unease. I'm sure Hephaestus thought it would be faster this way. "I am afraid Hephaestus is in the mortal realm gathering a few more materials before they can make good on their deal. We shall have to postpone our visit."

"Yes, I suppose you shall." Orion nods. "I must be getting back before the rush hits us. Oh, one last thing. We are getting a new wine that Dionysus found. He said it will be a huge success. It should be on our shelves within the next week."

"Then I shall be there to offer my critiques," I say cheerily.

As soon as I'm out of Orion's line of sight, I hurry as fast as I can without drawing attention from the crowd. I'm not sure where I'm going, but I have a good enough idea.

Once I break the city's edge, I walk so fast my calves burn. I have to catch him before he leaves.

Eventually, I find the large building I'm looking for. It

reminds me of my estate in that it is built of pale limestone and seemingly on its own on a large piece of land. But that is where the similarities stop. In the distance, I hear the waves. It is like a siren song calling me home.

I bound up the stairs, only stopping when I find two guards at the front doors. "I am here to see Ares. He is aware of my visit. I'm his sister-in-law."

The guard on the right, who must be six foot two and built with hard muscles, eyes me skeptically. His brows scrunch then he looks over at the other guard, who looks remarkably like him. They stand in silence for a moment before the one on the right speaks, "Very well. He is inside."

I nod thanks and hurry in. I'm not sure what I was expecting Ares's estate to look like, especially since he's rarely inhabited it, but it wasn't this. Every piece of furniture—the little that he has—is covered with sheets. Not a single piece of art hangs on the walls. Candle fixtures are few and far between. There is hardly anything to make it a home. Everything seems so cold.

"Ares!" I call out, ambling through each room, hoping I find him. Each room looks emptier and emptier the further I go. I decide to turn around and try the room adjacent to this one.

As I reach the foyer again, I hear, "Aphrodite?"

Relief fills me when I see the fiery red hair I'd be able to recognize anywhere. "Ares, oh thank the gods."

"What are you doing here?" he asks. "I was about to walk over to the Muses."

"We cannot go to the Muses," I shake my head, taking a few steadying breaths.

His brows furrow. "Has something happened? Are you alright?"

I nod. "We cannot go to the Muses. Hephaestus's apprentices are there."

"I see."

I huff at my stupidity. "I don't know why I didn't think of it sooner. We cannot be seen together in Olympus. People will talk. If we meet, we must do so in private where there are no watchful eyes."

Ares is silent. His eyes wander over what I can only assume is my frantic expression. His arms cross over his chest. "What then, do you suppose we should do?"

I wrap my hands around myself. "We must meet in secluded parts of the city or our estates. Of course, mine will depend on Hephaestus's whereabouts."

"So we will meet here mostly?"

"Yes," I cast my eyes over the vacant foyer. "Although your estate could use serious furnishings. I feel like I'm in a deserted building, not the estate of an Olympian."

I pace along the edge of the room to take in the minute details. The crown molding, the intricate detailing that lines walls and door frames.

"I'm afraid it does need some work. I let it go empty during my extended time in the mortal realm. Although it is clear that was not the only major change here in my absence."

Ares is already looking at me when I meet his eyes. His eyes bore into mine, and it feels as though he can see every part of me. I look away before he can see much else. "We will need a reason for why you are always here, if this is where you truly wish to be."

I trace the regal paneling along the wall. "We will say I am helping you refurbish your estate. After all, that will not be a complete lie."

"You're going to help me fix up this place?" he asks with a skeptical brow.

"I am. Unless you would not like me to come here. After all, I don't see how this would be considered better than my home. No matter how tempting the company is," I tease.

His eyes trace my frame. "Very well. You shall be my aid in turning my estate into a home."

"The matter is settled then."

"It is." Ares glances at the molding on the ceiling. "Would you like to take a stroll through the city?"

I turn slowly to face the god of war. Was he not listening? "Did we not just settle the matter on why we must meet in private?"

"We did." Ares grins mischievously. "But we will also need people to overhear why you are visiting my estate. After all, if you were to make frequent visits with no explanation, people would think we're having an affair. And we wouldn't want that, would we?'

"Ares," I warn. I sigh because he's right. The people need to hear why I'll be visiting him. "How do you suppose we leak the news?"

"We could tell people when they ask."

I shake my head. "I don't want anyone to have to question our interactions. Speculation of my motives is what got me into all of this mess."

Ares offers an arm for me. "Then we shall walk around Olympus, go into a few shops that sell fabric or art and tell the shop owners, loudly enough for others to hear, that you are aiding me in design. I am sure by week's end, the news will have spread." I nod. It's not a bad idea. "So, what do you say, seductress? Shall we take a stroll?"

You'd think since he is the god of war, I'd have given Ares more credit for his strategy. My arm loops through his after I offer him a defiant glare. "I say lead the way, soldier."

* * *

"SHALL we do one more shop for good measure?" I ask.

We dropped each other's arms before we reached the city. But I must applaud Ares. His plan has been perfect thus far. We've been in three shops, and the owner of each shop bought our tale and each has offered discounts if we choose to shop with them.

Ares shakes his head. "We've been in three shops. I'm sure that is sufficient enough to spread the news." I do send him a look and he sighs. "Very well. One more shop won't hurt."

I somehow already have him in the palm of my hands. "Wonderful. There is a shop I'd like to visit up here."

We enter the last shop on my agenda. I barely make it to the first product before Ares says, "A florist?"

"Yes."

"What would I need with flowers? I am the only one that lives there, save one butler."

I grin. "You put me in charge of remodeling your dismal-looking estate. I am a woman, therefore, I will put a feminine touch on it. Besides, a woman would enjoy feeling welcome when she visits and flowers have the power to do that. You will thank me one day when you win the favor of a woman and she mentions how welcoming your estate feels."

Ares looks at me with narrowed eyes, catching onto my double meaning. Then he looks at the shop owner who grins while arranging a bouquet. "Very well."

"Excellent," I say. "I prefer roses, but those are symbols of love, so that won't be right for you."

"I pulled a new bundle of peonies today, Aphrodite. Perhaps those would be more his taste," the shop owner offers timidly.

"May I see them, Miss—"

"Chloris," she finishes. "And they are right on this wall."

I follow her to where peonies in pink, red, yellow, orange, and white line majority of the wall. All of them are as vibrant as the next. "These are exquisite. I believe these shall look wonderful under a new painting in your dining room."

"Aphrodite, I am the god of war. I have no idea how to tend to flowers," Ares rebuts.

Chloris says, "I have a special feed packet that slows the decay of flowers. I'd be happy to include it in your bundles."

"Then it's settled. We shall take two bundles." I give Ares a look that dares him to argue before I face the peonies again. "Oh, and if you could do an assortment in shades of red. Ares is rather fond of the color, if you couldn't tell."

Chloris smiles. "I shall have them done as soon as I can. Should I bring them to your estate, sir?"

"There will be no need," Ares answers as I make my way

back to him. "I shall send someone with the payment to retrieve them when they are ready."

Chloris offers her thanks before we exit the floral shop. I feel rather satisfied with our endeavors and more at ease than I've felt in months. The sun above Olympus has set and the streets are filled with less children than before. And yet, I am not ready for this to be over.

I walk toward a shop I am very familiar with. "Aphrodite, where are you going?"

"One more stop," I say over my shoulder.

Ares catches up to me in a few steps. "We have already been to four. That is plenty."

"Relax," I say, opening the door that sends the smell of sugar and fruit into my nose. "It will not take long."

"What are you—" Ares finally takes notes of where I've led him. "The bakery? Why are we in the bakery?"

"Because this is your house warming gift from me. Even if your estate is not finished, it's good manners."

I step up to the counter.

"Hello Kyra, how are you?"

Kyra smiles as she runs a dark hand over her swollen belly. "As well as I can. It's harder to get around these days. My husband insists I stay home and get off my feet."

"Perhaps he is right," Ares adds from somewhere behind me.

Kyra merely waves her hands. "Oh, please, women were made to create life while still living their own. I'd go stir crazy if I stayed in my home all day, no matter how much I like it."

"I'd likely be the same."

"Raspberry tarts? I know they're your favorite. Unless you're getting blackberry for Hephaestus," Kyra rambles, grabbing a lilac box.

I half turn toward Ares. "Actually, I'm gifting Ares some as a housewarming gift. So whatever he prefers."

Ares stares at me with an unfamiliar look in his eyes before the corner of his lips twitch. "The raspberry tarts are my favorite."

I can't help the blush that creeps up my cheeks. I turn back toward Kyra, fighting the fluttering in my stomach. "Then the raspberry tarts he shall have."

CHAPTER 11

ARES

"What have I gotten myself into?" I whisper at the boxes, which Aphrodite referred to as "a few starter items." I haven't seen her in a few days, but the things she ordered have been arriving. Boxes now fill my foyer in what once had been empty space that she said felt "dismal."

Be that as it may, I can't help it as the corners of my mouth pull up that this little project she's taken up—even if it is supposed to be our cover—means I'll be seeing her quite a bit.

"Sir, a note has arrived. I believe it may be from your father."

I offer my thanks, taking the note from my butler's hand. Leave it to my father to be the one to dampen my mood. A tingling spreads in my chest and the muscles in my neck tighten. I open the note, only feeling my mood dampen further.

Visit our new training facility. It will not grow to its fullest potential unless you make a plan to get it there. I trust you with this.

- Zeus

* * *

MY MOOD DOESN'T LIGHTEN after I reach our training facility. The main room is circular, not large but not small either. It's a nice size for the few soldiers we have. The floor is packed dirt. Good, I suppose, since that will mimic battlefields. The space is closed in by a small stone ceiling that forms a dome.

"Ares, I'm glad you decided to show your face. After all, you are in charge of most of our soldiers," a woman teases.

The woman is a few paces away. Her hair is jet black and fastened in a knotted rope on her shoulder. Her eyes are almost menacing because the blue in them looks so much like my father's. But she was blessed with enough green to set them apart.

"Come now, Athena. This is the first time you see me in years and you mock me? That doesn't seem very lady-like," I retort.

Her eyes narrow. "You should by now that when I am talking about or participating in training, there is nothing lady-like about me."

I raise my hands in surrender, knowing Athena is a threat when angered.

A gloating smile marks her face. "Well, now that that's out of the way. We are to work together to build our armies. I will not pretend I would not like to make an all-female army one day, but I know your father will not let that happen anytime soon. So I will help you build the male armies up in the meantime."

"Our father sent you to babysit, did he? I must say that is a step down from the goddess of war and strategy."

Athena's jaw clenches. "Do not remind me that I come from him. We were not raised together, therefore we do not need to act as siblings do."

"My apologies." She is right. I know as much about Athena as I do the bakery owner Aphrodite took me to visit. The image of her smiling at me when I said I wanted her favorite pastry fills my mind. *Aphrodite. My seductress—No, not mine.*

"When you're done smiling like a giddy girl, I'd love to get back to our plan," Athena breaks me from the weird trance I was in. "You will be able to command the male armies on your own, but you will not be able to train them all. At least not as many as Zeus wants."

My brows straighten. "Why does he want so many? Is he trying to start a war?"

Athena shrugs. "Not to my knowledge. But if we are being honest, he's probably doing it so he knows he's ready in the event that he pisses someone off enough and they wage war. We both know that is inevitable."

A sigh falls from my lips before I can stop it. Athena is

right. I'd be a fool to deny it. I examine our training facility. It is much too small to train large legions.

"We will need to make this bigger if he wishes for a large army. Perhaps start by taking out the roof. The trainees will need to get used to fighting in the sun and weather."

"Yes, I thought as much. But we will need to start soon. Expanding the facility to fit our needs will take time. I can tell Zeus after we finish for the day."

I cross my arms. "Then we will train in an open field until it is finished. We can store the weapons here to keep them from tarnishing."

Athena nods. "That sounds like a decent enough—"

"You asked to see me, Athena?" I stiffen, then turn and meet my brother's eyes. "Oh, I didn't realize *you'd* be here."

My jaw clenches in time with my fists. He has such a punchable face. Then he opens his mouth, and it only doubles in punchability. "I could say the same for you."

Athena huffs. "Enough. Both of you. This alliance will not work if you two are bickering every five seconds. This is larger than all of us. Hephaestus, I asked you here because Zeus told me only you are to be responsible for making our weapons."

He softens when he turns to Athena. "Yes, I am."

"Good." Athena looks over at me. "I believe we will need say ten of each of all the weapons we have in our arsenals?"

"Twenty," I counter her modest assessment.

"I'm sure." Hephaestus huffs.

"What was that?" I ask through a clenched jaw.

"You're making things more difficult because I am the

one making the weapons. I'm sure you would not do the same if it were any other blacksmith."

I step closer to him, towering over his short frame. And for some reason, I am even more angered that this man who has to look up at me is married to Aphrodite. And that he felt he could put his hands on her. I should wring his damn neck.

"Need I remind you I was instructed to train and rebuild our ranks by our father? I cannot do that without a surplus of weapons. If it makes it easier to deliver the weapons in bundles of ten that's fine. But we will need at least twenty of each weapon. Do I make myself clear?"

Athena says nothing, and I like to think I can picture her supportive expression.

Hephaestus glares, and I can see his jaw clench and unclench several times.

"Fine. Expect the first bundle by the end of the week. My apprentices will deliver them in bundles of ten."

"Good." Athena clasps her hands as I take a step back. "Hephaestus you may go."

Without another word, Hephaestus disappears from the training ring, and my muscles finally relax.

"That went well."

Athena rolls her eyes. "It's always dramatic with you two."

"Can you blame me?"

Athena seems to contemplate before she answers, "No."

I chuckle.

Athena says goodbye and leaves me to my devices in the vacant training facility. The air in here is humid and feels like it sticks to my lungs, clinging to any surface it can to not be expelled back out. It won't change my fighting, but it will for the recruits. Hopefully Athena can be persuasive with the renovation proposal.

"Ares."

I turn to find my father at the threshold. "Zeus."

His lips purse and he steps inside. "Good to see you here. I was worried I'd need to use more persuasion."

I shrug, annoyed with him. "I accepted my role as an Olympian, and I meant it. Just because it does not fit your timeline, does not mean I'm wrongfully carrying out my duties."

He holds his chin higher. "That's where you're wrong, dear boy."

"Meaning?" I cross my arms over my chest, quirking a brow.

He hands me a loose slip of parchment that reads,
Our Laws.

i. Slander of the Olympian institution
   shall result in trial and likely
   death.
ii. Once sworn in, Olympians may not
   denounce their position unless they
   wish to die a tortuous death, unless
   otherwise pardoned.
iii. If tasks are not done to the liking
   of Zeus and Hera, trials may be
   organized. Full-ichored gods and
   goddesses will be assessed by the
   entire council of Olympians. Demi-
   gods and goddesses will be assessed

```
    by Zeus and Hera with the remaining
    Olympians as witnesses.
 iv. Any ill talk of Zeus will result in
    banishment from Olympus.
```

I stop reading after the fourth law. "You made it a law that people cannot talk poorly of you? Seems egotistical, if you ask me. Mortal kings never survive on the throne with laws like these."

"And yet it works." He snatches the paper from my hands and turns toward the threshold. "Besides, I'm not stupid enough to think everyone likes the way I rule. But laws like that will keep people from public uprisings. Their private talks will do nothing."

"If that is what you wish to believe…"

He pivots with absolute certainty gleaming in his eyes. "Why do you think I'm building armies? Those selected to train will think it a great honor. Therefore, they will either stop their talk or alert us of any they hear in the streets."

It's not a terrible plan, but I won't tell him that.

"Brush up on your political understanding of Olympus, Son. This is a different world. You'll either sink or swim in it."

* * *

"WHAT ARE you doing in my home?" I'm still on edge after my father's drop-in visit. The last thing I need is someone snooping in my home.

My sister doesn't startle. Instead, her hand trails along a

table I recently took a sheet off of. She lifts her chin, and I can already tell she is about to say something that proves my theory that she was meant for much more than the daughter of our parents who's stuck in the shadows.

"I'd hardly call this a home. You've nothing on the walls. All but a few pieces of furniture are still covered in sheets. If I didn't know any better, I'd say you were secretly praying to return to the mortal realm and leave all of this behind. The peonies are a nice touch though."

"You can thank Aphrodite for those." I school my expression. I can't have Hebe thinking there is anything more than there is.

Hebe inspects them. "Why would Aphrodite bring peonies? What business do you have with our *dear* brother's wife?"

The emphasis on the word dear tells me she doesn't really care about Hephaestus but more about what I'm doing with our newest sister-in-law. Either way, I have to play my cards right. If I let the wrong one slip, the implications could be very messy.

"Relax, sister. I asked her if she could help furnish my estate. I was looking around the shops and a few of the owners said she had quite good taste."

"That is all?" she asks with a pointed look.

"Yes."

Hebe eyes me for a moment before turning and tracing the outline of the table with her finger again. "I suppose it gives her something to do. Pity though."

"Meaning?"

Hebe looks at me from the other side of the table, and I swear I see a twinge of fear in them. "Oh, it's…nothing."

"Hebe," I warn. She never stutters unless she's lying.

"Oh, look at the time. I must get back before father starts looking for me." Hebe tries to rush around me, but I stop her by her wrist.

"Hebe…" This time I try in a calmer tone that has a little bite to it. "What did you mean when you said, 'it was a pity'?"

"Nothing." She yanks her wrist out of my hand. "Hephaestus always seems to be in the mortal realm—"

"How does that make it a pity that she is only refurbishing my estate?" I press.

Hebe sighs. "I'm sure she gets lonely. I only ever hear of her being around Dionysus."

I believe I know where Hebe is going with this and by the gods if we hadn't already worked this out. But she doesn't need to know that.

"Hebe, you know the hell that would be unleashed if I were to do what you are suggesting. I would face mother's wrath, and we both know that is far more dangerous than father's."

"Yes, but—" Her eyes grow wide like she was about to spill a dirty secret she was sworn to keep.

I try to sound as calm as possible. "What do you know?"

"I… I—"

"Hebe, tell me."

She sighs. "You and Eileithyia always talk so highly of the mortal realm, and I wanted to visit. So I asked—"

I place a steadying hand on her shoulder. "Breathe. You're rambling."

"Hephaestus is having an affair!" she blurts, then covers her mouth.

Rage boils within me. It feels like it's spreading through every vein in my body. I swear if I clench my jaw any harder all of my teeth will crack. "With you? How do you know?"

"Some woman. I don't know if she's immortal or not. All I know is that she has dark hair. I saw them when Hermes took me to the mortal realm. Her dwelling is somewhere on the outskirts of Delphi." Hebe's traded her startled eyes for something frazzled and calm, an odd combination, none-theless.

"Who knows?" I ask through my clenched jaw, fighting every urge to find the bastard and slit his throat before he ever has a chance to realize I'm there.

"Just me. Hermes dropped me off in the mortal realm because I told him I was meeting Eileithyia. Even when I did eventually find her, I said nothing. You are the only one that knows. I don't think Hephaestus even knows that I, well we, know." Hebe's shoulders sag in relief as if that secret had been weighing on her and the only way to relieve it was to tell someone.

I stand silent for a few moments, trying to figure out what to do.

"Does she know?"

Hebe stays silent but the shake of her head is enough for the urge to kill my own brother to come to the forefront of my mind. But I can't do that. No matter how much I want to, it would upset my mother too much. And probably my father only because he'd say it shows a sign of weakness amongst the Olympians.

I run my hand over my face, letting it settle on the stubble that has popped up on my chin. "I will tell her."

Alarm returns to Hebe's otherwise calm eyes. "Ares, you can't. She will act out. It will cause an uproar."

"If you were married and your husband's siblings knew he was having an affair, I would hope they would tell you. I'm going to tell her and I'm willing to bet she won't act out," I clarify in a harsher tone.

Hebe must note a certain look in my eye because instead of arguing with me, her face smooths and I see a glimmer of understanding in them for a moment. "Very well. I should be going. It's getting late and I'd rather not be yelled at by father."

I bid my sister a goodnight before filling a clear glass from my makeshift bar with a strong spirit. I slam the entire drink down in one sip before refilling it.

I suppose I should be glad my brother is such an ass. Afterall, it will likely make Aphrodite more apt to further our meetings. But how am I supposed to tell her that the marriage she is so determined to make work is a lie? What if the truth is too much for her to handle?

CHAPTER 12

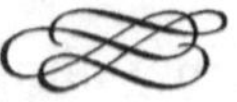

APHRODITE

"This painting will go above the small table in the foyer. Thank you," I offer a friendly smile. The first few items I ordered for Ares's estate, aside from small things like flowers, are arriving today. Ares is supposed to spend the day scouting for recruits in our ranks. So here I am all alone at his estate. Well, there are the delivery boys, of course.

"Where would you like me to put the rest of the decorations, Goddess?" A smaller boy, no more than eleven asks.

I smile at him, not knowing the strange feeling that pulls at my heart. I've been feeling that around children a lot recently, now that I'm thinking about it. "The dining room table is fine. I will put them in their rightful places. Thank you."

I circle around the foyer and the first floor, making sure all of the heavy pieces of furniture are where they need to be. Once everything seems in order, I send the delivery boys off, giving each of them a baked good from Kyra's before they walk out the door.

When I'm finally on my own, I take a deep breath, seeing what needs to be put up and where. I grouped the deliveries to arrive based on the rooms they will be in. All of today's deliveries belong in one of the drawing rooms on the first floor and one of the spare rooms that I plan to make into a study for Ares.

By the time I finish putting up the vases and other smaller decorations in the two rooms, the sun has begun setting over the horizon of the sea. I never knew any of the Olympian's estates looked out over the ocean. But now that I do, I never want to leave Ares's balcony. It's perfect.

"Aphrodite," Ares's voice carries into my ears like a siren song.

I turn to him with a smile, my arm still bracing the cold limestone balcony behind me. "Yes?"

"I wasn't sure if you would still be here, but I brought us some dinner back. I figured if you had left then I would give it to someone around the house. Would you like to eat?"

A flutter fills my stomach. He brought me dinner on the off chance that I was still here. "I'd love to. Could we possibly eat out here?"

His skin is golden in the setting sun. I feel my breath stolen from me just from the sheer godliness dripping from him. "Yes, I suppose that can be done. I'll go grab a bottle of wine."

I take a seat at the table just a few paces in front of me, watching the sunset while I wait for Ares to return with our food and wine. As I watch the sun sink lower and lower behind the waves, I'm filled with this overwhelming sense of home. I haven't felt that since I arrived in Olympus.

"Do you like the view? Eileithyia and I nearly fought for the estate with the sea view. We eventually reached a compromise that I got this one and she got one just a little way west that still gives her a partial view of it," Ares says as he sets our plates down and pours each of us a tall glass of wine.

"I love it actually." I smile at the waves. "It reminds me of a different time."

"A different time?"

"I was born from the waves. I spent some time amongst them; simply existing around what created me. My life was simple then. I lived amongst the waves, playing with some of the creatures. The turtles and dolphins enjoyed my company most. The only time I left was when I felt my powers pull me toward a certain couple that needed me," I smile at the distant memory before taking a large gulp from my glass. I take a piece of lamb steak in my mouth and force myself to hold back the hum of satisfaction that wants to escape at the delicious flavors melting on my tongue. "I was still living in the mortal realm when you met me."

"How did you end up here then?"

I stare out at the vast sea, but my mind is elsewhere. "One day, I felt the pull I'd felt so many times before. I followed it until it led me to a younger man who was by himself. It turns out it was Hermes. Zeus had caught word that I may be joining them when the time was right. He'd instructed Hermes to wait for me every day until I showed up."

Ares sits silently chewing his lamb steak before finally speaking, "How did he know you'd come to Olympus?"

I shrug. "To this day I still don't know. But if I'd known what would await me up here, I would have stayed in the mortal realm."

The corner of Ares's lips pull upward the slightest bit and it causes my own to mirror them. "I quite enjoy the mortal realm as well."

"You are a man of taste then."

"Yes," he pauses, his eyes dipping to look at my lips before meeting my own again. "You could say that."

Goosebumps erupt on my skin.

* * *

"HAVING TROUBLE WITH YOUR WINE?" I grin, catching Dionysus off-guard as he sniffs and swirls his wine chalice with a displeased face.

He matches my grin with his own. "Ah, I did not hear you come in. You could surely aid me in my problem. I just imported this new wine from the Underworld, but it seems a bit sour for my liking. Perhaps it spoiled on its travels up here."

"I'll be the judge of that," I smirk, filling a chalice of my own. Dionysus watches me with an amused eye as I take a sip. I hide my grimace at the sheer acidity attacking my tongue. "Refreshing."

"I tried to warn you," he laughs, signaling one of his

servants over. "Take this to the chef. He should be able to make a salad dressing out of it. After all, it is vinegar now."

I'm still clutching my throat from the acidity of the spoiled wine when Dionysus offers me a glass of water and ushers me over to the couches. I chug nearly the entire glass until I no longer taste acid in my mouth.

"So, how have you been? It feels like ages since I've seen you."

"Oh, I've been fine, I suppose," I say, running my hands over my skirt-covered knees. "Hephaestus has spent more time in the mortal realm ever since the deal was struck between him and Ares."

Dionysus cuts me a look I know all too well. "I don't care about Hephaestus. How is Ares? Have you ridden him like a horse again yet?"

It's my turn to offer him a glare. "No. All I'm doing is helping him renovate his estate. The place is dreadful right now. Well, dreadful isn't quite the right word. It's actually very—"

"Enough with the story you're feeding everyone else in Olympus. What have you two been doing?" Dionysus presses with an eager look.

An annoyed huff leaves my lips, "I am not having an affair with him, Di. I am honoring my marriage just as Hephaestus is."

He sighs. "Fine. Then what is it that you and Ares do?"

"We talk," I admit, running the fabric of my gown's skirt in my hands.

"You talk?" Dionysus asks, doubt clear in his tone.

"You don't believe me?"

A joking smile pulls on his lips to take away the seriousness of his next words, "Aphrodite, you had sex with the man two years ago and the few times I've seen the two of you in a room together, he looks like he wants to fuck your brains out in front of everyone. Forgive me if I do not believe that the two of you only talk during your frequent meetings."

I stand from the couch, not wanting to be patronized any longer. "Well you're going to have to believe it because we haven't shared anything since that night two years ago. We talk and that is all. I talk and he listens because he wants to hear what I have to say. We have taken romance out of the equation and found friendship in its place. Now, if you'll excuse me, I'm going back to my estate."

I'm almost out of the drawing room when Dionysus finally speaks after my outburst, "What if Hephaestus found another lover? Would you allow yourself to be with Ares?"

I turn to him, not missing a beat as I say, "That'll never happen. Hephaestus would never have an affair."

Later in the evening I allow myself to play out the fantasy of what it would be like to be with Ares. But just like I told Dionysus, it will only ever be a fantasy because Hephaestus is even more duty-driven than I am. I toss and turn in my bed for what feels like hours before I finally decide to let my thoughts out in my journal.

Dear Journal,

I felt comfort for the first time since my marriage. And I am saddened to say it was not from my husband but from the sea. The sea outside of his estate reminds me of the one I find myself missing when loneliness wins and I remember I never felt lonely when I lived there. But I am beginning to think it was not only the sea but the owner of the estate in which I saw it from. He did not laugh when I said I missed the mortal realm like so many others do. He listens to me because he wants to know everything about me. And I can't help but admit to myself that I want to know everything about him as well.

CHAPTER 13

ARES

My days with Aphrodite have become rather routine. I work with Athena scouting trainees while Aphrodite works on redecorating my estate. When I'm done, I bring dinner back and we share a peaceful meal. Even though it may seem as monotonous as some mortal married couples, I look forward to each of our days as if it were something new.

"So, how are the refurbishments coming along?" I ask, spooning a mouthful of a new desert Kyra's bakery is selling. She calls it a cheesecake flavored with raspberry puree. Apparently she'd made it completely by accident but ended up liking it so much she started selling it.

Aphrodite nods with a mouthful of the dessert. "They are going well. I'm almost done with the bottom floor. I want to take my time with the second floor since those are where all of the bedrooms are. They should feel welcoming but still represent who we—excuse me, who you are as an Olympian."

I still at her brief use of *we*. I may not be able to have her to myself but by the gods, that brief moment in which it even sounded like I did was enough to suffice for now. "You are always welcome here. You know that. I hope you take me up on that offer."

"Yes." Aphrodite nods timidly and I can see the wheels turning in her head. "I must be getting back. Hephaestus is back in Olympus so I'm afraid this dinner was quite the risk."

"Aphrodite, wait," I stop her before she can make more than three steps from the table, grabbing hold of her hand in a gentle touch. I soon realize how bad of a decision that is because now I never want to let go. Her seafoam eyes find the spot where our hands are joined, and I see her breathing halt for the slightest moment. I meet those dazzling blue eyes with my own. "I didn't mean to scare you. I only meant that I would not have a place that feels like home if it weren't for you."

"You are very generous," she whispers while my eyes dip to her plush lips. I'm sure hers are on mine.

I lean forward, closing the distance between our lips little by little. I just want a taste. I've thought about that night in Cyprus almost every day since. I need her. She leans forward to meet me. Our lips are mere centimeters apart. Just a little bit more and I can finally have what I've been craving since I met her.

Aphrodite pulls back with a shark intake of breath and panic in her eyes, "I can't—"

My head hangs for a second. "I should have never—"

"No, you shouldn't have," Aphrodite snaps, wrapping her himation around her shoulders. "I am married to your brother."

Something in her sudden coldness ignites a flame of anger in me. "You leaned in too."

"It was a mistake! This cannot happen. We cannot happen. No matter how much temptation plays a role in our little arrangement. You agreed that we would just talk if that's what I wished. That has not changed. Our arrangement will only work if you remember that. Goodnight, Ares." Aphrodite still has fire in her eyes when she walks around me and toward the door.

Before I can even stop to think, I say, "Why are you so hellbent on honoring this marriage? Surely you know affairs happen all of the time. Especially amongst the Olympians that are married. Look at my father. He has them all of the time."

Aphrodite immediately stops in her tracks, turning to me with more fire in her eyes than I ever thought possible coming from her. "Because if I partake in this affair, I will prove everyone right. I will be everything they say I am. A whore. A slut. A homewrecker. You name it and I will be it. Do you want to know why I was married off to your brother?"

I stay silent when I notice a tear of anger falling down her cheek. I reach to wipe it, but she beats me to it.

"I was forced to marry your brother because people thought I was too tempting to remain unwed. Women started complaining that I was trying to seduce their husbands when all I did was walk down the street. Your mother was worried I would tempt your father into another affair, so she had me married off. I was forced into this situation because my powers radiate from me. People aren't attracted to me. They are simply feeling the effects of my powers. Even when I tried explaining that, it wasn't enough. Then one night your father cornered me at one of Dionysus's parties. Your mother gave me an ultimatum after that: marry your brother or spend the rest of my immortal life running from the Olympians, especially your father. Nothing was enough," Aphrodite whispers the last sentence with more tears streaming down her cheeks.

The sheer emotion on her face and behind her words show me a side of her I've yet to see. This is the true Aphrodite. The woman that has been betrayed by the very thing she is supposed to bring. That's why she's so concerned about her image as an Olympian. I'd give my mother a long talk about what she's done if it wouldn't raise suspicion, but I know it would. But just because Aphrodite has been dealt this unfair hand doesn't mean I can't help her find a way around it.

"What would happen if Hephaestus stepped out first? You would be viewed as the wronged party. Therefore no one would blame you for stepping out," I ask, feeling the wheels turn in my head. This could work.

She shakes her head with a huff. "It doesn't matter. That will never happen. Hephaestus will never step out on our marriage. He understands our duties more than anyone. So stop trying to figure out a way out of this. I have already accepted that I'm stuck in this for eternity. You should too."

I panic when she starts walking out, knowing that if she passes the threshold of my estate it will likely be the last time she visits. Before I can think better of it, the words slip from my tongue, "Hephaestus is having an affair!"

Aphrodite freezes mid-step. The fire that was just in her eyes turns to ash. "What?"

I walk closer when I'm sure she will not run from me. I stop just two steps in front of her. "Hephaestus is having an affair."

I watch the light extinguish in her eyes and I hate myself for being the one that has caused it. Her head begins to shake. "You're lying. You're just saying that so you can get what you want. Hephaestus may not love me, but he knows our duties. He wouldn't—"

"Aphrodite," I pause, placing a steadying hand on her shoulder. Her glassy eyes meet mine and I can only hope she can see the sincerity in my own. "I would never lie to you. Especially about this."

Silence rings between us and I'm sure she's ready to bolt until she finally speaks in a low methodical voice. "How do you know?"

I sigh, letting my thumb trace the soft skin on her arm, "Hebe told me after my first day at the training facility. I—"

"You've known for weeks?" Aphrodite snaps, backing out of my touch. "What were you just hoping that during all of our dinners I'd change my mind and let you fuck me again? While you knew that my husband was sleeping with another woman? I can't even look at you right now."

"Aphrodite, wait." I try to stop her, but she continues to

storm toward the front door. "I did not withhold it from you for those reasons!"

"Then why did you?" Aphrodite snaps through gritted teeth, turning on her heel and marching toward me until we're almost touching. I can feel her breath on my chest as she looks up at me with narrowed eyes.

My eyes close with a sigh, before I meet the storm that awaits me in hers. "I wanted to make sure it was true. I spied on the woman's house that Hebe claimed was the mistress. Each time you'd mention Hephaestus was in the mortal realm, I'd go there when you left. The first time he wasn't there. But the next two times I watched the house, he was there. I'm sorry. I should have never kept it from you. I just wanted to make sure—"

"Take me to her house."

I say nothing, simply gauging if her emotional state is well enough for what she asks.

"Ares, I said take me to her house. It is the least you can do. Or so help me, you will never see me again," she orders.

I nod stiffly. "Very well."

During our entire walk to the stable on the far end of my estate, Aphrodite is silent. I don't say anything, but I notice the way her fingers anxiously tap against each other at her sides.

"Why are we here? You are supposed to be taking me to the mortal realm," Aphrodite asks, looking around the stables I had custom made for my horses. My house may not be considered the best, but I made sure Althon, Phlogius, and Kanobos were provided with the best shelter for all of the work they do for me. Each of their stalls are the size of two normal horse stalls. I try to visit them once a day otherwise they get spiteful. A quality that much resembles myself I'm afraid.

"How else do you think I got to the mortal realm on my own? I can't just spawn there." I prompt, holding my hand out in the direction of my chariot.

Aphrodite walks forward, tracing her fingers along the gold detailing of one of my most prized possessions. I wouldn't be as successful as I am without my chariot or my horses for that matter. "I wasn't sure. To be completely honest I've never thought about it. I've never cared to wonder how people got out of Olympus because I was so sure I'd never leave."

Something in the brazen manner of her tone reveals to me just how trapped she truly feels here. I suppose I caught a glimpse of that feeling myself when my parents ordered me to stay in Olympus. But I always knew I'd be able to escape eventually. Aphrodite can't.

I'm so used to leaving in a rush, the horses are strapped in and I'm whispering my intent to go to the outskirts of Delphi in just under five minutes.

My horses take off in a sprint through the open stable doors but before we pass them, a gust of wind sweeps past us, and my skin starts to tingle. My horses slow their trot, eventually coming to a halt just outside of the temple the mortals have dedicated to me in the city. While I appreciate how quickly I'm able to get to the mortal realm, it would be nice if my horses were able to go to my exact location rather than the closest temple to my destination. But alas, all magic has to follow some form of checks and balances.

Even at night, the air of Delphi that surrounds us is warm and humid. I hop off of my chariot, extending a hand to help Aphrodite off. I want to chastise myself for the bolt of pure electricity that shoots through my hand when hers touches mine, but I decide against it. I've known we have a connection, but this is just bad timing.

"Where is her dwelling?" She asks with a clipped tone. I know Aphrodite doesn't love Hephaestus. So I also know her spiteful tone is not geared toward the woman we are going to see. No, this attitude is something deeper. Something unknown to me. But yet, I wish she will allow me to aid her through whatever the turmoil may be.

I point up the dirt road in front of us. "Just up here. You have a glamour, yes? It will be easier if no one can see us."

Aphrodite nods before closing her eyes and breathing deep. Goosebumps erupt on my skin and the hairs on my arm stand up so I know she's activated her glamor. I activate mine without another word and lead her forward with my hand in hers. I allow my thumb to trace her soft skin, hoping she will find it soothing in this troubling time.

We reach the house after a few short minutes, and a pit grows in my stomach. I wish I did not have to be the one to show her this. But if I didn't do it, no one would. And she deserves to know.

I search her blue eyes for a sign of hurt after seeing the house, but they are void of any emotion. "Are you sure you want to go in?"

Pure sincerity gleams from her, "Ares, I need to do this."

Without another word, I nod and lead her into what seems like an empty home. I'm sure it is the right house. I wouldn't forget something this important. "It appears the maiden must be off somewhere. We can come back another time if—"

"No," Aphrodite shakes her head, pacing around the room as if she's looking for something. "If this is the woman Hephaestus cares for, there will be something, a trinket perhaps, that proves he's been here. I don't need to see her."

"Very well," I nod, looking over the room with the same detail I do for a new battlefield. I hadn't come inside the last time I was here, but this is as much as I expected. Most of the home is just off to the side. It's not a very large home, but only those of great wealth can afford to live anywhere bigger than this.

While Aphrodite is searching the main part of the home, I grab one of the oil lamps and search the bedroom. There isn't much in here either. But I'm determined to find whatever is needed for proof. I don't want Aphrodite here any longer than she needs to be.

Just as I am about to give up on this room, a glimmer of gold catches my eye. I pick it up, not really knowing what it is. The first piece is shaped like some type of flower warped into a semi-circle. A second piece in the shape of a solid rod slides through to create some type of fasten. I almost set it back down until I see a small inscription on the stem that makes my stomach drop. *Agapi mou.*

I make my voice sound as calm as I can, "Aphrodite."

She turns to me with a questioning look before she sees the trinket in my outstretched hand. "Is this what you're looking for?"

She takes the clip from my hand without a word,

inspecting it with a careful eye. She hasn't seen the inscription yet and part of me hopes she never does. But that would be impossible.

Curiosity still fills me despite the anger my brother's stupidity has brought. "What is it?"

Aphrodite is silent for a moment, and I can see the exact moment she finds the inscription. Her eyes enlarge for half a second before something dark fills them. She takes a deep breath before meeting my eyes. "It's a hair pin. Almost identical to the one I was gifted by Hephaestus for our engagement. Only mine was a rose because he knew they were my favorite. This one is a fennel flower. Otherwise known as his favorite. Mine also didn't have a—"

She pauses and I swear I see her eyes become glassy. I take a step toward her but before I can get to her, she wipes the tear from her cheek and speaks, "I've seen enough. I want to go back to Olympus. Now."

CHAPTER 14

APHRODITE

Dear Journal,

I've played this scenario out in my head a thousand times. The ultimate what if? But I never thought it would become my reality. I was so sure that I didn't care about Hephaestus, and yet his betrayal has robbed me of something. I feel...like a fraud.

I walk down a lone corridor until I find Dionysus's library. It's my favorite room in his estate because the art he has hanging on the walls is exquisite.

I let the door click behind me then I take several deep breaths. The party going on behind me has grown sweltering with the mingling of bodies and the amount of people present. I wipe the bead of sweat from my brow and jump when the door opens behind me.

"There you are. I've been hunting you for hours."

"Zeus." I take a step back with unease clawing at me. Something about the look in his eyes is making all of my powers retreat, curling into a small ball like a frightened doe. "What a surprise. I didn't expect to see you here tonight."

He takes another calculated step towards me. "Oh? It seems like the only way I could see you."

"Why would you want to see me?" I take another step back. I jump again when my back meets a bookcase.

"Because you've been toying with me for too long." He cages me in against the bookcase. He leans in to press his lips against mine.

I turn away. "I can assure you, I haven't done any of that. You're married."

His lips press against my neck and it's never felt more foreign. "Don't try to deny it now. I've seen the way you act around me. Like you need to be properly fucked." He rips my peplos and panic starts to line my veins, claiming them one by one.

"Get off of me!" I shriek, clawing at his skin. All he does is grip my bare thigh, suffocating the flesh. "Stop!"

I'm seconds away from accepting my fate when a loud thud makes Zeus loosen his grip on my body. Zeus slumps on the floor between Dionysus and I.

Dionysus shakes his hand. "Are you okay? I saw Zeus slither out of the party room not long after you. This is why I never invite him."

Tears prick my eyes. All I can do is nod.

Dionysus steps over Zeus, engulfing me in his arms. He strokes *the back of my head and I cry silently. "I promise you he will never do that again if I'm around."*

It's amazing how a wound from one man opens wounds from another. I've done my best to forget about Zeus. It could have been a lot worse, and that should stand for something. But I still can't shake the dread that claws at me when that memory resurfaces.

My fifth glass of wine goes down like water. The past five days have been the same. Wake up and leave before Hephaestus awakens, drink wine until I almost can't see straight and wonder how I ended up here then sneak back into my estate once I'm sure Hephaestus is asleep

"Is everything alright?"

I set down my chalice, finding Orion's concerned eyes behind the bar. I push my cup forward, silently asking for a refill. "Of course, why wouldn't it be? I'm an Olympian and the Olympians' lives are perfect."

Orion pushes my glass back toward me without refilling it. "You've been drinking more. You only do that when something is troubling you. What has happened?"

My eyes narrow as my annoyance grows, "What has happened is that you're not doing your job. Now please give me another glass."

Orion takes my glass in his hand, placing it with the other dirty ones under the bar. "I'm afraid I can't do that."

"Why not?"

"Becuase I am the bartender and I get to decide when people are cut off. I will not let you drink yourself into oblivion another night. So you are cut off."

"Fine," I sigh, placing my money on the bar. "I will just have another glass at home."

Before I can take more than two steps Orion stops me. "I don't know what you're dealing with but I'm sure it will get better. Even if it doesn't seem like it now."

I pull the best appreciative smile on my face as I can, despite the pain the reminder of why I feel the way I do brings, "I can only hope you're right."

I waste no time pouring another glass of strong wine when I get home. I take a gulp as I draw closer to my bedchamber. It's empty when I enter but I can't help but feel relieved. I walk to my wardrobe, running my finger through the soft fabric of my night dresses.

"Where have you been?" Hephaestus's voice is filled with condescension from wherever he is behind me.

"Wouldn't you like to know," I scoff, continuing to examine my nightwear.

I hear a step behind me. "What was that?"

I stay silent, delighting in the fact that I'm drawing some emotion from him for once.

His next words are clipped, "Answer me."

I turn around, letting my own words drip with matching condescension. "I said wouldn't you like to know. Did you hear me clearly enough?"

Hephaestus's eyes narrow when I meet them, "What is that supposed to mean? I haven't seen you since I returned from the mortal realm. As my wife I should know where you are."

I roll my eyes, crossing my arms over my chest, "And where has it that you've been?"

"The mortal realm. You know that. I've been making the weapons for my brother as my father—"

"Do not lie to me," I snap. "I am your wife. Therefore I have a right to know. Where have you been?"

I see anger start to ignite in his eyes. "I have been in the mortal realm as I said. Do not turn this around on me. You have not been home in days. Need I remind you of your duty as my wife—"

"Oh, do not speak to me about marital duty. That is something you know nothing of," I chastise, reveling in this new wave of confidence.

"I know nothing of it? Do you care to know what one of my apprentices shared with me?" He prompts, not even waiting for me to respond before he continues with narrowed eyes. "He said that you've been at my brother's estate nearly every day for weeks. Now tell me, wife, how does that show marital duty? Because that surely looks suspicious to me. I should have known you would step out of our marriage. I was warned of your whorish ways before we were wed; having sex with any man that batted an eye at you. But I never thought you would betray me in such a way."

Anger boils deep within me. How dare he insinuate that I'm a whore. I have done nothing but be a faithful wife. "There is nothing going on between Ares and me. I am renovating his estate. The shop owners recommended my help when he seemed lost in his own efforts. I have never stepped out on our marriage. I meant my vows when I said them."

"You're lying."

"No," I laugh at the irony of our situation, turning to my jewelry holder. "But you are, *husband.*"

Silence rings out between us when I hold out the fennel flower pin. "I believe this belongs to *your beloved.*"

"Where did you get this?" Hephaestus's voice is dangerously low before he snatches the clip from my hand.

"Where do you think?" My eyes narrow to match his. He stays silent while his eyes bounce between mine and the clip. "And you say I know nothing of marital duty."

I turn back toward my wardrobe when I think Hephaestus is finally done speaking. But just before I reach it, he says, "How did you find out?"

"You're not as clever at hiding it as you think. You're fortunate the people that do know realize how important it is that our marriage upholds. And I am fortunate that they are kind enough to think I had a right to know."

"Ares told you." His name drips off of Hephaestus's tongue as if it were poison. "You do realize he likely only told you that because he wants to fuck you? It's what you're good at. Seems to be the only thing."

I slam my wine glass down on my bedside table so hard it shatters and stomp over to Hephaestus. "Oh and I suppose that is suitable for you to say since you have never tried to know me! You're only ever around me when you want to fuck me. Which I'm sure now was only to give your mother the grandchild she says she longs for."

"I did try," he tries to interrupt.

"No, you didn't. I tried! I learned all of your favorite things. I bring home your favorite dessert from the bakery even though they are my least favorite. I ask you to eat with me when you're in Olympus and yet you find a way to cancel every single time. I made a vow to myself that I would honor our marriage because you deserved that no matter how many people told me I shouldn't. Meanwhile, you've made me look like an utter fool for gods know—"

My words fall short when a sting of pain erupts on my cheek. "You will not speak to me like that."

I clutch the cheek that Hephaestus just struck. I can instantly see the regret spark in his eyes and yet there's still that monstrous level of anger lurking deeper within them. "Aphrodite, I'm so sorry. I—"

"This marriage is over," I say without another thought, putting much needed distance between us.

"What? Aphrodite, you know we cannot—"

I drop my hand, leveling him with a stare I don't think I've given to anyone else before. Furry at what my life has turned into clouds my eyes and all I see is red. "We cannot divorce but this marriage is over just the same. To the eyes of Olympus we are still married but we are done. You can live your life with your mistress, and I will alert you when you are needed up here. We will send away our servants here so that they will not know about your absence."

Hephaestus is silent for a moment, bracing his hands on his hips. Eventually he lets out a sigh, "What will you do then?"

I haven't thought of that yet, but the thought of freedom causes a bubble of hope to rise within me. "I don't know."

"Aphrodite, please do not go to him."

A scoff leaves my lips before I can stop it, "You lost the privilege to make requests on my actions. I will not do anything that makes either of us look bad."

"Aphrodite," Hephaestus pleads with a pained tone I've

never heard from him before. "Please, that is all I ask. You may choose anyone else. Just not him."

I stay silent for several moments and I know he is waiting for an answer, so I offer the smallest nod.

"Okay, I shall be going to the mortal realm then." Hephaestus seems as though he is in another place mentally as he slowly strolls through the door.

Just as I grab one of my nightgowns from my wardrobe, Hephaestus's now quiet voice sounds, "What will we do about the matter of producing a child. My mother will still expect it, and the city dwellers will start being suspicious if it does not happen soon."

My body freezes at the thought of him touching me again. But he's right. "I still don't know if our efforts last time were successful. Eileithyia says it can sometimes take months for us to find out compared to the mortals. But we may try again once you're back."

"Very well," he nods. "Goodbye, Aphrodite."

As soon as the door clicks shut a sputtering breath bursts from me and I clutch my hand to my lips. My eyes sting with the tears I've been trying to keep at bay, but now I can't get them to stop.

I walk to my mirror, seeing a bruise already grazing my cheekbone. The center of it is significantly darker than the rest. The clip must have still been in his hand. The sight of the new bruise causes a fresh wave of tears to burst from my eyes. Only now I can't seem to breathe. No matter how deep of a breath I try to take, it seems impossible to take an effi-cient breath.

A knock sounds on my door, "Goddess?"

My panicked eyes turn to meet Alexandra's as she peers through my door. Without another moment's notice she closes my door, rushing to my side.

"Oh, Aphrodite," she whispers, her hand reaching out to trace my bruised cheek. "What has happened?"

I shake my head, not ready to replay the events. "I will need— your bruise cream."

Alexandra nods, "It will not be ready until tomorrow, but I will bring it as soon as I can."

I nod, still finding it hard to stop my tears, "Is Hephaestus still here?"

A sympathetic look fills her eyes, "He just left."

"Then I need to leave. I can't be in this house tonight. I will be back in the morning for the cream." I insist. "Thank you, Alexandra."

"Of course," Alexandra dawns a small smile before I offer her the best one I can muster. Although I'm not sure how convincing it is with the rest of my puffy, tear-stricken face.

The darkness of the night aids me as I rush to the one place I've felt comforted since my arrival in this godsforsaken city. The streets are nearly deserted at this late hour which means I can walk as fast as I can without drawing attention to myself.

My breathing is somewhat back to normal by the time I reach my destination, but tears are still steady on my cheeks. The guards are gone which means I have to pound on the door. It feels like I'm pounding for hours. I almost give up before I finally hear the lock click.

Ares's shirtless frame opens the door with a startled look

that immediately relaxes when he notices it's me. "Aphrodite? What are you doing here?"

I turn to fully face him, now displaying my fresh bruise. Even in the darkness of the night, I can see something dark overcome him. Anger, no doubt.

"Ares," I say in a hoarse whisper.

His face softens and for a moment that darkness is gone, "Aphrodite."

I burst into a fresh set of tears when he pulls me flush against his warm chest. My unmarred cheek pressing against his skin and I'm enveloped by his balsam scent.

"What happened tonight?" Ares asks in a soothing voice. He rubs calming circles on my back as he engulfs me.

"I— I can't go back there," I mutter through sniffles.

Ares's arms tighten around me to bring me closer to him, "You will stay here with me then."

CHAPTER 15

ARES

It's been three days since Aphrodite stumbled onto my doorstep in tears. Three days of her staying here. And for those three days I've had to discipline myself more than ever.

The second I saw the screaming purple blemish on her cheek, it took everything in me not to scour every realm—Olympus, Mortal, and Underworld—until I found Hephaestus to tear him limb from limb. I continue to fight that urge every time I hear her sobs through the door. The only thing that stops me from it is how my brother's murder would affect my mother.

She waits until she thinks I'm asleep in the room across from hers but I'm a trained soldier. Every sound wakes me. Her cries are no exception.

Even now as I pace the corridor between our rooms, I fight myself not to storm in. She needs her own time to overcome this. I'm afraid I'll scare her off if I jump too soon.

I'm pulled from my endless stream of fruitless plans when the knob to her door turns and the creak of it fills the corridor. I wretch my eyes up, immediately schooling my disappointment when they find a set of brown ones.

"How is she?" I ask, my voice more strained than I expected it to sound.

Her maid's eyes gleam in some sort of sympathetic look. "She is doing better than she was. The cream I gave her has virtually removed the bruise, but she has a small cut that still needs to heal."

My jaw clenches and I take a deep breath, pushing my thoughts of murder away. "Has she eaten yet?"

Worry fills the brown eyes that face me, "I'm afraid not."

It is now my turn for worry to ebb its way into my veins. I sigh, "I see. Well, I cannot thank you enough for your help with all of this. I don't know what to do. I'm afraid everything I do will scare her off and the only place she has to run is that awful house."

A sympathetic smile pulls on the maid's lips, "She is a friend. I'm happy to help. Now, I must be going. She will not be happy to hear I'm lingering just because I'm worried about her."

I nod, "Very well. Have a good day."

The woman's steps echo in the silent corridor. I barely take a step myself before her voice sounds one last time, "One more thing, Ares."

"Yes?" I turn.

"She is much stronger than you think. I've seen her take on many troubles and I've seen her slowly dwindle since the beginning of her marriage. Even through all of that, the one thing she hates most is pity. Don't pity her and you may find a more resilient woman."

And then the maid is gone.

Something in the woman's words strikes something within me and it is as if the plan I've been trying to work out for days is staring me in the face.

I chase after Aphrodite's maid, catching her just as she reaches the gate to my estate's land. "Goddess! Goddess, wait!"

Curiosity mars the face of the brunette woman in front of me, "Yes?"

"May I ask for one more favor before you depart? It is for Aphrodite," I add, not knowing if she'd be willing to do something for me if she thought it was for me alone.

"Very well," she nods. "But if we are now on the terms of doing favors for one another, you may as well know my name. It is Alexandra."

"Pleasure to finally make your acquaintance." I nod. I may not be known for my manners, but if this woman is close with Aphrodite, I need to remain in her good graces, lest I risk scaring Aphrodite off.

Once I send Alexandra off, I rush to one of the last of my staff that I keep at my estate most days to complete my plan. It takes several moments but after I make sure everything is perfect, I storm into Aphrodite's room, not missing the dark circles under her eyes from her malnutrition.

"Ares," Aphrodite says with alarm, standing from her

mattress. Her gown fits looser than it did before. Yet another sign that she has not eaten since she arrived.

Without so much as a word, I sling her over my shoulder, holding tight to her legs so that she does not fall.

"Ares! What are you doing?" She protests, wiggling in my embrace to escape it.

"You will see when we get there." Is all I offer for solace.

"Put me down at once!"

I fight a laugh, only allowing a smirk to dawn my lips, "I'm afraid I can't do that, seductress."

I feel her huff of air more than I hear it, "You're impossible."

"Perhaps," I smirk, placing her down when we finally reach our destination. "But my being impossible is what's going to save you. Now, you are going to eat."

Aphrodite's eyes narrow before she finally realizes where we are. Her body immediately relaxes and I swear I see her ears perk up to the sounds of the waves just behind me. Her head drops, watching as she squishes her feet in the soft sand beneath us. Her eyes close and she takes a deep breath of the salty air that envelops us.

"Why are we here?" She asks, her voice almost mystified.

"Because—" I pause, holding back my grunt as I sit on a blanket covering the sand "you have said you are most at ease by the water. If you are at ease then you will be more inclined to eat. So eat."

She joins me on the blanket, separated only by the vast food spread between us. I had my cook whip up as much food as he could in such short notice. Her eyes stay fixed on the waves washing over the shore a few feet in front of us, "I am not hungry."

"You need to eat. You will not get any better without food."

"I do not need your sympathy," Aphrodite snaps.

There she is. Even if it was just a glimpse, my seductress is still in there somewhere. "I am not pitying you. I am not one to pity anyone. But I will not let you starve to death. You are already showing early signs of starvation. I will not let you waste away. Eat."

She remains silent, letting the sea breeze run through her hair. She still says nothing, and I suppose I should be surprised by her stubbornness yet I'm oddly not. "Aphrodite, so help me, if you do not eat. I will force feed you. We will not leave until you eat at least something. Even if that is a singular raspberry tart from Kyra's."

Her blue eyes whip to mine, "You got raspberry tarts from Kyra's?"

"They are your favorite. Are they not?" I ask, holding one for her to take.

For a singular second, a grin pulls at the corner of her lips. It was so fast that if you blinked you'd miss it. A sigh leaves her lips, "I suppose I can eat a few bites."

It is my turn for a grin to grace my face. Only mine lasts longer. "That is all I ask."

A breath of relief leaves me when Aphrodite finally takes a bite of a raspberry tart. Her hum of satisfaction intensifies my relieved feeling.

"If I am to eat then you should as well. It is only fair."

I eye her with a skeptical glance until she levels with a

daring stare. A breeze must have rushed over us because goosebumps erupt on my skin. I grab a fork from the napkin next to me, spearing the fish below me, before taking a bit. Various flavors of lemon and other seasonings burst on my tongue. I spear another piece, holding it out toward her, "Your turn."

She shakes her head, holding her lips tightly together.

I level her with a commanding stare, "Aphrodite, you need to eat something more than a pastry."

Her head shakes again, "I do not eat fish. I was born from the waves. I once considered the fish my friends. So–"

"You do not eat fish," I finish for her. Eating the bite myself, I move onto the various sides my chef prepared. "Very well, then you can eat the vegetables and potatoes then."

A defeated sigh fills the air between us, "As you wish."

A thankful grin pulls on my lips when she leans forward, allowing me to feed her the potato wedge on the fork. I take a bite of my own while handing her a fork of her own. "I would have brought wine out but I'm afraid you need water more than wine right now."

"That is fine. I think I've drunk enough wine for a life-time in the past two weeks." A note of sadness and something else is present in her voice but I can't quite put my finger on it.

I reach my hand out, resting it atop hers. I watch as her breath catches, and her eyes find where we touch before they meet my eyes. "You did what you thought you needed to do to get through that. What matters now is that you learn to move on from it. To heal from it because that pain won't go away on its own."

"Wise words from a soldier," she pauses, pondering. "How did you become so wise on overcoming obstacles?"

I look out over the waves, my jaw clenching and heart beating just a little faster. "I've lost many friends in my years as the god of war. It never gets easier."

"Does it not scare you? The thought of losing someone each time?" Aphrodite spears another potato. Her line of questions feels like a punch in the gut, but I will take it if it offers just enough distraction to make her eat.

"It terrifies me."

"So how do you do it?"

I shrug, not really knowing what else to do. "It's what I was made to do. I had to learn that if you can't beat fear, do it scared."

"Do it scared," she mimics. I look over, finding Aphrodite looking mystified at the ocean.

"Do it scared," I confirm. At that she looks back at me and grins the smallest grin. And for the first time in days, I truly believe she will be okay.

"WELL IF IT isn't my favorite brother."

I turn away from my balcony, already knowing who is behind me before I even see her, "Eileithyia, what are you doing here?"

"Can I not simply drop in for a visit? I thought we were

close enough for that." My sister dawns an expression that proves her offended tone is merely a facade.

I level her with my knowing stare, "Of course you can. In fact I wish you were around more. But you and I both know that our duties leave us with little free time."

"I'm afraid you're right. I do not have enough free time anymore. In fact, I'm traveling to the mortal realm now."

"How long will you be gone this time?" I ask, turning back to face the sea again.

"I'm not sure. A mortal woman is due with twins in the near future. That is a difficult labor as it is. But they are also father's twins and birthing a demi-god is even harder for mortal women than their regular babes." Eileithyia joins my side on the balcony, finding what—or rather whom—I've been staring at.

Collectively, our eyes watch Aphrodite, walking at a leisurely pace through the waves on the shoreline. Ever since our picnic on the beach a few days ago she's been eager to stay on the shore until she tires of it.

"I didn't realize she was here," Eileithyia breaks our silence, never letting her eyes leave Aphrodite in the distance.

My eyes do the same, silently thanking whoever will listen for letting her find something that gets her out of her bedchamber. "She's been staying here."

"What?" Eileithyia's alarmed eyes whip over to me. "Ares, have you gone mad? She cannot—"

"Stay in the estate she shares with Hephaestus," I finish for her before she can say that Aphrodite can't stay here with me.

"Don't be stupid. Hephaestus is her husband," Eileithyia warns.

"The same husband that beats her," I snap, feeling that dark anger ignite in me for the first time in days.

My sister suddenly cowers next to me, "I did not realize that he did that. If I had known—"

"She didn't want anyone to know. Just as she doesn't want anyone to know about Hephaestus's affair. She doesn't care if he continues it, she just doesn't want anyone in Olympus to find out."

"Hephaestus is having an affair?" Her eyes grow wide in shock.

I nod, "I thought Hebe would have told you by now. His mistress is mortal."

My sister shakes her head, "She said nothing. But that still doesn't answer why Aphrodite is staying with you."

"Were you not listening? Hephaestus has beaten her. That should be enough."

"And I believe it should be. But that does not change the fact that if someone finds out—if mother finds out—that will not be a good enough excuse."

I sigh, "The night she confronted him, he beat her again. She had a cut on her cheek and a large bruise. She was so shaken up she couldn't even breathe when she knocked at my door. Hephaestus decided to stay in the mortal realm and have Aphrodite alert him when he is needed here. The alliance of his weapon making for me allows a suitable enough cover for that. Both of us have sent all of our staff away. Well, I had none to begin with. Nonetheless, including you, there are only two people that know she is staying here."

Eileithyia is silent for several moments before she sighs, "At least she has found solace somewhere. Not everyone is granted such mercy. Now, I'm afraid I must be going. I will see you when I return, brother."

"I look forward to it," I grin, offering my sister a departing hug before she disappears back into my estate and through the grounds.

* * *

Sweat is still slick on my brow line when I clamber up my limestone stairs toward my bedchamber. I just finished my first training session in what feels like ages, but my muscles remember it like it was yesterday.

My estate is oddly quiet. Usually, I hear Aphrodite clambering with some decorations that came in that day or my chef fixing dinner before he leaves for the night. The room across from mine is ajar and I see candlelight peeking through the crack.

Allowing my curiosity to win out, I push the door open until I find Aphrodite straightening out a new set of linens on a bed I'm sure has never been used. The bright blue linen is the shade of Aphrodite's eyes and is trimmed with gold just like her hair. The furniture that finishes the room matches it with gold and white.

"Fancy seeing you in here," I smile when her eyes meet mine, fighting the shiver that threatens to spill on my skin.

Her hand smooths the last wrinkle on the bed before she walks closer to me, letting her eyes trace the new furnishings. "I wasn't planning on doing the bedrooms yet. But I figured if I would be staying here for an extended amount of time, I needed a place to sleep."

"A place to sleep," I repeat, an inquisitive tone leaving my lips, toying with her.

"Yes." She nods. "I cannot let you sleep on your couch anymore. You were already too generous to allow me to sleep in your bed for one night. Let alone as long as I have been."

I smirk, choosing to indulge her, "Well I thank you for giving me my bed back. However, that does not mean that you have to abandon it too."

Aphrodite freezes before she continues closing the blue and gold curtains on the other side of the room. "That is not necessary. I am a guest here. I shall take the guest room."

"If that is what you wish," I say, turning on my heel to walk out of the room. "I am going to bathe but we may share dinner when I'm done if you'd like."

"Yes, I'd like that," she smiles as I depart.

The sun has sunk well below the horizon a long time ago and yet Aphrodite and I can't seem to move from the outdoor couch we share on my balcony. We watched the sunset as we ate our dinner—a roast that is apparently Aphrodite's favorite—and now we've been watching the stars while sipping on my whiskey and her wine.

"So," I pause, tracing my fingers over Aphrodite's bare calves while she has her legs propped up on mine. "How have you been feeling?"

She finishes the last few steps of her wine, reaching forward to place the empty glass on the table in front of us before settling back down. "Much better since being here, I think. That house haunts me with memories of what has happened and how things should have been."

I continue circling soothing circles on her smooth legs, sometimes reaching higher on her thigh. "I'm happy that you've been able to become yourself again."

We sit in silence for a while, simply enjoying each other's company while watching the stars. It's weird. I've been a soldier my whole life, living a rather lonely life and yet I always felt content. Now, I sit in silence with someone I met not so long ago, and I can't think of anything else I'd rather do.

"I was thinking," I pause, twisting my fingers in my palm before placing them back on her calves. "I know you said you miss Cyprus and the animals. So, I thought that we could go on a day trip to visit. But only if you want to of course. I wouldn't want to—"

I cease talking when I realize Aphrodite is sound asleep at my side. Carefully, I remove her legs from mine before I scoop her in my arms. When I am sure she is still asleep, I carefully make my way back into my estate and up the stairs. I open the door to the room she set up for herself as quietly as I can. No matter how much I wish she was still sleeping in my room since it makes my sheets smell like her, she insisted that she sleep in here now. And I have to respect that.

Once I finally have her settled on the new bed, I take a moment to just look at her. She's been through so much since I met her, and even before that, and yet right now she looks more at peace than I've ever seen her. Her lips look plump and luscious. Her skin looks creamy in the little moonlight that spills through the curtains. And her hair looks like golden silk. She's perfect.

I brush a strand of hair behind her ear, placing a gentle kiss on her forehead, "Goodnight, seductress."

Before I can take more than three steps away, a hand reaches out, stopping me in my tracks. Soft fingers wrap around my own, and a voice just as soft fills the silent air around me, "Stay."

And just like that I realize I'd do anything for her.

CHAPTER 16

APHRODITE

Dear Journal,

Do you ever wish something isn't as good as you've made it out to be in your head? Yeah, me too. I was wrong. So so wrong. Now, I'm so fucked. Again.

The scent of balsam with hints of mahogany draws me from my sleep. It is remarkable how much his linens still smell like Ares despite the week and a half it's been since he's slept in them. I roll onto my back, deciding it is time to open my eyes. Only, instead of the crimson and gold I've come to be so familiar with in Ares's room, my eyes meet light blue—almost like that of shallow waters—and gold.

I'm not in his room.

A deep breath sputters next to me. I turn, finding Ares at my side. I should have noticed the arm across me, but when I am waking, it often takes me a few moments to gain recognition of everything.

Even sleeping, he oozes power and strength, and beams of sunlight break through the curtains onto him. His hair looks like flames. His brows, which I usually see creased in thought are relaxed. By the gods, this is the first time I've seen him calm.

When it is just us he is calmer than normal, but he still seems as through he is trying to solve a puzzle. And yet here he is, completely at ease by my side.

I place a gentle hand on his cheek and whisper, "Good morning, soldier."

And as if some cynical god is listening, I realize how right this feels and how wrong it is for it to feel right. Self-deprecation burrows in my gut.

I slowly crawl from the best sleep I've had in close to a year, praying that I do not wake Ares. I shouldn't be doing this.

I can't.

Ares has been generous in letting me stay here so long. But his generosity will end eventually, and I'd rather leave before it does. However, I will dignify him with a goodbye.

I leave the bedchamber as quietly as I can. I'm afraid my thoughts are loud enough to wake him.

The sun is bright through the house but once I reach the balcony, I see dark clouds creeping in. It won't be much longer before the clouds cover Olympus. Demeter is gracious in keeping Olympus in mostly fair weather, but we need showers every once in a while to keep the plants alive.

I eat a place of fresh fruit and eggs on the balcony before I return inside and take a seat on a plush couch in the drawing room while I wait for Ares to wake. In my boredom, I picked up a journal that accounts for the last war and Ares's role in it. Reading about how strong the man is who has let me put peonies in his home, I find him even more admirable considering how many mortals he helped save.

"There you are," Ares says, slowly approaching the couch.

"Here I am." I smile back, hiding any hint of my plan.

"I've been looking for you." He stops at the edge of the chair.

"Have you?" I ask, closing the journal in my lap.

A smile graces his face. "I want to show you something on the grounds."

"It is going to storm." I point to the dark clouds that cover the grounds.

"We will be done before it starts." He extends his hand toward me. "Come on."

I take his hand. "Very well."

We walk out onto the vast grounds. Even after there is no need for me to hold onto Ares, I can't seem to let go. It's as if my soul wants to cling to him until the very last moment.

"Over there I plan to build an outdoor training ring. Not as sophisticated as the one we train recruits in but it will suffice for my personal training," Ares points to an open area between the estate and a set of trees. "Over there—" he points closer to where the stables are "—I will have an indoor training ring built."

"Two training rings? My, you must be quite rusty since the last war." I giggle.

He levels me with a joking glare. "Someone has to be big and strong to protect you and the mortals."

That same sinking feeling from earlier returns, and I stop walking. "Ares?"

"Yes?" He stops, his brows form that same crease I've come to know means he's worried.

"I…" I brush my hand over my hair. "I'm leaving. You've been generous but—"

"You can't." He shakes his head.

"Ares… I have to."

"Where will you go?" He eyes me fiercely.

"I will go back to my estate," I admit.

His hands brace his hips. My eyes stay on his when I notice the way his muscles flex. "You said last night that place is nothing but a reminder of the pain you've been through. Why would you go back? Of all places."

"I don't know, but I can't stay here. I will stay with Dionysus if I can't handle my estate, but I can't stay," I ramble, feeling as though each word I say is putting another nail in the coffin that is us.

"Why?" His voice raises, but not in anger.

"Because!" I shout, but I can't tell him the truth.

Before I can make an excuse, the sky falls out and pours onto us. I'm soaked from head to toe within seconds.

"Follow me. We can take shelter in the stables," Ares shouts over the rain.

"Why can't we go back to the house?"

"Because the stables are closer." He extends a hand toward me.

I shake my head, knowing what his touch does to me. "Ares."

"Would you quit being difficult for one minute? We can continue this conversation once we are under shelter," he says.

I take his hand and sprint to the stables. We're soaked to bone.

"You can't leave." Ares holds my elbows while I hold his biceps. My torso is a mere centimeter from touching him.

Being this close to him makes it harder to breathe. "I must."

"Why? Give me one good reason, and I will let you go without another argument," he pleads.

I take a step back. "Because this is too dangerous for us. We cannot stay in such close proximity. I will stay with someone else."

He takes the smallest step closer, and I match that with a step back until I hit one of the stalls. "I have heard you say that we shouldn't do this because you were married to my brother. That has ended. So if that was an excuse, and you simply never cared for me, then leave. I know you worry about your ruin."

"Ares—"

"But I have never heard you say you do not care for me. I have felt a connection to you since I met you. I've always been drawn to you. I stopped eating fish because of you for the gods' sakes.

"Say you do not care for me, and I will let you walk out

that door, no questions asked." Ares closes the gap, and I'm forced to look and meet his eyes.

My breathing is shallow, and I feel that magnetism I felt in Cyprus. It's always there when he's around, but I feel it stronger than ever now. "Ares."

"Say it, Aphrodite," he orders as his hand snakes around the back of my neck to pull me closer. Our torsos are flush. I can feel his heart beating rapidly in his chest, matching my own.

Our lips are centimeters apart at this point and yet my eyes stay transfixed on his, "I can't."

Before I can take another breath, it is stolen by Ares. He kisses me so fervently that it feels as though my legs are made of water.

He works his fingers through my pinned-up hair, and it falls in seconds. His tongue pushes past the barrier of my lips and invades my mouth. I gasp while his knee forces its way between my legs, letting his thigh settle against me.

I roll my hips forward on his thigh, only for him to grab the small of my back and pull me toward him.

His lips taste like transgressions. But if this is what being unrighteous feels like, then I'll gladly fall from grace.

I roll my hips, desperate for friction. He dips and presses his lips to my neck. I throw my head back, and when his tongue licks a strip on my skin, I rasp, "Yes."

Ares separates from me. The absence of his body against mine feels cold. His eyes look almost black with desire. His lips are swollen as I'm sure mine are.

"Hold on," he warns.

Before I can respond, Ares grabs my legs and hoists them

around his waist. Then his mouth returns to my neck, and he walks us toward his chariot. He sets me on the small seat-like ledge in it, squeezing my thigh.

A low moan rumbles in my throat when his calloused fingers run up my bare thigh, higher and higher. I hold tighter to his shoulders when his fingers find the ache I've been desperate to relieve between my legs. "Gods, seductress, you're soaked. I knew you felt the spark between us, but not how much."

He gathers the liquid with his fingers while watching me like a hunter who found big game.

I can't stop my moan when he pushes two fingers inside. He drags them in and out, only curving them when he's fully inside to play with that spot that only makes me slicker.

"Look at you, making a mess on my fingers," he teases, removing them completely. I meet his dark eyes.

I've felt desire plenty of times, witnessed it even more, and yet I have never felt it as strong as this. "Ares, do not tease me."

His smirk grows. "Oh? But I thought that's what you liked. After all, it is all you've done to me since we met."

I look at the little space between us and see just how much he wants me. I level him with a playful stare as I move my hand between us to cup his larger-than-I-remembered cock and move my hand up and down with a firm grip—just once.

He sputters before he regains his composure.

"Is that what I've been doing? Teasing you?"

I move my hand two more times when he doesn't answer me. His voice tightens. "Aphrodite."

"Ares," I return seductively, moving my hand again.

"By the gods," he says it like a curse, then he moves my hand away and hitches my skirts to my waist.

He moves so quickly I don't even see him remove his breeches. But I feel it when he runs his hard dick against me because a whimper escapes me at the friction. He does it a few more times and I crack.

"Ares, I need you," I whine, feeling overcome with need for him. I am ravenous, overcome by my need to be filled.

"Finally, you admit it," he says before entering me, which is slow at first until he's fully seated within me.

We gasp when his hips meet mine. I've never felt so full and yet I still feel as if I need every part of him. I inch my lips forward to meet his.

As if my kiss ignites something within him, his hips retreat and push forward with more force than the first time. I moan at his forceful entry. He retreats again, only to come back in harder and faster than before.

My mouth falls open and my head drops back. "Oh gods."

"I will be the only god you remember when I'm done with you," he purrs while pulling the top of my gown down. He takes the hardened peaks of my breasts into his mouth while he drills his hips into me.

His tongue laps over the hardened peak before his teeth scrape it, inducing chills all over my body. My right hand pulls at his fiery locks while my left claws down his back. The grunt that leaves his throat vibrates against me.

Just when I think I can't feel any more pleasure, his lips return to mine and his finger circles my clit while he speeds up his thrusts. The only sound that can be heard is the mingling of our moans and the obscene smacking of flesh against flesh.

The pressure low in my belly builds at an alarming rate. I feel it blossoming and spreading from where he rubs my clit. Each time he drives into me, he rubs that perfect spot inside me, and it has me on the cusp.

"Ares," I whine against his lips.

His eyes meet mine, and I can see his desire shining in them. "Your mouth says you want to leave, but the way your pussy is suffocating my cock says otherwise."

My mouth falls open when he nails me with a hard thrust. I am teetering on the edge of snapping. "Ares, I'm going to—"

The pressure snaps when he bites my bottom lip. He continues thrusting, riding out my orgasm until he finds his own, groaning my name.

I sag against him and see stars. Sweat clings to our skin, and we are silent for what feels like ages, simply gaining composure. Once we've both calmed our breathing, he lifts my chin until I meet his eyes.

"That"—he places a chaste kiss on my lips—"is why you can't leave."

CHAPTER 17

ARES

It was painful to leave Aphrodite's side this morning. She looked perfect sleeping. I fought the part of me that wanted to wake her up by trailing my lips down her soft skin until she let me greet her good morning with my tongue. If I didn't have to meet with my mother, I would've. The past three weeks have been nothing but sex and love.

And now, I'm cursing myself for thinking about all the ways I can pleasure Aphrodite when I get back before I meet my mother.

Someone clears their throat, drawing my attention from the filthy images in my mind. The same man that greeted me the first time I met with my parents stands a few paces away.

He looks slightly more muscular and tanner than when I last saw him.

"Forgive me, but I do not think I caught your name the last time we met," I say.

"I'm Hermes, sir," he says with a polite nod. "I'm one of the Olympians. I was sworn in when you were away."

I internally roll my eyes at how my father has instructed him to behave. "I see. Please, you do not need to use such formalities with me. We are equal rank."

"Very well," he says. "She is ready for you know."

I nod in thanks, then walk toward the new throne room. "Thank you."

I am surprised when I find my mother inspecting flowers along the wall of the thrones rather than sitting on her throne. "Mother."

She does a double take before she realizes which of her children is greeting her. "Ares, I'm so glad you made it."

"You requested to see me," I add, although I pair it with a playful grin so she knows I'm not bothered.

Her light-brown eyes narrow. "You used to love spending time with me. Of course, when you finally learned what a sword was, that became your favorite pastime."

"And now I am the strongest warrior in all realms," I remind her.

My mother sighs. "Yes, very well."

"Are those new flowers?" I ask, pointing to the bundles she was inspecting.

"Lotus flowers. Demeter delivered them. I suppose she's still sucking up after the affair she had with your father."

"Mother," I warn.

"I know, I know. He very well forces most of them, but that does not take the sting away."

"I know." I place my hand on her forearm to let her know I support her. "Where is the man we speak of anyway? It is unlike him to not be meddling with something here."

My mother walks away from the flowers, stopping in the middle of the room. "Demeter insisted he visit Persephone. This is the second time he's seen the baby since she was born, so I do not blame her. Oh, but I did not ask you here to talk about your father's newest child."

"Then why did you?" I ask. My mother can be very charismatic when she wants to be.

"Hades is hosting a solstice ball in the Underworld. We are not usually invited because he doesn't like your father. However, we are trying to form an alliance and therefore, have received an invitation."

I hope she does not mean what I think she does. "I'm failing to understand how I fit into a ball."

Her chin lifts the slightest bit and she suddenly looks every bit the queen she is. "You are to attend on the Olympians behalf."

I sigh, "Mother—"

"I am not finished," she warns. "You will attend with Aphrodite at your side. The two of you are the newest members of the Olympians and therefore should be given your first task. You will do well to remember you represent an institution that has been in place since the fall of the titans. If the two of you do well, you may seal the alliance for us."

I suddenly don't feel so queasy anymore at the idea. "I see."

"So you agree?" my mother asks, leveling me with a stare that makes me think I don't have much of a choice. I think a getaway to the Underworld with Aphrodite would be rather pleasing. The thought of her causes my mind to replay the sound of her moans. The way she feels against me— "Ares."

I clear my throat, ridding my mind of the dirty images again. "Why do we need an alliance with Hades? He controls a different realm. One we never interact with, might I add."

My mother sighs. "Your father wants our institution to be impenetrable. By uniting with Hades, the Olympians will have control over our realm, the mortals, the sea, and the Underworld. So, will you do it?"

Ah, so it's all just a power move for my father. He wants Hades in the palm of his hand the same way Poseidon is. That won't stop Aphrodite and I from having a secluded weekend away from Olympus though. My cock goes half-hard at the thought of all the nasty things I can do to her. "I suppose."

"Wonderful." My mother smiles. "You two will leave in seven days."

I leave my mother at the Mount and make my way to the training ring. Athena is already there and polishing weapons when I arrive. A few recruits stand along the wall chatting.

"Ares, I was beginning to think I would not see you today," Athena jests while laying out the last sword in line with the others.

"You know as well as I do, they need what we have planned for them. Being one of my personally selected soldiers has gotten to their heads. They need to learn their lesson," I say, but I do not look at Athena. Instead, I stare at the relaxed nature of what will someday be my ranks.

"They are getting cocky. I will fix that." Athena looks as if she's hatched a master plan.

"What do you mean 'you?" My brows scrunch.

"They are too comfortable thinking they have a guaranteed spot in your army. We need something to show them their weaknesses. And what better way to humble an arrogant man than a woman who is stronger than them." The look in her eyes looks downright sadistic.

"Do your worst," I encourage.

"Ares, my worst would simply be unfair." She saunters toward the middle of the ring.

"Everyone, listen up."

Her voice booms, and the recruits are silent against the wall. The training facility hasn't been expanded yet, but the roof has at least been removed to provide the openness I wanted.

Athena paces in front of the line. "Each of you will be completing a new task designed to test you to your limit."

"The room's a little small for that, don't you think," one of the recruits shouts.

My eyes narrow but before I can say anything, Athena says, "Since you're so sure you know what the task is, come to the center of the ring. Now."

The other recruits—a mix of lower gods and demi-gods—look around as if they think her orders are comical, but the one that spoke walks forward. Athena was right. They're getting too cocky.

"Grab a sword," Athena orders, already holding hers.

"Why?" the recruit asks, his brown eyebrows scrunching.

She levels him with a stare, "Because we are going to spar."

He chuckles, "What, me and you? I'm not fighting you. You're a woman."

He looks back at me but I level him with the same glare Athena does. "Ready your sword, soldier. She gave you a command."

His face flushes when I do not grant him assistance. In silence, he grabs a sword, walking back to the center of the ring where Athena stands ready. The other recruits eye the pair skeptically, but I can see they find it amusing that Athena believes she will win.

"I will go easy on you," the recruit half-teases.

"That will not be necessary. Though, I will go easy on you."

"That will not be necessary," he mocks.

Athena grins devilishly. "Very well."

Athena swings her sword wide, nearly landing a killing shot right then and there. The recruit ducked at the last possible second.

With each swing of their swords, I watch the recruits reactions at Athena's strength. Underestimations like that will lead to their deaths if they don't fix it.

The fight is almost comical. With each maneuver of Athena's sword, my soldier is forced lower and lower to the ground. In as little as five motions, Athena is able to disarm my recruit and land what would be a killing shot.

"So," she says through light pants, "still think you don't need to improve?"

"Perhaps you should have gone easy on him," another recruit jokes from the wall. The others chuckle.

Athena turns, no longer paying any mind to the man she beat. Instead, she gives the rest of the recruits a calm and collected stare. "That *was* me going easy on him."

Their laughs silence, and I see the moment they realize how much of a threat Athena is. This is what they needed. Humbling them is the only way to get them to train hard enough to become the soldiers I need them to be.

A malicious smile pulls on my lips as I walk to her side. "Who's next?"

CHAPTER 18

APHRODITE

Dear Journal,

The past several weeks have been better than I've ever had in Olympus. I've felt alive for the first time since I moved here. Something in his touch just sets me on fire. I'm like a moth to a flame, waiting for everything to burn up around me. My powers have never felt stronger. I've never felt more me. And I have him to thank for that.

I'd be lying if I said my heart didn't leap when Hera told me I'd be going to the Underworld with Ares. From what I've heard of the Underworld, its inhabitants don't keep up with the day to day affairs of the Olympians. That means Ares and I can just be us. No hiding—afraid of whispers that might erupt. Just us. My stomach flutters with butterflies at the idea.

But Hera made it perfectly clear her expectations for our behavior. We are to act and dress our best to represent who the Olympians truly are. I fought a giggle when Hera said that no matter how little we know of each other, Ares and I were to act as close friends. "The closer our members appear, the stronger we will be perceived," were her exact words.

"Goddess?"

My eyes refocus, snapping me back into the modiste's, "Yes?"

"I noticed a small run in a piece of fabric down here. That will be another thing for me to fix before your dress is delivered. But do not worry, it will be done before you leave for the ball."

"That sounds perfect. I'm sorry for my lack of attention today. I've been worried about the ball," I offer.

The modiste meets my eye in the mirror. "Well with this dress, you will certainly be the belle of the ball. It is a pity Hephaestus won't be in attendance. I'm sure he would want to rip all of my careful work from you until they are tatters on the floor."

My hands run over the soft fabric on my hips, and I meet my own eyes in the mirror. The corner of my lips lift slightly. "A pity indeed."

✳ ✳ ✳

I PLACE the fresh bundle of flowers I purchased in a vase, ridding it of the old ones before I find Ares on the balcony, watching the sun sink.

I saunter over when he meets my eye. "What are you doing out here all alone? Surely, you could get a maiden to keep you company."

A smile dawns on his face. "And yet, the only company I want spent the day away from me."

Before I can object, he lifts me, placing me on his lap bridal style and plants a chaste kiss on me. "I missed you, seductress."

I plant another kiss on his mouth, this one gentler than his had been. "I was only gone a few hours."

He gives me a playful stare. "You were gone for most of the day."

"I had my last fitting at the modiste for the gown I'm wearing to Hades's solstice ball. Besides, what is it that you think I do when you spend all day at the training facility?" I challenge, looping my arms around his neck.

He squeezes the side of my thigh. The calluses on his palms burn through the fabric of my gown, feeling deliciously rough on my skin. "Long for the moment I get home?"

I roll my eyes and push off his chest to stand. I make it barely an inch before Ares's hand encloses my own, and I'm flush against his chest again. "I'm only joking. You mentioned a new dress?"

"I did." I ignore the way his hand grazes my arm.

"May I see it?"

I shake my head.

"Will you tell me about it?"

I shake my head again.

"You won't even oblige me in the smallest of details?"

I ponder his question for a moment, allowing a wicked grin to line my lips. "I believe tatters were mentioned…"

His eyes grow a shade darker, and his hand tightens on my thigh. "Anything else?"

"Nope."

"You cruel, cruel woman."

I inch closer, hovering over his lips. "You love when I'm cruel."

"I can't deny that," he whispers before seizing my lips in a searing kiss.

* * *

I HAVE an extra pep in my step as I walk into the Muses. It's surprisingly empty for this time of day. But that doesn't stop just the person I wanted to see from sitting at the bar.

"I knew I'd find you here." I plop in the seat next to Dionysus. I don't even have to tell Orion what I want before he has the glass poured and in front of me.

"Am I that predictable?" Dionysus quirks a brow.

We each take a pull of our wine before I offer, "Great minds just think alike I suppose."

"You seem extra chipper today."

"Have you heard about my most recent task for the Olympians?"

Dionysus takes a long pull of wine. "Mhmm, so you were selected for the Underworld ball. Last I heard Zeus and Hera were looking for two Olympians to represent us. Who's your partner?"

"Ares." I smirk.

Dionysus's eyes go wide. He sets his wine glass down, looks around, then leans closer to me. "I don't know who I have to thank for that arrangement, but I pray to any higher gods than us that you two finally fuck. The two of you ooze sex whenever you're in a room together."

"About that." I hide my mischief behind my wine glass.

He chokes on his drink. "You're joking."

I shake my head.

His eyes brighten. "Aphrodite, you dirty dog. Was it good?"

I clench my thighs at the memory of the way Ares worshipped my body just before this. "The best in my life."

"Can I watch next time?"

I hit Dionysus's arm, laughing as I start to feel the wine's effects. "In your dreams."

"Damn straight it is."

CHAPTER 19

APHRODITE

Dear Journal,

Something about the darkness the Underworld exudes brings out the darkness within me. It makes my desire carnal. It makes me want to play with him the same way he's toyed with me. And yet, even our games only make my love for him grow stronger. Something about his predatory claim over me drives me wild. I've always wanted someone to care for me the way he does.

The air is cold when Ares's chariot stops in the courtyard of Hades's acropolis.

Well, what should be an acropolis.

I'm not entirely sure what you'd call Hades's manor. It looks far grander, or rather, more official than an acropolis.

I lean into Ares, feeling as though I need to whisper for some odd reason. "Why is his manor so different from all of ours?"

His tan shoulders shrug. "Hades is known for his flair. I'm not sure I've ever seen a building like this though."

The dark arches and sharp edges of the building make it feel more uninviting than I could have imagined. I take a deep breath, fighting the urge to grab hold of Ares's hand. "Well, best not keep the man waiting."

I feel the calluses on his palm reach for mine before they pull back. Ares must feel the same urges I find myself fighting. "And into battle we go."

I hug my himation closer, trying my best to shelter myself from the cool air without covering my peplos. Appearance is everything. Midnight-colored carpet covers the stone beneath our feet, stretching across the steps leading up to the doors. I take each step one at a time, holding my chin high like I've seen Hera do dozens of times. I keep my eyes level, not letting them cower when we pass the guards that line the sides of the steps.

The closer we get to the top of the stairs, the more the nervous bubble in my gut grows. I can't mess this up. Our alliance hangs in the balance of how well Ares and I charm Hades.

I put on the best smile I can when I notice Hades standing at the doors.

"Well, well… I was wondering when my brother's puppets would arrive," Hades purrs. His shoulder length dark hair is slicked back. His skin is pale compared to Ares's. The hair on his face is short and well kept. I've heard rumors from some women in Olympus of his numerous love affairs. I'd be lying if I said I didn't see the appeal.

"Hades," Ares greets him with a somewhat friendly smile, but something is strained in it. "It has been a while."

"Indeed it has, nephew." Silence fills the gap between us while he and Ares hold a strained stare for a few seconds. It's not a secret that Hades has no blood relation to Ares. Zeus and Hades don't even share blood. They are bound by their relation to Poseidon—who shares a parent with each of them. The three just call each other brothers to set themselves apart from the rest of the gods and goddess.

Hades's claim of Ares doesn't negate my attention. Something is happening here and I want to know what. But before I try to introduce myself to break the tension, Hades dons a devilish smile. "And you must be Aphrodite, the goddess of love I've heard so much about."

"All good things I hope," I say, not fighting it when Hades grabs my hand and places a gentle kiss on the top of it.

He meets my eyes with his dark, almost black irises. "Marvelous things."

Ares clears his throat. "I was told you would provide a place for us to sleep tonight after the ball."

Hades drops my hand and straightens. He rivals Ares in height. "Of course. I will have my guard, Leon, take you to your rooms. I am sure the goddess would appreciate more time to get ready. The festivities will start in a few hours."

"Thank you for your kind hospitality, Hades," I remark as I follow the guard through the corridors. The same midnight shade of carpet covers the interior floors. The gray stone walls stretch high, forming an arch in the ceiling.

The sound of metal clanging on metal draws my attention away from ogling the strange architecture. The sword our guard wears at his hip clangs against the metal armor on his thigh. I see Ares making note of the same thing when I cast a glance at him. He's probably already made note of every exit.

The guard with tight dark curls makes an abrupt stop in front of us. His golden eyes look as though they shine against this dark skin. "This is your suite, Goddess. Ares, yours is the next door over. If you have any trouble, let me know."

"Thank you, Leon," Ares says before the guard leaves us.

"Do you know him?" I ask, watching him leave.

"We've crossed paths. It was long before I was forced to stay in Olympus," Ares clarifies, snapping back into focus and opening my suite door. "Shall we?"

"You do not need to follow me. You have your own suite to inspect," I tease.

When we enter, I run my hand over a gold-plated chair.

"I will, *after* I make sure your room is free of traps," he says, already inspecting every drawer and wardrobe.

I sit on the bed as I wait for him to finish his ministrations. The mattress feels amazingly plush beneath me, so I run my hand over the soft silky fabric. The burgundy color of the silks match my peplos. "Do you think Hades would set a trap for us when he is in the process of forming an alliance with us?"

"I've seen men fall to their deaths with similar set ups," he admits absentmindedly while searching the bathroom. He walks back out seconds later, looking satisfied.

"No traps?" I tease.

"No traps. I need to go check my room. Don't move until I get back."

The door clicks, and I flop onto the mattress. I shut my eyes, taking a few calming breaths to fully relax in the odd quietness before I need to get ready for the ball.

My limbs relax more with each breath that I take. I almost drift into a peaceful slumber but my door bursts open, drawing a shriek from me.

"What the hell are you doing?" I shout, clutching my chest to soothe my rapid heart. I stand.

Ares stands with his hands on his hips. "It appears we have adjoining rooms."

"You don't say."

"Interesting choice of arrangements on Hades's part. I would have thought he'd want to separate us."

"And why is that?" I ask, sitting back down now that my heart rate has returned to normal.

"The further we are apart, the weaker we are." Ares turns back to me after his eyes trace the intricate gold details on the ceiling.

"You are not weak, Ares."

His sun-ripened honey eyes meet mine, and I swear something mischievous flashes in them. He stalks over to me like that of a predator closing in on its prey. "Maybe not to others…"

"Not to anyone," I correct, leaning back as he cages me in.

"That is where you're wrong, seductress," he whispers,

then places a strategic kiss under my neck. "You make me weak. But I'd never be strong again if it meant I could always be in your presence."

Shivers run down my spine after he places another kiss under my chin, then on it before his eyes meet mine. His eyes have darkened since the last time, as I'm sure mine have. I trace his stubbled jaw. "Then be weak."

Ares seizes my lips. I melt into his touch, feeling my self-control slipping more by the second. I rake my hand through his fiery hair, pulling at the root ever so gently. His calloused hands glide across me with ease, almost as if my touch sets him ablaze, as his does to me. Before I realize it, the hem of my gown is being pushed higher, creeping to meet my waist.

"Ares," I gasp.

He traces the bare skin of my thigh, inching higher. "Yes, seductress?"

"We—" Another gasp leaves my lips when his fingers ghost around the pooling ache between my legs. My body yearns for his touch, but we can't here. "We have to get ready for the ball."

"We have hours," he whispers, his warm breath covering my chest before his lips meet my neck again.

"We have two hours."

"And?"

"Ares." I push at his shoulders. "I need to get ready. You may not need that long, but I do."

He sighs and his head drops. "Very well. I will leave you to your womanly duties."

I place a chaste kiss on him before wiggling from beneath

him. "I will see you when I'm ready. Now go before you distract me anymore."

"As you wish."

Almost exactly two hours later, I clasp the last gold chain around my waist and ensure it is tight enough to hold my peplos to me. The white fabric drapes off of each of my shoulders, pooling low on my back to leave the rest of the skin on my back exposed. A slit runs up my left thigh, just high enough to remain tasteful. I fasten the top half of my hair with a golden laurel leaf pin Hephaestus made me ages ago. I step into my shoes right as a knock sounds on my door.

"It's open." I know it's Ares without even looking up from fastening my second sandal because the door clicked open before I was done speaking. "You are incapable of staying away, aren't you?"

"I wanted to give you something before we go downstairs." I hear footsteps closing in on me from behind. When I stand, I meet Ares's golden eyes in the mirror.

"And what might that be?"

"Something that represents who you are." I narrow my eyes at his evasiveness.

Ares brings a dainty gold chain around my head. "Hold your hair for me."

I do as he says, my breath catching when his fingers brush my spine through the open-back of my gown. Goosebumps erupt on my skin when he places a warm kiss in the same spot he'd just touched.

Releasing my hair, I lift the dainty chain."An opal?"

He wraps his arms around my waist and leans down to

rest his chin on my shoulder. "It's more for the stone that rests above it. The aquamarine reminded me of your eyes. They were the first thing I fell in love with.

You bare your soul in those eyes. The second I saw them, I was ensnared."

I place my hands over his, which is still wrapped around me. "It's beautiful."

His arms tighten around me, and they remind me what genuine love feels like when it blossoms in my chest. "It has nothing on you."

I smile and turn in his arms to face him. "I don't know what I did to deserve you."

"You deserve so much better. I'm afraid I'm too selfish to let you have that though, " he whispers, kissing my forehead while his thumb rubs soothing circles on the back of my neck. "Now, shall we be going?"

"We should."

Each corridor is lit with candles, leading guests from wherever they are coming from toward the ballroom. Ares and I walk with arms linked, hoping it portrays a unified front rather than romance. Luckily for us, those two can overlap here without drawing much suspicion, if we play our cards right.

My fingers tighten on his muscled biceps when we finally reach the crowd waiting to enter the event. Partygoers of all sorts form a line, each talking and laughing amongst themselves before it is their turn to enter.

"Breathe, seductress. Everything is going to work out," Ares whispers. His breath tickles my ear with each word.

"How can you be so sure?"

His arm tightens around mine in a reassuring squeeze. "Because Hades is strategic. He would not invite us if he wasn't already planning on agreeing to the alliance. Olympus is my father's kingdom, but this is Hades's home."

"Ares, there you are. I've been looking for you." Leon closes in on us from the other side of the corridor. "It is almost time for the two of you to be announced."

"We have to be announced?" I ask. From the stories I've heard about Hades's ego, I would have suspected he wouldn't want to draw any attention away from himself.

Leon leads us up a small set of stairs to a large door with a small line in front of it. The loud chatter of partygoers fills my ears each time the doors open for a new guest announcement. "You are here to represent the Olympians, of course you have to be announced. Hades has all high-ranking members of his court introduced at his high-profile events."

"Is that a new badge?" Ares asks, pointing to a golden pin on Leon's black chiton.

A proud smile fills his face. "A lot has changed since the last time we saw you. I'm head guard now."

A strange, vacant look crosses Ares's expression. "Indeed it has. Congratulations. You earned that rank."

Leon offers one more smile before turning around and heading toward the door. He gives the two guards working the doors a nod before the rush of talking and music fills our ears long enough for him to cross the threshold.

"I thought you said you've met him only in passing," I say, meeting Ares's eyes with my own confused look.

"It has been a long time since we have seen each other. I

will fill you in when we get back to Olympus," Ares whispers before it is our turn to walk through the doors.

The light of a thousand candles meets us when we walk onto the grand staircase at the entrance of the ballroom. Hundreds of guests dance and talk on the floor below.

A single man in the corner of the balcony waits for us to take a few more steps before his voice echoes through the stone room. "Ladies and gentlemen, representing the Olympians for the evening, the god of war and goddess of love, Ares and Aphrodite."

A hush falls over the crowd. All eyes find us. I practically hear Hera warning us of what will happen if we fail tonight.

I take a deep breath and hold my chin high before I whisper to Ares in the lowest voice I can, "Let the games begin."

CHAPTER 20

ARES

Eyes track our every move down the stone steps from the balcony into the ballroom. Some scowl, others track the woman at my side with wonder-filled eyes. I don't have to look to know Aphrodite is smiling at each individual she passes, looking every bit the leading goddess she is.

The hungry stares of men and even some women does not escape me. This is what Aphrodite was telling me about. Her power oozes from her, drawing nearly everyone in. My stomach twists when I remember that is the very reason my mother married her to Hephaestus.

Her fingers tighten around me, hidden by the himation she has wrapped around her arms. Aphrodite schools her face well, but I know her enough to see the worry in her eyes and the small crease in her brows.

I run my hand soothingly over her back. "You're not what my mother implied. Everything is okay. We are in control of our lives."

Her icy-blue eyes whip toward mine. "How did you know—"

"You squeezed my arm around the same time I noticed the intense stares of Hades's guests. It does not take a genius to know where your mind went."

Her eyes soften and her lips purse. But before anything can happen, the booming voice of the announcer pulls our attention from each other and toward the balcony as Hades makes his debut. A man with pale skin and even paler hair, almost like that of ice, hands the two of us goblets of wine.

Hades smiles when he casts his gaze over the large crowd. He grabs a goblet of wine. "Here we are again my friends. This is a night I look forward to every year. A night where we can come together and celebrate our success and unity. And tonight, we celebrate the growth of that unity.

"Too long we have been at odds with the Olympians. We have suffered and lost. But through this alliance, we may never suffer and never lose again. So please join me in giving our two Olympians a warm welcome. To Ares and Aphrodite."

"Ares and Aphrodite," the crowd echoes, raising their glasses in a toast.

At once, the string music begins again and guests take to the floor. She doesn't notice it, but I stare at Aphrodite watching the couples with a smile on her lips. Her eyes are bright like the Aegean when the sun first shines on it. If it weren't for my role as war general, I would allow my smile to shine.

The first song ends, and I extend my hand to her. "Care to dance, seductress?"

Her ice-blue eyes melt. "Absolutely, soldi—"

"Ah, just the goddess I was looking for." Hades glides through the crowd as if he's floating on ice. "Aphrodite, it would be my pleasure if you would honor me with your first dance of the evening."

Something dark and fiery ignites at the way his eyes devour Aphrodite. I know that stare because I do it all the time. It's hard not to when I can see her eyes darken just looking at me.

The dark fire grows stronger when her hand slips from my arm and she reaches for Hades's extended hand. "The honor would be mine."

Hades shoots me a wink before turning with Aphrodite on his arm. I have to ball my hand into a fist so tight I feel my nails carving crescents in my palm just so I don't wring his damn neck. I'm sure my mother wouldn't like that very much. No matter how much I might.

* * *

HADES HAS DANCED with Aphrodite for the past four songs. With each song, his hands have drifted lower and lower, until they've now reached the top of her ass.

He meets my stare with a smirk across the ballroom, winking before the song's final commencement. He bows, then kisses her hand before another man asks to cut in. Aphrodite smiles at him and envy whispers dangerous things in my mind. Things I'm sure would make the average person cower.

Hades offers me a glass of dark liquid. "So, Ares, how are you liking the ball? I haven't seen you take to the dance floor yet." I down the contents of the glass without asking what it is. To my surprise, a well-aged whiskey meets my tongue and not the dreadful drink used for the toast.

"We appreciate your invite. I'm sure Zeus and Hera are eager to finalize your alliance negotiations," I say, placing my empty glass on a tray but not before asking the waiter for another.

"Yes, I'm sure." He nods. "Those negotiations will take place in the coming weeks. After all, I am a very busy man. Speaking of busy, I hear you're living in Olympus permanently instead of gallivanting around the mortal realm."

My jaw clenches. Both at Hades inquiring about my new living arrangement and at the man dancing with Aphrodite. His hand has slipped the same way Hades's had. But this time, Aphrodite doesn't mask her unease. My fist tightens around my fresh glass of whiskey. "You've heard correctly. It was time I accepted my role as an Olympian. Something you will join me in soon, oddly enough."

"It's insurance, my friend. But with eye candy like that to look forward too, I may be eager to sign the alliance treaty tonight." Hades looks at Aphrodite before looking at me. The devious look in his eyes tells me he's baiting me to get anything out of me.

I take a deep breath, recollecting my thoughts from

murder to more civilized conversation. "I'm afraid she is no longer on the market, *my friend*."

His smirk turns feline. "That never stopped me before. Besides, are you telling me you've settled down with a woman? I heard she is wedded to your brother, Hephaestus. Unless I'm mistaken?"

My thoughts of murder shift from victimizing Hades to victimizing my brother. "You are not mistaken. Aphrodite is married to my brother."

"Pity." Hades tuts. "I'm sure she's an animal in the bedroom. The perfect little brat."

"I would advise you not to talk about her like that. She is—"

"Your sister-in-law," Hades interrupts. "Enjoy the ball, Ares. There are plenty of women to pick from if you get bored."

I down my whiskey with one quick pull, then down the second one that Hades ordered but never drank. Gods, I forgot how much Hades enjoys getting under people's skin. He's a master at tormenting people. That's why he's the ruler of the Underworld.

I get ready to interrupt Aphrodite's dance with the random man when a familiar head of brown hair catches my eye. "Eiliethyia? What are you doing here?"

"Oh, hello, Brother." My sister stops. She's wearing a cobalt blue peplos adorned with silver, jewel-encrusted detailing. Her hair is pinned with the same silver embellishments as her peplos.

"What are you doing here?" I ask again. "I thought it was just me and Aphrodite representing the Olympians?"

"It is." She looks over her shoulder as if trying to find someone. "I was invited. I aid deliveries in Hades's court, so he invited me."

"Do Mother and Father know you are here?"

"Of course not," she retorts. "They do not need to know my every move. And I would appreciate it if you do not tell them about it."

"I won't. I thought you were going to the mortal realm."

"I am, but I wanted to attend the ball first. I'm leaving after the ball is over." Her eyes focus on something behind me. "Sorry, I must be going. Tell Aphrodite hello for me." Before I can say goodbye, my sister is gone into the crowd.

Thankfully, my talk with her led us to the end of the current song, allowing me to interrupt Aphrodite and her new dance partner. Although I don't give a damn about being rude, I know Aphrodite does. The once smug looking man who is touching Aphrodite starts to look scared as I approach. *Just how I want him.*

"Aphrodite, do you mind if I speak with you? It's an urgent Olympian matter," I ask, placing a gentle hand on her shoulder but never breaking eye contact with her dance partner.

"Yes, of course. Perhaps you should ask her for a dance." Aphrodite points to a lone woman on the edge of the dance floor with a gentle smile. Her previous dance partner offers his thanks then bids us goodbye.

I guide Aphrodite out of the ballroom with my hand on the small of her back. Simply touching her soft skin makes me more at ease than I had been before. *My seductress.*

"Ares, is everything alright? What has happened?" she asks as we turn down an empty corridor.

"Nothing," I mutter before grabbing both of her cheeks and slamming my lips against hers. Her lips sync with mine, and it causes ichor to rush straight to my cock.

Hell, I've been half-hard since I first saw her in her gown. Her slit goes just high enough to let my imagination run wild without showing anything. It's downright provocative. I make a mental note to personally thank her modiste when we get back.

She moans into my mouth when I meet her tongue with mine. "Ares."

"Yes, seductress?" I kiss the outline of her chin, then the shell of her ear, then her neck.

"Ares, not here." She lets out a puff of air when I repeat the process on the other side. "There's too many people who could see us."

"You're right. We can't do it here." Her eyes are a shade darker from lust. Without warning, I hoist her over my shoulder, and jog to our rooms.

"Ares! Are you mad? This will draw even more attention."

"Relax, darling," I say, smacking her ass that's perched on my shoulder before finally putting her down. "We're at our rooms. We need not worry about someone finding us."

She looks down the deserted corridor before she turns her gaze on me and smirks devilishly. "Good."

Aphrodite snakes her hand down her waist and unhooks the gold chain that fastens her dress. Her peplos opens down her middle. My mouth waters at the hint of her breasts subtly peeking through, and the sliver of her pussy that shines. My cock hardens so much it almost hurts.

"What's the matter, soldier?" she teases while turning the doorknob behind her and disappearing behind the door. I let out a silent curse before following and locking the door behind me.

"You have been playing a dangerous game, seductress." I stalk over to where she's stopped in front of the bed.

"Have I?" She arches her brows, pulling the left strap of her peplos down in one languid movement.

I pull her into my chest by the small of her back. I suck on the soft skin beneath her ear. A whimper leaves hers. "You've been teasing me with all of these other men, letting them touch you the way I touch you."

She gasps when my hand coasts down the open slit of her peplos. "Did seeing me dance with another man make you jealous? Watching Hades's hands drift lower and lower on me?"

A flame of anger ignites at the memory of Hades, but I extinguish it because she was only playing her part. And now, she's using it to get me riled up. Maybe Hades was right. Maybe she is the perfect brat. Damn that bastard.

I run my fingers through her silky hair until I get to the roots, then I pull them until her head jerks back. "You have no idea the violent things I wanted to do to him for touching you. You're mine."

Aphrodite smiles and my cock twitches. "Prove it, soldier."

I rip the peplos from her and hoist her legs around my

hips. I groan at how delicate she feels against me. A juxtaposition to me in every way.

"That was my favorite peplos," she whines against my mouth.

"Your modiste said it would end up in tatters, did she not?" I lay her on the bed gently before kissing my way down her body.

"That does not mean I wanted it in actual tatters."

"I will take it to the modiste myself, if I have to. Quit worrying about the damn gown and let me tongue fuck you."

Aphrodite doesn't have time to utter a word before I lick a long strip up the slit of her pussy. Her back arches and she moans. I map both her thighs with kisses. And circle back with a gentle kiss on her clit before taking it between my lips and giving it a harsh suck.

"Ares—"

"That's right, seductress. Let them hear how I pleasure you."

I lick another long strip before delving my tongue into her pussy. She squirms at the intrusion, but I steady her hips. Her moans get louder and more frequent. I tongue fuck her until she's on the cusp of coming. Then I remove my tongue.

"Ares." She huffs. "Don't tease me."

"I'm just getting started. By the time I'm done with you, the mortals will be envious of the way I've worshipped you."

CHAPTER 21

I haven't been able to sleep. I've been plagued by my thoughts all night. Nothing about mine and Aphrodite's relationship is fair. She's been patronized by my family since she moved to Olympus. I can't help but wonder how different everything would be if I had just been there. I could have saved her from all of it. Our love wouldn't be whispers in abandoned corridors, it would be loud—they way she *should* be loved.

"Obol for your thoughts?" Aphrodite asks, then kisses my chest.

"Good morning, seductress?" I kiss her forehead before looking back at the window. "I was wishing last night could be how all of our days are."

She shivers and I pull her closer. "What? Fucking me until I shake?"

"No, but that would be a plus." I grin, but it falls after a second. It's still a shock when such vulgarity comes from her perfect mouth. "I mean us being us. No masks, no hiding. You and me together."

She frowns when I look down at her. But it is vanquished just as fast as my grin. "We knew what we were getting into when we started this, Ares. I think that's something that makes it beautiful. Our love is not for others to see, but a promise between us. By removing the outside expectation, we are left with the only thing that truly matters, our love."

All I can do is stare at her. Some emotion I can't quite pinpoint takes hold of me—and maybe that's okay. "You're right."

Her body visibly sags and light returns to her eyes. "I usually am."

"You tease me."

"I seem to recall a certain soldier teasing me all night last night."

I shift and nip at her skin on her neck. "Hmm, I do not recall such a thing. Are you sure it wasn't one of your fantasies?"

"No, I'm quite positive," she says, but her voice comes out breathier than earlier.

Tugging her naked body against me, I nip at her skin again. "How did it start?"

"Well, you kissed the length of my body—"she gasps when I start doing it again.

"And then?" I trace her thighs with kisses. Each one makes her pussy glisten more and more in the moonlight. She tries to clench her thighs, but I hold them open.

"You—" she huffs when I blow cool air over her wet pussy. My cock pulses at the sound. "You feasted on me."

I look up at her grinning like a devil. "Good girl."

And then, I feast.

* * *

I welcome the warmth of Olympus air when my chariot pulls into my stables. I take Aithon and Konabos to their stalls with ease. When I walk out of Aithon's stall, I find Aphrodite running her hand over Phlogius's mane. Phlogius leans into her arm, letting his eyes close.

"He likes you," I say, running my hand down Phlogious's mane before he, too, is guided into his respective stall.

"How so?"

"Phlogius is my most aggressive horse. He doesn't like other people." I pet the horse one more time before kissing between his eyes and giving him a carrot like I did the rest of them.

She smiles. "Well, I appreciate it, Phlogius."

The horse huffs again, and we both chuckle. I wrap my arms around her shoulder and guide us out of the stables and back toward my estate.

She begins to lay her head against my shoulder but stops when I remove my arm. My skin feels cold in the absence of her touch. I squint. "Is that Hebe?"

She looks up to find Hebe running at us frantically. I take

off to meet my sister in the middle. Aphrodite runs some-where behind me, but not quite fast enough.

Hebe is already rambling and out of breath when we meet in the middle of my field. "Ares, you have to—"

"Hebe." I grab her shoulders. Alarm bells ring in my head. I've never seen Hebe act like this. She's always the calmest of my siblings. "You have to breathe. What has happened?"

"Eileithyia is in trouble! Mother told her not to help the delivery of twins in the mortal realm, but she did anyway. Now, Mother has her imprisoned somewhere in the mortal realm."

Fire ignites and I ball my fists so tight I'm sure my nails have cut crescents into my palms. "She did what?"

"I heard her talking with her maid about Eileithyia being locked in an iron cage inside a cave. She never said where though," Hebe continues.

"Hebe, where is our mother at this moment?" I say through my clenched jaw.

Most people in Olympus, even myself, loath my father's egotistical ways. But most don't realize that my mother can be worse when pushed hard enough.

"She's at home. She's planning some sort of dinner for father tonight. Ares, you have to save Eileithyia!"

"I will, but first I have to interrogate our mother to find out where she's at." I turn toward Aphrodite, and I'm surprised at the worry in her eyes. I never thought she was close to Eileithyia. "Wait here. You're coming with me when I figure out where she is."

She nods without hesitation. "I was going to go whether you liked it or not."

"I'm going too," Hebe insists.

I turn toward her, shaking my head. "Hebe, you've only been to the mortal realm once. I would be too worried about you to focus on finding Eileithyia."

"I am not a child, Ares. Eileithyia is my sister too, and she is in trouble. I am coming. Besides, I will stay and keep Aphrodite company when you go to Mother."

I sigh. Being the god of war, I have to know when to pick my battles. Fortunately for Hebe, this is a battle I know I would lose. "Very well. Stay with Aphrodite until I get back from visiting mother."

* * *

I MAKE it to my mother and father's estate in record time.

I shoot each guard one look, which makes them cower and move from the threshold. I burst through the door, letting the wooden door slam against the stone walls.

I hear my mother's voice wafting from the direction of her sunroom. "Zeus, I have told you a million times not to take your anger out on the house!"

"Hello, mother," I say.

"Oh, Ares." Hera smooths her peplos. "What are you doing here?"

"What am I doing here?" My anger turns into a blaze. "Where is Eileithyia?"

Her demeanor slips, and I see a sliver of darkness grow in my mother's eyes. "She was acting out, so I punished her."

"Punished her? Hebe says you've locked her in a cage!"

"I warned her not to aid the birth of those twins."

178

My fists tighten again as my mother waters her lotus plant. "You are her mother! Have you no shame?"

My mother stiffens, then gazes out of the window. She tends to her lotus flowers again. "I think it's the opposite of shame, really. I am trying to save this family from more scandal."

"How does imprisoning your daughter—an Olympian— avoid scandal?" I ask. My brain hurts trying to figure out my mother's logic.

"Because," she snaps. She stomps over to me and prods at my chest with her finger. "Your father has created too many illegitimate children. They threaten the strength of this family. We do not need any more. Persephone was bad enough."

"You cannot punish Eileithyia for doing her duty. It is not her fault father is unfaithful."

"I don't give a damn! I told her not to go, and she did anyway. I am your mother. You all will listen to me!" Mother shouts, her anger draws tears to her eyes. "We are supposed to be a family."

Something cracks within me because I see a glimpse of what might have become Aphrodite's future if I had not come to live in Olympus. She would have been drawn into the same madness my mother has fallen into. "Mother, we *are* your family. Your children—including Eileithyia—care about you. Even if father does not."

A tear cascades down her cheek, and I pull her into my arms. My mother sobs in my arms, and all I can do is hold her. Growing up, my mother was a symbol of sanctity and togetherness. "Where is Eileithyia?"

Hera pulls away from me, wiping the tears from her cheeks. "She is in a cave in Cyprus. I don't know which one specifically."

At that, I bid my mother a goodbye and head back to Aphrodite and Hebe.

CHAPTER 22

APHRODITE

Ares arrives with fire in his eyes. "Get in the chariot. We're going to Cyprus."

Hebe and I walk as fast as we can to catch up with Ares. "Mother told you where she was?"

"No." He guides us into his chariot. "But she told me which city. Fortunately for us, I saved the King of Cyprus's life not so long ago. He should be willing to let us stay with him until I find Eileithyia. I'll turn the whole island upside down to find her if I have to."

The humid night air of Cyprus kisses my skin as the chariot comes to a halt on a random side street in the heart of the city. The laughter of its inhabitants wafts in my ears from neighboring roads. Ares takes turns helping us out of his chariot before turning his horses loose and telling them when to return.

"How are we supposed to get to the King? Last I remember, mortal kings have a lot of guards," I whisper, though I'm not sure why. It feels like we're doing something wrong and yet all we're doing is walking down the street.

"Relax, seduc—Aphrodtie." A blush creeps up on my cheeks at the near-slip of my nickname. I don't know how much Hebe or Eileithyia know, but I would like to keep them ignorant, if possible. "We are within the bounds of his palace. I am the reason they won the war, and that was quite recently. If he were anything like me, or the old me, he will still be celebrating."

Ares leads us through a limestone archway, which takes us into the palace. I'm rather shocked at how easy it was to enter, but perhaps Ares knew which entrance to use.

"Ah, here we are." He turns back to us and holds the unlocked door open, waiting for me and his sister to pass the threshold. Music and voices fill the room at an alarming volume when we enter.

Hundreds of men who look like they just walked off the battlefield line the room. Almost all of them are entertained by women who look rather bashful in front of them.

Another blush covers my cheeks and a tendril of heat fills my belly when I notice a man and two women being rather lewd in the corner. It brings a memory of Ares and I last night and the heat intensifies.

"Is that…" A man with dark brown hair and a matching beard pauses. His well-sewn ice-blue chiton is adorned with many war medals. "It is! Ares!"

"Alexander." Ares claps the man on his back.

"What are you doing here? I thought you'd be off saving more mortals," Alexander says with an appreciative grin.

"A god needs his rest too." Ares extends his arm to show me and Hebe behind him. "Alexander, meet my sister Hebe, and Aphrodite. Mind if we join you in your celebrations?"

"Your majesty." Hebe curtsies to show her respect for the mortal king. I do the same.

"*The* Aphrodite? We are in for a treat tonight. You must meet my wife." Alexander calls his wife over. She has equally dark hair and an exquisite peplos that stretches over her swollen belly.

"You've been busy since the war, Alexander. Congratulations." Ares smiles before shaking the Queen's hand.

"Cressida, and thank you, Ares. I cannot possibly show how thankful I am for saving my husband." The woman rubs an idle hand on her belly.

"Do you have a name?" I ask with a smile. *Oh how I long for the connection I can feel between Cressida and her child.*

"Alec, if it is a boy. Cora, if it is a girl."

My longing intensifies. "Both are lovely."

King Alexander hands each of us a glass of spirits before turning to Ares. "How long will you be in town?"

My breath hitches at the way Ares's throat works as he

sips the liquid. "A few days. I need to retrieve my other sister and then we will be on our way."

"You must stay here," Cressida insists. "We have plenty of spare rooms. We've yet to accept any guests overnight since the war, aside from my nephew, of course. We are eager for new company."

"Then we shall stay here." Ares shakes King Alexander's hand.

"How many rooms will you need? Two? Three?" Alexander asks.

Ares looks at me, then at Hebe. He winks before answering, "Three is fine. One for each of us."

Hebe has long been distracted by someone far off, so she does not notice her brother's hand snake around my back. Ares pulls me in to him, letting me know he has no intention of using the third room. My powers ignite the longer I look at Hebe. A tether grows between her and someone in the ballroom. I look to see who has her so transfixed and that tether snaps into place when he finds her. Love.

I lean closer to her, breaking away from her brother's hold. "You should go speak to him."

Her face scrunches and she whispers back. "But he's a mortal. I have no business falling for a mortal."

"One conversation won't hurt." I nudge her side.

Hebe doesn't take her eyes off of the man across the room. "I will find my way to my room later."

I watch Hebe walk to him and clasp my hands in front of me. Warmth spreads in my chest as the tether I feel between them strengthens.

"Very well. I shall lead you to your rooms so you know where they are when you're ready to stop the party." Alexander smirks suggestively before guiding Ares and I through his palace.

CHAPTER 23

APHRODITE

Dear Journal,

I may have lost control in Cyprus...but it wasn't my fault. It's been so long since I've physically interacted with the mortals. My basin shelter's negativity in favor of mortals who need me at that moment. It's been too long since I've been in the mortal realm. Today was proof enough. I just hope no one finds out about this incident.

"How do you know when two people will be a good match for one another?" Hebe asks as we stroll through the streets of Cyprus. Ares said he was spending the day trying to find Eiliethyia. So that left the two of us to our own devices. The air has the same salty humidity that I remember from living here. It clings to my skin like a lover's embrace.

I shrug. "You have powers. Yes?"

She nods, her light brown hair is slicked into a smooth updo against her neck. "Yes, but my power of restoring youth is quite selective. Someone has to do something great for me to grant them eternal youth."

I ponder how our powers differ. "I suppose the way we assess people is similar. I get a feeling when love has finally found them or is coming. I feel it in my body. If they need aid to secure it, I give them a little push. But I ultimately decide how I will help them."

Her lips purse. "Yes, but how do you know they are right for one another? How do you know that love is not fleeting?"

"I don't." I look over to find her slightly displeased so I say, "You never know if love is permanent. In fact, love takes more work to maintain than anything people experience, mortal or immortal. It changes with the seasons. You have to be willing to weather the storms with your partner."

Hebe focuses on the street ahead of us, keeping an extra keen eye of the couples that pass us.

"Is there a reason you're so interested in my powers?" I already know the answer without asking. That tether I felt snap into place for her and the gentleman at Alexander's party has only strengthened. Usually, that means the love will last.

"I—" she sighs. "I believe I've met someone. Although I'm sure you already know that."

I nod. "Yes, I felt as much. Is it the man from Alexander's party?"

A blush creeps up her neck and cheeks. "Yes. His name is Cassander. He's Cressida's nephew."

"Ah, a man of nobility, I see. Seems you are quite attracted to men of power," I tease.

A new spark of electricity starts to warm my hand. It reaches for the man I'm currently passing. My fingers graze his linens without him ever noticing my touch. My fingers heat again as a woman shopping at the fruit stand across from us comes into view. I lead Hebe in her direction. My fingers graze her linens the same as I did for the gentleman before. I pick up a fruit to hide my grin when my hand cools. Soon enough, they will meet.

"I am not attracted to his power. I am far more powerful as a goddess than he is as a future mortal king, even if I'm not an Olympian."

"Ah, but you are attracted to him," I say in a sing-song voice.

Hebe blushes again, this time with wide eyes. She quickly schools her expression the same way I've seen Hera do a hundred times. It must run in the family. "Even so. He's a mortal. I don't see how I could ever love a mortal. It's like asking to have my heart broken."

I guide Hebe back onto the street after I'm satisfied in my efforts to match the mortal couple up. Even with her excuses, the tether of her love does not waver. "Hebe, you have the power to restore his youth over and over again."

Something somber takes hold of her. "That may be, but it won't save him from some freak accident. Mortals perish so much easier than us. I don't think I could put my love into something to have it ripped away from me like that."

"Your fear is admirable. It's a sign that you have a big heart." I loop my arm with hers, patting it while we walk back towards the palace. "But a word of advice? You can't go into love deciding how it's going to end before it's even begun. Love is a journey, not a destination."

The somberness that had taken hold of Hebe dissipates and a light returns to her. "A journey," she echos.

We walk in silence for the rest of our journey towards the palace, simply taking in the beauty of the city. Gods, I've missed this place. I've felt more at home here with Ares and Hebe in the past two days than I have in the last year in Olympus. I hate that it took Eileithyia's capture to get me here, but I needed this trip.

My own love for my home city engulfs me like a hug, soothing me like sleep to the freezing. But that warmth is extinguished when we pass the temple the mortals have dedicated to me. Outside of it, a group of women block the entrance. They shout indecencies and my blood starts to boil.

"Aphrodite is no goddess worth worshipping!" One woman shouts.

Another follows her. "The worship of Aphrodite will lead you nowhere!"

"She's not a real goddess!" A final one says.

Hebe eyes me carefully, alarm clear in her eyes. My jaw hardens in time with my fists clenching. All I see is red. I walk up to them without another thought in my mind. Hebe attempts to grab me but I break free of her with ease.

"What has the Goddess done to you to make you deny her divinity?" I ask.

The first woman that spoke scoffs. "My husband left me for another woman. If there truly was a goddess of love, that shouldn't have happened."

"I've never been married. I've tried to worship her, and yet nothing has worked." The second one adds.

"It's the same for me," the third and final one agrees.

I scowl. "The Goddess cannot prevent you from being with the wrong person. You have free will to go against any of the God's wishes. Whose to say you haven't done that?"

The first woman grimaces. "What are you, some sort of Aphrodite-sympathizer? She's not worth it. Don't waste your time worshipping a Goddess who can't do anything more than have sex with anyone she comes across."

My entire body starts to vibrate. Hebe tries to grab me again, urging me to leave. I take my half-glamor off. It's easier when dealing with the mortals to mask my full divinity but right now they need to know who they're talking to. The crowd that had gathered around us gasps. The women in front of me grow pale.

"I *am* Aphrodite."

The first woman, who was confident in her assessment of my duties, starts rambling. "Goddess, I do not mean—"

"You meant exactly what you said," I snarl. My eyes narrow. "Since all three of you are so sure you know my duties and my powers, I have a gift for you. You believe all I do is bed anyone I come across, so now that is all you will do.

"You will never know love. Your hearts will grow cold as the men of Cyprus take you to bed again and again. As they grow colder, they'll also grow harder, until you're nothing but stone."

They try to plead with me but I silence them. The curse is already set. As the curse filters out of my body to cover each of them, I feel lightness return to me.

I turn to Hebe with a relieved smile to find her with shock-ridden eyes. She's looking at me like I've gone mad. I grab her arm, looping it with mine as it had been before we ran into the women. "Shall we be heading back to the palace? I believe you must find Cassander."

CHAPTER 24

ARES

"So tell me, Ares, how has life been treating you since the war?" Alexander, asks, placing his glass of bourbon next to him. He'd found me wandering the corridors and offered me a drink. Who am I to turn down a free drink? I'd also been looking for him, so I can find Eileithyia.

"I can't complain, Alex." I take a pull from my glass.

"Has the god of war finally decided to put an end to his promiscuous ways?"

I look over to find Alexander grinning smugly. I roll my eyes. "You were quite promiscuous the last time I saw you, Alexander. Don't act all high and mighty now.

"Tell me, how long have you and your wife been together? I can't imagine you came home from war as the new king only to get married right away."

"No need to act, Ares." He chuckles before he says, "I did get married rather quickly. Cressida and I grew up together. It took almost losing my life for me to realize I wanted to spend every last second of my life with her. That's who I was writing to the night you saved me. I regret admitting it took such an extreme, but that's behind me. I have a beautiful wife who is giving me my first child in a few short months."

"She is lucky to have a husband who cares. Many are not so lucky," I say as something dark stirs in me at the thought of my brother mistreating Aphrodite or how my father treats my mother.

"Yes, well… Despite your murderous ways, I'm sure you would rather die than join those who mistreat their wife. It was you, after all, who told me character makes a good soldier, not strength."

"I'm wise." I lift my amber glass to my lips and down the rest of its contents.

"I can't thank you enough for saving me. That woman was…well inhumane. Have you ever seen a woman murder that many men so quickly?"

I hate to admit it, but I shiver as I recall the night I saved Alexander. The fighting had slowed, so most of the men had gone back to their camps for the evening. Most were resting, until yelling broke out.

A woman that Alexander's uncle found and took to his tent turned into some sort of beast with talons instead of fingers and teeth that could shred skin and bone. She'd killed every man in Alexander's family before I managed to stop her. He went from being fourth in line to the throne to being king in a single evening.

"No, I haven't. But I hope we never see her again."

We cheers to that.

"So what really brings you here? I find it hard to believe you're here to celebrate."

"I can't drop in on an old friend?"

Alexander's face turns stoic and his arms tense in his chair. "Ares, I have a child on the way. Tell me with sincerity, is my kingdom in danger?"

"No," I say instantly. "Your heroic demonstration in the final days of battle—even after the rest of the men in your family were slaughtered—solidifed your role as King of Cyprus. For now."

He sighs at the last part and takes his turn downing the bourbon in this glass. "Okay, if you aren't here to tell me my kingdom is in danger, then why are you? I invited you to celebrate as soon as the war ended, but you declined. Why now?"

I refill my glass as I say, "My sister is in danger."

"Hebe? She seemed fine." His brows scrunch.

"Not Hebe, Eileithyia. My mother locked her away because she wanted to aid the birth of my father's newest twins."

"And I thought my family was a dramatist's wet dream."

I chuckle at that before remembering why our private talk is so important. "Yes, well, there's a reason everyone knows not to cross my parents—that's beside the point though. I need you to tell me what cave you would hide someone in, if you didn't want them to be found."

Alexander contemplates my request. I almost groan at his lack of immediate response. If it were me, I'd know every centimeter of my kingdom, down to the type of rocks in each part. I advised him to do as much at the end of the war.

"There is one, but I don't think you're going to like it."

"Why?"

"It's guarded by cyclops. That would be the only cave fitting enough to hide an Olympian goddess."

I'm already standing before I say, "Tell me how to get there."

* * *

I FOLLOW Alexander's instructions to a tee, jumping over rocks and running through the rich vegetation of Cyprus. I opted to leave Hebe and Aphrodite at the palace because I knew they'd only serve as a distraction. Any second, I should be arriving at the cave, if I have the right one. I skid to a halt at a booming laugh.

I duck behind the last exterior wall of the cave. Even with the raging sea on my right, the cyclops's voice is all I hear.

"Such a pretty goddess," the cyclops taunts.

A woman's scream rips through the air, and I run in.

It is risky given the size of my enemy, but I have to save my sister. Rather than continue my rampage like an untrained soldier, I slow my run, stealthily using stray rocks as shields to get closer to my sister and the cyclops.

The deeper I get into the cave, the more the scent of burning flesh fills my nostrils. I peer over the rock I'm crouched behind and see a body in the middle of the fire.

"Don't touch me!" Eileithyia shrieks, fear dripping from her every word.

Gods, how long has this gone on? What has she had to endure?

The cyclops pokes my sister again through her cage and laughs when she shrinks in the corner. "Do you want another playmate?"

The cyclops turns and shuffles with something in the corner. I take the opportunity to grab a stray rock. I aim at the cave's opening, throwing the large rock with enough force for it to bounce off the furthest cave wall.

The noise distracts the cyclops, and for the first time, I'm able to see his face.

Brontes. He's supposed to be one of my father's loyal aides.

Brontes walks to the front of the cave, his steps making the ground shake. I run as fast and quietly as I can to my sister's cage.

"Ares?"

Holding my finger to my lips, I assess the lock on the cage. It's a simple latch, but it's made of cyclops crafted iron, too heavy for a mortal to lift and one of the only materials that can harm an Olympian.

I try lifting the latch, and my skin burns as I do. My neck strains trying to hold my yell in.

"Ares." Eileithyia's eyes grow wide, and she tries to scoot further back in her cage. "He's coming back."

I don't have time to turn around before a hand grabs me and steals my breath. Brontes spins me in his hand, dangling me by my feet. "What do we have here?"

He sniffs me, and I hold my breath to keep from smelling his stench. "Ah, another Olympian. My lucky day."

"You're supposed to be an aid to the Olympians, Brontes. I don't think Zeus will like what you've done to his daughter."

Brontes chuckles, and it makes my body shake along with it. "I don't care what Zeus thinks. He doesn't care about anyone but himself. I can't imagine what he'll think when two of his children are murdered and delivered to him on a silver platter."

The smile he wears is sinister. My sword turns loose from the grips of his fingers around my legs and towards the ground. "Not if I can help it."

I don't give Brontes time to digest my threat before I catch my sword then squeeze my core and pull my torso to his fingers. I use my free hand to swing my sword, slicing his fingers as I do.

He howls in pain, releasing me from his hold.

I land on the hard dirt, and I'd be lying if I said it didn't wind me, but I don't have time for my breathing to come back.

If I don't kill him now, it will be Eileithyia and I who take our last breaths today.

I run around Brontes, using my sword to slice through the tendon on his ankle. Blood sprays onto my face, and his howls pierce the air. Brontes's howls bring me back to the battlefield, and I'm reminded why the mortals call me merciless. I use the wall to help me onto his back.

Brontes swings his arm, trying to catch me, but I jump onto the limb instead. He tries to catch me as I climb his body, closer and closer to his head. I made it to the top of his shoulder before his hand comes down on me in a rather heavy hit. It knocks me off balance, and I'm forced to catch his beard to keep from falling.

My sword clambers to the ground.

"Ares!" Eileithyia wails behind us.

Brontes laughs. "What's your big plan now? Little Olympian against a cyclops with no weapons…I wonder how it will end."

"Aw, Brontes, you should know me better than that." I smirk, and I know it's sinister by the way it makes my chest warm.

In a fluid motion, I hold onto his beard with one hand while the other finds my short sword in my chiton. I pull my free arm back, using the same agility I did with the rock to throw my sword.

Brontes rears back when the blade pierces his eye. I release his beard and absorb my fall in my legs. He stumbles, tripping over a loose rock.

The ground shakes when his large body falls to it. Before he can think about standing again, I scoop up my sword, run along his body until I'm standing on the center of his chest, and ram my sword directly into his heart. Blood sprays my face again.

I wait until I feel his lungs stop expanding before I step down.

"Ares." I run to my sister, looking around for anything that will help me get her out. I silently curse when I realize there's nothing that will help me.

"I'm going to get you out of here." I take a deep breath and grab the iron latch with my bare hands.

My sister shrieks. "Ares!"

I groan through the searing of my skin. My jaw clenches, but I fight through the pain. I can hear the iron sizzling my hands, but I don't stop.

The latch finally lifts, and I slide it out of place. My sister pushes through the door and into my arms. Her cheeks are wet against my shoulder. "Thank you."

I wrap my arms around her. Blisters cover the reddened skin, but I ignore it for now. All that matters is that my sister is safe. A few new scars won't change my relief. "Let's get you home."

CHAPTER 25

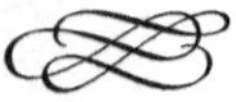

APHRODITE

Dear Journal,

The journey it took to save Eileithyia was eye-opening in many ways. I met the dark side of myself again that I usually keep locked away. I've forged new relationships and strengthened others. But most of all, I learned the one form of love I've yet to master...motherhood. I'm scared that my womb will forever be scorned by the hostility I've faced. I can only pray that those anxieties remain just that...anxiety.

"How long have you and Alexander been married?" I ask Cressida. Eileithyia and I have joined her in her drawing room. Ares had apparently promised Alexander something in exchange for the location of the cave Eileithyia was trapped in. I sent Hebe to the palace gardens when I found her gentleman sitting in them. That left Eileithyia and I by our lonesome.

"About six months. We conceived immediately, so the belly tells all." She laughs and her belly bounces too. A green-eyed monster clouds my vision, but I will it to cease. The envy turns melancholic.

I wonder if my womb will forever sit barren. If I will ever experience the eternal love between mother and child. If Cressida and Alexander could conceive right way, why couldn't Hephaestus and I? We've been married almost double the time. A surge of panic takes hold of me when I start to question whether Ares and I will be able to have a child. We've been together for months.

"Would you like to know what you're having?" Eileithyia asks, pulling my focus back to my company.

"You can do that?" Cressida and I ask in unison.

Eileithyia smiles. "I can." Her gaze falls on to me before she says, "I am able to tell the moment a babe has taken to a womb. It's like there's a timer, letting me know when you will need my aid."

"What it must be like to be a goddess…Please tell me, Eileithyia. I've been so eager to know if this child will be the heir to the kingdom," Cressida begs. "I will keep it a secret from Alexander if I must."

"There's no need to keep it a secret. Although I would keep it a secret from neighboring kingdoms because you are carrying the next heir to the throne."

"It's a boy?" Cressida asks with an elated smile.

Eileithyia nods. "It's a boy."

"Oh, praise the gods! Well, you all I suppose."

Eileithyia and I giggle.

A knock sounds on the door before Ares enters, finding my eyes in an instant. "Is everyone ready for Olympus?"

* * *

"KYRA, how are you? When Ares and I returned to Olympus last week, the shop was closed. Is everything okay?" I ask, when I enter the bake shop. The sweet smell of fresh pastries soothes my stomach. I'd caught a whiff of fresh game on my way over here and almost upturned my breakfast.

Kyra greets me with her usual friendly smile but something softer melts in her eyes. "Everything is perfect." She bends down behind the counter and rises with a bundled blanket in her arms. "Aphrodite, I'd like you to meet Stella."

The babe's rich, dark skin practically glows in Kyra's arms. Her jet-black hair lays in tight curls against her head. She's asleep soundly in her mother's arms.

"Oh my word, she is beautiful, Kyra."

"Would you like to hold her?"

"I wouldn't dream of doing anything else." I take the newborn in my arms. She stirs then settles back to sleep. I can't take my eyes off her as I graze the tops of my fingers on her soft head. "How is motherhood?"

"It is like nothing I could have dreamed of. Other mothers in the village talk about how they never thought the amount of love they felt could grow until they had children. I love my husband, but I fear they may have been right."

"They are." Stella grabs hold of my finger. "I can feel the love flowing between you. You may not feel it from her yet, but it's there."

"I know I've asked before, but do you think a baby will be on the horizon for you? Your eyes lit up when you saw Stella," Kyra remarks from the pastry section.

"Perhaps. My womb is the one who will have to make that decision. If it were my heart's choice, I'd already be with child." My heart nearly bursts when Stella coos and a grin crosses her lips even in her slumber.

Kyra places a lilac pastry box on the counter, then takes Stella from my arms.

"Perhaps you should take the raspberry and blackberry tarts I've given you and practice making one."

I follow Kyra's gaze to the entryway of her shop. Hephaestus stands there, stoic as ever, and my stomach fills with lead. "Aphrodite."

My nausea returns. It takes everything in me not to release my stomach contents all over Kyra's floor. I swallow my thick saliva before saying, "Hephaestus, what a lovely surprise. I was purchasing some fresh pastries. Shall we walk home together?"

He eyes me with something unreadable before nodding. I bid Kyra and Stella goodbye and without another word, take Hephaestus's arm out of the shop. We walk through the rest of the village, smiling at passing city dwellers.

What is supposed to be a short walk feels as though it takes hours with our weighted stillness. Neither of us exchange a word until we reach the fortitude of our estate. As soon as the door clicks shut, I remove my arm from his and practically throw the pastry box on our entryway table. "What are you doing here? I thought we agreed you would stay in the mortal realm."

"We did," he says. "I heard what my mother did to Eileithyia so I came back to check on her. She may not like me as much as Ares, but she is still my sister."

He may not be a great husband, but I must commend him for being an admirable brother to Eileithyia. "When will you be leaving?"

"I was on my way out when I stopped by Kyra's. I wanted to bring some of her blackberry tarts to—" He stops.

"You were bringing them to her?" I ask, filled with an unknown rage. I don't know where it came from. I've known about Hephaestus's mistress for nearly two months. I've been loved by someone else for months now. Why do I care?

"Yes." Something dark stirs in his eyes when I roll mine. "Do not get angry with me. You were the one that called off our marriage except the title."

I huff. "That does not change the fact that you were cheating on me when we were still married."

Hephaestus's jaw clenches. "Do not try to act all high and mighty. I'm sure it only took a day for you to return to your whorish ways that forced us into this union."

"Do not speak to me like that!" I snap before I say something I regret almost immediately when it comes out of my mouth. "I'm sorry only a mortal woman could love you. I'm sorry *all* of your siblings love me and not you. I was never a whore, and I'm still not one now."

Hephaestus is on me before I can blink. Pain explodes in my head and back as he shoves me against the stone wall behind me. His blue eyes look crazed, as though madness has engulfed every ounce of his body. He holds my chin so tight I know a bruise will color it. "It's Ares isn't it? The man you're having an affair with? I thought I told you not to fuck him."

He pushes my head against the wall harder and I wince. "Hephaestus, you're hurting me." Fear digs its ugly claws into me, claiming more and more of me by the second.

His free hand moves to my neck and squeezes. My heart races and ichor rushes against his hand. "Did you fuck him? Did you sleep with my brother?"

It's hard to breathe. Seconds tick by. A tear falls from my eye before I croak, "No. I haven't slept with anyone while I wait to see if I'm carrying your child."

Hephaestus releases me and steps back. His eyes are less crazed, but I refuse to look at him as I crumple to the floor. "How much longer until you know? My mother is getting more insistent."

Tears fall freely from my eyes as I clutch my throat. "Eileithyia said it could be any day but may take another week."

"Then I will be back in two weeks. I'll see you then, wife." Hephaestus leaves, taking Kyra's pastries with him.

The click of the door triggers a wave of sobs. I curl into a ball on the cold floor, practically shaking from fear. *What have I done?*

I jump when a gentle hand touches my back.

In my panic, I hadn't even heard the door open.

"Aphrodite, what happened? I saw you and Hephaestus in the village. I followed you here because I figured you'd need me."

"Get Ares!" I sob, barely able to speak through my panicked breaths. "I need Ares."

I don't know how long I sat alone, sobbing on my floor before Ares burst through the door with frantic eyes. It only takes a second for him to find me and scoop me in his arms.

"He did this to you?" he asks, his eyes deadlier than Hephaestus's had been.

I choke with a tear falling down my cheek. "Please not now."

The fire in his eyes extinguishes. His lips press against my forehead before he looks behind us. "Alexandra, I need you to run a bath for Aphrodite and make sure it's filled with soothing salts. After that, take as many of her things as you can back to my estate. We will join you later."

"Of course."

Alexandra's steps echo in my ears as she bounds up the stairs behind me. I stopped sobbing, but I still can't stop the rogue tears.

Ares hugs me tighter to his body, rubbing my back in soothing circles. "You're safe. He will *never* touch you again or so help me he will never breathe again. Consequences be damned."

CHAPTER 26

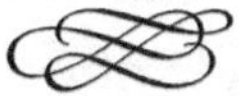

ARES

From the moment I burst through the doors of Aphrodite's and Hephaestus's estate, I saw red. Her neck and chin had visible marks. The fear in her eyes was enough to wake the sleeping beast that I only let out during war. But the moment she asked me to stop my reign of terror against my brother, the beast sat, bowing to my seductress.

I tried taking Aphrodite upstairs to bathe in hopes that the warm water and soothing salts would aid some tranquility. But the further I took her into their estate, the more frantic she became. Finally, I decided she would come home with me.

I knew she wouldn't want to be seen, so I wrapped a himation around her head and neck like a veil and walked her down all of the backroads of the village. Thankfully, no one saw us.

At home, she begged me to sit with her, so I did. As the seconds ticked by, the urge to murder my brother increased exponentially. I'd let him slide before, but this was too far.

I kiss Aphrodite's forehead before clicking the door shut and striding to the threshold of my estate. I barely make it to the foyer before Eileithyia struts in.

"Where's Aphrodite?" she asks.

"Sleeping. Do not disturb her," I order, only stopping when she levels me with an intense stare and disrupts my path.

"I need to see her. *Now.*"

I cross my arms. Annoyance floods me. "With all due respect, she needs to rest. Besides, I don't think she wants you to see her in her current state."

Hard-set brows and steeled eyes meet mine. "Ares, I need you to tell me right now what happened. Did you do something to her?"

My fists tighten and that darkness returns. "How dare you accuse men of doing anything to her! What about her abusive husband?"

"Hephaestus did something to her? Why?"

I shake my head. "I don't know. I haven't asked her. I just got her to calm down. Why are you so concerned? You weren't the first time he hit her."

"Because she's—" Her eyes growing timid. I don't even have to say anything before she sighs. "She's pregnant, Ares."

My breath stills. I can hear my ichor pumping in my veins. "What? How—"

"She's only a few weeks," my sister answers. "I'm not sure she knows. She's probably only starting to get symptoms."

"Is it—" I gulp with a shaky breath. "Is it mine?"

Eileithyia sighs. "If I had to guess, yes. I'm not sure when the last time she and Hephaestus were intimate, but I'm guessing it's nowhere close to the last time the two of you were. I felt the connection to the babe when I ran into you in the Underworld."

"You're sure it wasn't earlier?"

This time she huffs. "Ares, I am very capable of understanding my powers. This is your baby. That baby was in distress earlier. Please, let me check on her."

The monster inside roars to life. "She's in my room, upstairs. Don't tell her I know about the baby. I want her to tell me when she's ready. If she asks for me, tell her I will be back shortly."

"Where are you going?" Eileithyia asks as I cross the rest of the foyer in mere seconds.

"Hephaestus beat the woman I love while she is carrying my child. Where do you think I'm going?" I don't let her answer before the door closes behind me.

My horses make it to the familiar cottage outside of Delphi in record time. I burst through the door, to find my brother enjoying what I'm sure was a peaceful dinner.

"Ares—" Hephaestus doesn't have time to finish before my fist connects with his jaw.

"Hephaestus!" his mistress shouts. I don't have to look at

her to know she's scared. All I see is rage, and it's targeted at my brother.

"Have you lost your gods-damned mind?" I shout, punching my brother twice more in the face. His bones crunch beneath my fingers.

"Get off of me!" my brother shouts. He tries to strike me, but I block him. What a pussy.

"You think it's okay to beat on your pregnant wife?" I say through clenched teeth, then deliver another harsh blow.

Hephaestus stills, looking at me with what I'm sure is the same shock. "Aphrodite is pregnant?"

"Yes, you asshole. Do you feel any better since you hurt the woman you made vows to? Not only her, but the unborn baby she carries too?"

I take the chance to knee his ribs before he answers. "I didn't know!"

Gripping him by the fabric of his chiton, I bring him so close, I can practically smell the fear dripping out of his pores. "You think that makes it any better? You're a coward. Maybe you shouldn't be in this child's life."

At that, his eyes harden. "How do I know it's mine? That whore could have slept with anyone."

This time I headbutt him. "Ask Eileithyia. She's the one who told me about the baby after Hebe found Aphrodite." I may be lying about the circumstances in which Aphrodite was found but I don't think either of my sisters nor Aphrodite will mind. Hell, the look in Eileithyia's eyes when I tried to stop her from seeing Aphrodite almost made me bow down to her. "Stay away from her."

"Or what?" Hephaestus grins with ichor-covered teeth. I

must applaud him for how stupid he is for egging me on. Frankly, the politics that would follow murdering my brother wouldn't be worth it. No matter how much of a scumbag he is. "She'll never flock to you. We made a deal. She can fuck whoever she wants as long as its not *you*."

If I wasn't so hellbent on protecting Aphrodite, I would rub it in his face that the child she carries is mine and not his. At how eager she is to take every inch of my cock. But I love her too much to do that. "I'm here because our sisters begged me to find you. Stay away from Aphrodite or I swear to all gods more powerful than us that you will not wake to see another day."

I go to take my leave when I see Hephaestus's mistress cowering in the corner with a tear-stricken face. "Now you know the true nature of your beloved."

* * *

"What the hell happened to you?" Eileithyia marches toward me when I return. Hebe is alarmed in the foyer.

"Where's Aphrodite? Is she still sleeping?" I ask, trying to force myself past my sister.

"What did you do, Ares? Your hand is covered in ichor." Eileithyia grabs my hand, inspecting it like some sort of mother hen. I wince when she presses on my knuckles. "Gods, you've broken your hand. I need to clean this and bandage it."

I yank my hand away. "My hand is fine. I need to be with Aphrodite—now."

My sister huffs. "She is still sleeping. You have plenty of

time to be with her *after* I bandage your hand. But if it helps, Hebe can sit with her in the meantime."

Hebe nods in agreement. I eye my sisters, noting how different they are. Where Eileithyia's features are dark, Hebe's are light. It only takes my sister touching my already-bruising knuckle once for me to agree. "Fine. But get me immediately if she awakes."

Hebe nods, then walks with the same regal cadence my mother has while looking every bit my father's daughter. "Very well."

"I assume your bandages are still in your bathroom?" Eileithyia asks.

"Yes," I respond.

I pour a tall glass of strong wine while I wait for my sister. I down it and go for a second. With the night I've had, I might drink the whole damn bottle.

My sister doesn't have to speak for me to know she's behind me. I can feel her disapproval.

"Wine?" I ask.

"Perhaps. I need to bandage your hand first." She ushers me over to the plush couch on the opposing side of the room.

I pour her a glass before sauntering over to the plethora of bandages she's laid out. She takes my bruised hand in her smooth, clean one.

"Gods, Ares, I thought you knew how to protect your bones when fighting," she mutters. She takes a damp rag to the ichor on my knuckles.

"I do," I counter. "I do when I'm not completely blinded by rage. You can't say Hephaestus didn't deserve it though."

My sister sits with a solemn look on her face. Once my knuckles are ichor free, she takes turns pressing on each of them to see how many of them I injured. "That may be so, but you did not need to harm yourself to do it. Gods, what an awful family to bring a child into."

The anger that was directed at my wretch of a brother vanishes. Instead, something foreign spreads within me.

Fear. Perhaps a mix of happiness too.

"I'm going to be a father."

"You're going to be a father," Eileithyia echoes.

I rub my face with my free hand, feeling the weight of today's news, "What am I going to do? I'm at war so often, and Aphrodite has to remain with Hephaestus at least publicly. How will a child—our child—grow up in a stable home?"

My sister wraps my hand with a clean piece of cloth, ensuring the bones are set properly with each wrap. My immortality may grant me speedy recoveries, but if the bones aren't set correctly, I'll be stuck with pain in my hand, lest I choose to break it again.

"It won't be easy, but you'll figure it out. You always do. You'll be a good dad."

Nerves rise like magma, slow yet deadly. "How can you be sure?"

"You were always there for Hebe and me. We both know that mother and father are anything but parents. All they did was give us life. If anyone noticed when Hebe and I were upset, it was you, and you never let us remain upset for long. You're a great brother, and you'll be an even better father."

It's my turn to smile. "Do you really mean that?"

My sister nods. Her constant aiding in deliveries has given her quite the knack for first aid. But it doesn't take long for me to notice something is wrong with her too. Eileithyia's eyes are distant, as though her mind is taking her somewhere else. Based on the clench in her jaw, I'd say it's nowhere good.

"What's going on in that head of yours? And don't say nothing because you have that crease in your eyebrows you get when you're anxious."

Eileithyia sighs while tying off the last bit of my bandage. "I'm leaving Olympus."

"What?"

"I can't stay, Ares." She shakes her head, and I watch her eyes grow glassy. "Every day that passes, I feel that iron cage looming over me. I can't sleep without nightmares of the cyclops. What kind of a mother subjects her daughter to that?"

I can't blame her. "Where will you go?"

She picks at the skin around her fingers. I place my hand over hers, willing her to stop before she draws ichor. "The Underworld, I suppose. Hades has offered me a place to stay plenty of times. He's caught wind of what mother did, and he's not pleased. He wrote to me this morning asking if I wished to stay with him."

"Did you tell him yes?"

Eileithyia shakes her head before sipping on the wine poured for her earlier. "I haven't written back. I'll write to him tonight, telling him I will come to the Underworld after the baby is born."

I shake my head. "Eileithyia, I can't ask you to do that.

You've already told me how horrible you feel here. I can't ask you to stay for the duration of Aphrodite's pregnancy."

"Nonsense. I'm not staying for you. I'm staying for Aphrodite and the baby. Besides, I've got to get the last few months of heckling you in before I leave Olympus for good."

"You're sure about this?" I ask.

She nods. "Absolutely."

"Then, I wish you the best, little sister." I raise my glass to her. We cheer before taking a gulp of wine.

We get lost in conversation for the first time in what's been too long. We are so lost in conversation that neither of us notice Hebe entering the room. "Aphrodite is awake."

CHAPTER 27

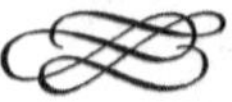

APHRODITE

Dear Journal,
I don't even know where to begin.

"I don't understand. Why must I marry Hephaestus? He does not love me, nor I him," I plead.

"Love does not matter, and it's time you learned that. You made the oath to be an Olympian." Hera leans over the table in her study, mouth pinched tight.

"Yes, I made the oath. But nowhere in that oath did I say I would marry Hephaestus. It would entrap both of us."

"You should have thought of that before you led so many men of Olympus astray. I will not allow this behavior."

"I haven't slept with anyone's husband! I haven't done

anything. Hera, I cannot help the draw my powers have on some people." I pick at the skin on my fingers.

"Enough!" She slams her hand down on the wood between us. "You may not have slept with another woman's husband yet, but you're on track to. Our institution will remain respectable. You will marry Hephaestus."

It's my turn to glare. "And if I leave Olympus? What then? I can't tempt husbands if I am not here." I should never have followed Hermes here. I could be living blissfully ignorant in the mortal realm.

Hera leans closer, her glare almost daring me to do it. "You made an oath to the Olympians. Leaving us would guarantee a life of torment and death. I will not pardon you.

"If Zeus were to ever find you, he'd have his way with you no matter how many times you screamed for him to stop. I'm afraid none of Zeus's mistresses have a happy ending either."

"So this is about Zeus?" I almost laugh at the irony, but I'm so angry. Of course this is about Zeus.

"You have two options: Marry my son or live your life running from us."

"What's stopping your husband from raping me now?"

Hera straightens. "My husband is many things, but he is still a father. It may be twisted, but your marriage to my son will ensure your safety from his advances."

I feel like screaming. In fact, every nerve in my body is telling me to, but I can't. How is this a choice? A stray tear of anger falls as my glare settles on Hera. My jaw clenches as do my fists. "When will we wed?"

The left side of Hera's mouth ticks. I was right where she

wanted me. "Three months from now. Any sooner and the rest of Olympus will think you're welcoming my son's bastard child."

I long to scream from frustration. "Very well."

"Welcome to the family."

I startle awake, feeling the same nerves I felt when Hera gave me the ultimatum. That day has haunted me ever since. I still wonder sometimes what would have happened if I had chosen to run. Ares's arm tightens around me. He has his other arm propped behind his head, showing off his toned chest and abdomen.

"Why do you look so troubled, soldier?" I ask, running a hand on Ares's muscled torso.

He turns to me. Who knew the merciless god of war could smile. Let alone over something as miniscule as a woman asking if he was alright. "Nothing, seductress."

"It is not polite to lie, you know."

In an instant, Ares hovers over me. He kisses my neck once, twice, and a third time before nipping at my ear. I gasp, and he pushes back up, grinning like a devil. "Polite isn't my style, seductress."

I groan at how easy it was for him to distract me. Yet, all I can think about is getting him inside me. Gods, the level I long for him rivals insanity. I need him like a fish needs water and a fire needs oxygen. "Ares."

"Aphrodite."

"Tell me what is wrong," I order.

He sighs and hangs his head. "Athena has requested I spend the day at the training facility. She says they're done with the construction of the main dome. She also stressed the importance of my presence if we have any hopes of our recruits being worth anything."

"Why does that trouble you?" I rub his stubbled cheek idly, thinking of how the textures of his skin and beard work so nicely together.

Ares kisses each of my cheeks. "I wanted to stay with you. After last night, I don't plan on leaving your side."

It's my turn to sigh. I maneuver myself from beneath him and sit up. "I am not some damsel in need of saving. I came to you because I trust you and you'd protect me. But that does not mean I need to be coddled. You're going to the training facility."

"But—"

"No buts. I will not be on the receiving end of Athena's wrath. I will be fine here. I will take a nice long bath. Alexandra will visit. Your sisters are here. There is no short list of people that will be here if for some strange reason I burst into hysterics."

I swear I almost see admiration gleaming in his eyes. Then something more frantic takes hold of them. My brows crease and he schools his eyes just as fast as it came. "You're sure?"

"Ares." I stand from the bed to start running a bath.

"Fine, seductress." He has me in seconds. He pulls my back flush against him. His hands sit somewhat possessively over my stomach. "Enjoy your day of relaxation. I will be back before sunset."

"Very well."

A knock sounds on my door after a long and luxurious

soak in a lavender and lemon scented bath. I turn, thinking Ares found a reason to neglect his duties. "Back so soon?"

Eileithyia walks through the door. "I'm afraid I'm not the one you are looking for."

"You are welcome nonetheless." I smile, tying one last knot on a new peplos Ares purchased for me before sitting on the couch.

"How are you feeling?" Eileithyia asks as she sits next to me.

"Better." It's not a complete lie. I had woken up from a nightmare of Hephaestus choking me last night and sat emptying the contents of my stomach for much longer than I wanted to admit. Ares rubbed my back the entire time. And I felt better this morning. Waking up in a house I knew I was safe with a man I knew would protect me, aided in calming almost all of my nerves this morning.

"That's good," Eileithyia grins. She toys with her fingers and avoids eye contact.

I narrow my eyes, skepticism bringing forth my nerves. "What are you not telling me?"

She stills her pale hands, rubbing them on her clothed thighs. "Why would you think I'm hiding something?"

"Eileithyia, your brother nearly killed me for thinking I'm in love with your other brother. Please don't lie to me."

Her right foot bounces against the left. Her nerves make mine ignite, and the anxiety makes me nauseous. After a few seconds, she sighs. "Do you remember when we were in the mortal realm I said I could tell the moment a babe took to a womb?"

I nod, suddenly feeling quite hot.

"Well, I felt it…with you."

My mouth runs dry and my stomach drops. "I'm pregnant?"

"Yes."

My hand shoots to my stomach. "You're sure? Hephaestus and I tried for so long and nothing ever happened. I began to think I was barren."

Eileithyia takes hold of my hand. "I'm sure. I checked on you when you were sleeping. Based on the baby's size, you're about eight weeks along."

"Eight weeks! You waited to tell me for eight weeks?" My voice comes out shriller than I'd intended, but it's hard to control my voice and digest this news at the same time while fighting the urge to vomit.

"Sometimes with goddesses, it's harder to feel the exact moment a babe has taken because you aren't on the same cycle as mortals. In your case, I didn't notice until your visit to the Underworld." She squeezes my hand. "This is a good thing, Aphrodite."

I take a deep breath and rub a circle on my still-flat stomach. I look down now with an astonished smile. "I'm going to have a baby."

"You're going to have a baby."

The moment Eileithyia left, I had Alexandra find Ares. I may be excited for the baby, but that certainly does not mean I'm short of any troubles. So I walk to the beach in the back.

I pace, clutching my stomach. A wave washes over my feet and I will my nausea away, listening to the sound of the water and allowing the salty air to filter into my nostrils.

"Aphrodite."

"Ares," I say and run into his embrace. He takes me in an instant and suddenly, my nerves subside a fraction. "I—I don't know what to do. I don't know what we're going to do. What is Hephaestus going to do?" My breathing turns rapid. My chest feels tight. It hurts to breathe.

Ares grabs my shoulders and meets me at eye level. "Aphrodite, breathe." He takes a deep breath, lifting and lowering his hand to signal me to do the same.

I do, and we do that three more times.

My chest no longer feels tight, but my eyes still sting. "Ares, I'm pregnant. It is our child. Gods, what is going to happen to me? Hephaestus almost killed me at the thought of me just being with you. What will he do when he finds out this is your baby?"

Panic starts to spread through me again. Rather than coach me through breathing techniques, Ares wraps his arms around me and rubs my back with soothing circles. "I will protect you the same way I always have. I don't care if I have to kill him. I will protect you and our baby with my life."

"We're having a baby," I say after standing in his embrace for some time.

I may still fear Hephaestus, but I know, without a doubt, that Ares will protect me. And I have to accept that victory, however small. It will not change the fact that I get to have a baby with the man I love.

"We're having a baby," he says and kisses the top of my head.

CHAPTER 28

ARES

I'd decided to dedicate my day to the training arena. Athena was not very pleased with my early departure yesterday, but the moment I saw Alexandra's worried expression, I knew something was wrong with Aphrodite. Every fiber of my being felt like it was on fire until I knew she was alright.

We spent the rest of yesterday on the beach, taking turns swimming and getting tangled in the sand. By the end of the day, light had returned to Aphrodite's eyes, rather than the tempest that had occupied them since Hephaestus attacked her.

I'd much rather be worshipping every inch of her, the same way I did last night, but it was time I acknowledged my duties.

"Ah, you're both here, wonderful," my mother announces as she saunters into the newly-furnished training arena. Complete with the open dome roof and sand floors, this facility is what Athena and I had in mind for the trainees. We'd have a fully trained army in no time. If we were careful with our planning, we'd also have a steady stream of new trainees every year. But that took planning we haven't even begun to acknowledge yet.

"Here we are," Athena answers from the weaponry wall.

"Mother." I grin though its facetious. "Fancy seeing you in the training facility. I can't imagine what for."

"Watch your tongue." Her eyes narrow before she regains her composure. "We will be hosting a state dinner in honor of the training facility's completion. It's in six days. You will both be there with the rest of the Olympians."

"It won't be here, will it?" Athena asks, walking to the outskirts of the ring where my mother and I stand. "We have too many weapons to host something like that."

"Of course it will be here. If we are to celebrate the newest advancement in the city, we shall need its inhabitants to see it. Put the weapons in the vault. That is what it's there for."

"We cannot have another stuffy ball or dinner, especially here of all places." I wave my hand across the room behind us.

My mother's brow raises. "You both are well aware how dire it is that we present a strong, united front to the rest of Olympus since our new institution is in somewhat early stages."

I nod. "I know you have a fascination with our reputation. But if you want the citizens of Olympus to care about our institution long-term, we need something other than balls and dinners. Eventually they will grow tired of the monotony. They'll start to question how they're any different than us. You have to remember that they are gods too."

"What do you propose we do then?" My mother asks but I can tell she's angry that I've challenged her authority.

I shrug. "We have a gladiator event. It lets the citizens see what skills they gain from training with us. It also lets Athena and I gauge where our recruits need work."

My mother crosses her arms across her chest with a skeptical look. Athena nods next to me. "That could work. It both challenges the recruits and could peak interest in joining the ranks."

"Fine." Hera uncrosses her arms. "But if something goes wrong, it's your fault. I will alert the rest of the Olympians about the change."

I roll my eyes knowing my pig brother will be there as well. "Yes, Mother. We understand." I sigh.

"I shall be there, Hera. I'm afraid I need to leave. I will spread the word about the challenge to the trainees. Our success is their success." Athena speaks with grace, but I refrain.

"I like where your head is at. I will see you at dusk." My mother smiles as Athena leaves us. She waits until Athena is out of sight before she turns back to me. "Why can't you be more like her and spare me the headache?"

I cross my arms across my chest. "Well, I am the product of you and father. It's not in my nature to go down without a fight."

She sighs. "Very well. Just be at the event and don't start any arguments with your brother like you did at the last family dinner. Our family needs to, at least, appear civilized."

"Speaking of my dear brother," I say before my mother has a chance to leave.

She turns to me with curiosity on her face. "What about him?"

"I need you to annul his marriage," I say.

She does something between a laugh and a scoff. "Why would I do that?"

"Because they are not in love." Out of respect for Aphrodite, I won't share that Hephaestus has a penchant for beating women. I know how much it pains her and how much havoc it would wreak on her emotionally if that information were to get out.

My mother's eyes harden the same way they did when she scolded me as a child. "Son, that hardly matters. The only thing that matters is—"

"Keeping up with appearances," I finish, not caring that I cut her off. "Mother, you cannot possibly subject someone to a life of unhappiness because you think she would tempt your husband."

Something dark takes over my mother's once-kind eyes. "Why I did what I did is none of your concern. Your brother is married to Aphrodite, whether you like it or not. I warned you about spending time with her."

Anger burns through my veins like the fires of the Phlegethon. "You don't understand—"

"It's time your visits come to an end and for you to find your own wife. Let your brother be happy with his." My mother's unmoving opinion only causes the fires to burn hotter within me.

"You have cost this family so much in your effort to keep up appearances. Your own daughter is leaving because she is terrified to be around you."

My mother stands, her eyes unmoving. We enter a silent standoff, neither of us sure what to say next. Finally, something cracks. "You're right. Keeping up with appearances is everything, Your request will never be anything more than that. Perhaps if you had been in Olympus, it would have been you and not Hephaestus."

She gives me a pat in the center of my chest and leaves without another word. The roaring flames subdue in exchange for a green-eyed monster.

* * *

I LAND in my usual bar stool, failure clawing at me. "Orion, give me a double, neat."

Orion walks to the other end of the bar to pour the strongest drink he has. He places the glass on the bar. "On the house."

I cheers and down the liquid in two gulps. I welcome the burn down my mouth and throat before settling in my stomach. "Give me another."

"Something on your mind, Ares? Your visits have been scarce recently. Aphrodite's too." Orion's lips pull up. *Cheeky bastard.*

"What's your point?" I ask, sipping the next drink.

"Nothing at all." He shrugs, poking his bottom lip out to

emphasize his feigned ignorance. "Just pointing out you haven't come in here looking like hell and in need of a drink for a long time. Same with a certain goddess."

I narrow my eyes. "Stay in your lane, Orion. Olympian affairs can be much messier than you may think."

Orion raises his tanned hands in surrender. "You need not worry about me. Most people in Olympus don't realize I'm able to spot their dirty laundry with the smallest glances. I think the number of secrets I know would make even you quiver."

We size each other up. I have him in almost every physical aspect, but as he's hinted, he knows very valuable secrets. I raise my glass. "Touché."

His tight lips turn to a grin. "Excellent. Now, are you going to tell me what's going on or should I keep guessing?"

I shake my head and tap my fingers against the glass. "I'm afraid I can't. I can't add anyone to that list of those who know. All I can tell you is I have to plan something—something big."

"Well, it shouldn't be too hard for the god of war to come up with a battle plan, should it?"

Orion pours me one more glass before tending to other patrons. I let his words simmer, taking his confidence as a strategist as encouragement.

With every sip, I think of every avenue in which my plan could blow up in my or Aphrodite's faces. With each hole I find in my plan, I drink more. Finally, after what feels like an entire bottle, I have what seems like the best course of action.

CHAPTER 29

APHRODITE

Dear Journal,
I don't know what God I pissed off, but they have a strict vendetta against me. Just when my soldier and I were getting happy, Hephaestus came to ruin everything. The news of my child is tainted by the looming threat of my husband. My child should know their father without a threat on their life.

"Ares, have you gone mad? There is no way I will agree to that!" I yell. My hand instinctively protects my belly. "This is your child. Not his. Our child needs their father."

Ares grabs hold of my shoulders, leaning down to meet

my eyes. "I know, seductress. But this is our best option. For all of us."

His calloused hand covers mine against my belly. My eyes close. My head drops to his shoulder. I sit for a while, willing the lump in my throat to go away. Gods, this baby makes me more emotional than I already was. "It's not fair."

He lifts my head. Cupping my cheek, he says, "I know, but if it means our baby will remain safe, then that is what we will do."

"You promise you will see us when he is not here?"

Ares nods, the smallest of smiles gracing his lips. "I wouldn't dream of anything else."

The lump in my throat dissipates. I tuck into Ares's arms, and he holds me there. "I shall tell Hephaestus about the baby before the gladiator event."

I may not like Ares's plan to tell Hephaestus this is his baby, but he's right, this is our best option.

"The sooner he believes that our child is his, the safer you and the baby will be." Ares kisses the crown of my head. I look up at him. His chocolate eyes are soft in the candle-lit room. He leans down, kissing me tenderly. His beard tickles my chin. "I love you, Aphrodite."

My heart skips a beat because for the first time I know someone means it when they say it. "I love you, Ares."

* * *

I KNOCK on the great wooden door in front of me. The last time I entered Dionysus's drawing room without knocking first I walked in on an orgy.

"You may come in." His voice faintly passes through the door. I enter. "Ah, Aphrodite. Long time no see."

"It's only been a couple of weeks," I say, but guilt claws at me, nonetheless. I hadn't seen Dionysus since before my trip to the Underworld.

"That's quite a bit of time when we used to see each other almost daily." Dionysus pours a glass of wine and offers it to me. I kindly decline before taking a seat on his plush couch. "You've changed since the last time we saw each other."

My brows scrunch. "I have not."

"The Aphrodite I knew never turned down a glass of wine." He sips from the glass he'd offered me. "And your cheeks look fuller. Your eyes are no longer dark around the edges. You don't look sickly."

"If you truly thought I looked awful, why didn't you say anything?" His harsh confession makes me question how many other people saw how my unhappiness weighed on me. Did anyone notice? Or did they simply not care?

He shrugs. "I did. You didn't like what I had to say."

"You told me to find a new lover. How do the two things correlate?" I snap. His eyes widen at my sudden rage. "My apologies."

"You did what I told you to, and it worked." I open my mouth to object, but he holds his finger up to stop me. "I know you've been staying with Ares. Don't try to deny it. I tried visiting you a few weeks ago. Alexandra was leaving your estate with a few bags."

"She told you?" My heart races. *She swore she'd never tell anyone. Who else could she have told?*

"No." He shakes his head, and my heart slows. "I followed

her to Ares's estate. That's beside the point, Aphrodite. You're happy. That's all I care about."

I twist my fingers in my hands. "Hephaestus stepped out first. I may have slept with Ares two years before we were married, but Hephaestus was sleeping with a mortal woman our entire courtship and marriage."

Dionysus grabs my hands with his smooth, tan ones. "You do not need to justify your actions. I'm glad you're not wallowing in your own pity anymore. Besides, I never liked him. He's too ugly to be as egotistical as he is. Shall we drink to that?"

I shake my head again.

Surprise lines his face, his eyebrows climb higher on his forehead. "This is the second time you've refused my drink offer. Has Ares put an embargo on your drinking? If he has, than I shall find you another fellow who lets you do whatever you like while pleasing you in ways you've never imagined."

I chuckle, my hand instinctively rubbing my mostly flat stomach. "Of course not."

His eyes grow so wide I can see the white surrounding his otherwise dark brown eyes. "Good gods, you're pregnant."

There's not use in hiding it. All of Olympus will know soon enough. "I am."

"No wonder your breasts look extraordinary."

I laugh. "Of course you'd look at my chest."

Dionysus smirks and even I have to admit I can see the draw people have to him. Regardless, we are friends and nothing more. "It's hard not to. I'm sure Ares loves this new development."

I roll my eyes and stand. I turn toward the threshold as I say, "Are you going to come with me to the modiste to find a dress for the gladiator event or would you like to keep making jokes about my breasts?"

"Lead the way."

The walk to the modiste, with Dionysus by my side, feels foreign. We've done it so many times before and yet it feels odd. Perhaps Dionysus was right. I have changed, and not just physically. My life before Ares feels like a distant memory.

"Oh, Aphrodite! How wonderful to see you." Theodora meets me at the door with an appreciative smile on her face. "I was wondering when you'd come in for the Olympian event."

"I hope you don't mind Dionysus coming along," I say once we've gotten our greetings out of the way.

Theodora ushers us further into the private room she usually helps me in. "Of course not. If there were any man I'd trust to offer his thoughts on a dress, it would be him."

"You're smart." Dionysus gives her a wink.

She blushes before turning back to me. "I was anticipating your visit, so I already started a gown. I hope that's okay."

"That's perfectly fine."

I slip into the silky fabric. I have to adjust my breasts a few times to fit in the peplos less scandalously. Wincing, I adjust the tender flesh one last time and walk back out to Dionysus. "What do you think?"

He rakes his eyes over me once, twice, then swirls his finger for me to turn. I see him do the same thing in the mirror before he says, "I think it looks marvelous. White suits you."

I smooth my hands down my hips, satisfied with the way it fits. "It's perfect. Thank you, Theodora."

"You outdid yourself," Dionysus tells her. "Although, I think it may be time to schedule some re-fitting appointments."

I cut my eyes at Dionysus. I'm not ready for anyone else to know about the pregnancy before I tell Hephaestus.

Theodora's eyes grow wide. "Congratulations, Aphrodite! I thought the bust area looked tighter than usual, but I wasn't going to assume you were with child until you confirmed it. Hephaestus must be over the moon!"

Dionysis and I lock eyes. I offer an appreciative smile. "Thank you. I'm afraid I haven't told Hephaestus yet. I'm going to surprise him at the gladiator event."

She clasps her hands at her waist. "Well, your secret is safe with me. Now, let's get a few appointments in my book to schedule your re-fittings every few weeks."

CHAPTER 30

APHRODITE

Alexandra takes the last of my curlers out and runs her fingers through my hair. She'd found the curling devices at a blacksmith shop in the village. She heated the round cylinders by fire, letting them cool slightly, and rolled my hair with them. While risky, since I am to leave for the gladiator event soon, it looks quite good.

"Some final touches…" Alexandra pulls the top half of my hair back and pins it with a gold rose hair pin. She walks to my wardrobe in the corner of the room and ruffles through my fabrics. When she returns she moves my hair to one side, then clasps the necklace Ares gave me around my neck.

I settle my hair back in place, turning toward her. "It's perfect. Thank you."

Alexandra squeezes my hand with a smile. "Good luck tonight."

I offer a timid smile before looking in the mirror. I smooth my clammy hands over my waist. I flatten my peplos over my belly. My heart warms. My baby is there.

When I hear a knock, the butterflies scatter. Hephaestus enters wearing a brown chiton that looks new. His usually unkempt hair is slick and brushed. "We should be leaving for the training arena."

"Very well," I say and brush past him.

I've never seen Olympus so electric. Ares was right. It seems everyone thought the constant state dinners and balls were repetitive. Our chariot has to travel much slower than normal due to the heavy traffic on the path to the arena. The entire ride thus far has been silent. I twist my neck to ease the twitch in it. The longer I stand here next to Hephaestus, the more nervous I get.

My heart races every time I look at his hands and the memory of them gripping my throat flashes through my mind. As our chariot halts, I turn toward Hephaestus. His lips open a fraction. "Aphrodite—"

"I'm pregnant."

He looks at me with something melancholic about his

eyes. For the first time I notice the yellowing bruises around them. It doesn't take much for me to realize Ares put them there. His hand was bruised for days after that night.

"I shall stay in Olympus more—for the baby."

"What?" My stomach drops and nausea washes over me.

Hephaestus's hand grasps mine in the chariot. "It is time I do right by you and our baby."

"Very well." I swallow, plastering the best smile I can on my face. "We shall tell the others tonight."

I take a deep breath, willing my nausea away as best I can and take Hephaestus's hand. No matter how much his presence puts me on edge, we are at an official Olympian event, and he is my husband, and the "father" of my child when we announce it later.

"Ready?"

I brace myself. "Ready."

The training arena is full of Olympians and villagers. Hephaestus and I offer kind hellos to those that greet us as we make our way deeper into the hall towards the observation deck.

Hera and Zeus stand in the center of the closed-off corridor that leads to the deck. Each looks rather tense as they talk with Eileithyia. When we draw closer, I see Hera's nostrils flare. "Oh, thank goodness, you two are here. It's almost time for our grand entrance. Come, we shall go to the weapons vault to wait."

Tension coats the air like sticky molasses in the Greek heat, slowly growing and suffocating. I steal a glance at Eileithyia. Her hard-set jaw and cynical look makes me wonder what she'd been discussing with her parents before we interrupted them. It isn't until the door that separates us and the villagers clicks shut behind Poseidon that anyone speaks.

Hera turns, facing everyone. "Tonight is very important for the Olympians. We need to uphold a united front. After the dismal and embarrassing ordeal with Hades refusing our alliance, it is more important than ever." Hera glares at me when she says the last sentence. That glare shifts when Ares walking through the door distracts everyone.

My breath hitches at his polished appearance in the new crimson chiton I picked out for him. His hair is brushed and pushed back to rest on his shoulders. His beard is just right. I feel a rush of warmth spread low in my belly. Ares stands next to Dionysus who's across from Hephaestus and me.

Eileithyia's voice pulls me from the flustered state I was headed toward. "Do not blame Ares and Aphrodite for Hades pulling out of the alliance, *Mother*. He was pleased with their visit. The broken relationship is your fault."

Everyone in Zeus and Hera's immediate family act calmly because they know things like this happen, me included. However, the other Olympians look at each other as if questioning what to do.

"Watch your tongue. If they—" Hera points at Ares and me— "had done a better job at charming Hades, we wouldn't be in this mess."Hephaestus grabs my waist, and I flinch. He releases me almost instantly.

"No, Mother. If you hadn't locked me in an iron cage with a cyclops, you wouldn't be in this mess." Eileithyia crosses her arms. "You forgot that women still have babies in Hades's court. Since I keep so many of them safe, Hades considers me one of them. Your stunt showed him that no alliance will give him the protection he wanted for his court."

"Hera," Zeus rumbles. "What did you do?"

Hera ignores him, and so does Eileithyia when she says, "That's also why I'm leaving Olympus—permanently."

Zeus's and Hera's eyes grow large. Hera tries to grab Eileithyia's arms, but she steps out of her mother's reach. "Eileithyia you cannot leave. Who will represent us for child-birth? You have a duty."

Eileithyia smirks, and I'd say it gives Hades a run for his money. "I thought you'd say that. That's why I arranged for those twins you didn't want born to join the Olympians. They are products of father and therefore will possess great abilities. Besides, the sister aided the birth of her brother before I got there. She shall take my place."

I swear I see literal fire burn in Hera's eyes. "You cannot do this."

"Hera, enough. If Eileithyia says they have the capability, then they do," Zeus counters. He looks at his daughter, and for the first time since I've met Zeus, he resembles something of a father. He looks proud. "When will you leave?"

Eileithyia raises her chin. "I have to get my affairs in order. I will make sure Artemis is ready to take on the role." Her eyes fall on me. "The first mother she will aid is in this room."

All eyes fall on me, and my nerves heighten. Instinctively, I cover my belly. Though every eye in this room is on me, mine find Ares. I take comfort in their protectiveness.

"Is it true? Are you finally with child?" Hera asks, taking a timid step toward me.

Hephaestus's hand creeps to the small of my back, and I force myself to look at him and smile but I can't look him in the eye. He answers for me. "Yes, Mother. Aphrodite and I are expecting a child."

The fire that was in Hera's eyes evaporates and a smile lines her lips. "Oh, praise all. Finally!"

Hera hugs us, and I am shocked at how hard it is to hold back tears. It should be Ares at my side. We should be celebrating *our* baby. Instead, he watches me from the corner of the room.

Hera settles next to Zeus, locking arms with him as she leads everyone to the door. "Let us get back to the event with that joyous news fresh on our mind."

CHAPTER 31

ARES

Having to hear Hephaestus claim my child as his own made me angrier than I expected. I was the first one out of the vault to put some much needed distance between me and my brother. Giving my brother a part two to the beating I gave him in the mortal realm would not be a good look for today.

Even now that we're well into the event my eye twitches every time I look at Aphrodite and Hephaestus. My brother takes on the role of a doting husband and it makes me want to vomit. To an untrained eye, he looks the part exceptionally. But for someone trained in studying behavior, I can see how awkward and foreign it is for him.

I have to force myself to stop white-knuckling the banister of the observation deck. An uproar of yells and grimaces fill the arena when one of the recruits currently battling slices the arm of their opponent. Blood sprays and flesh is shredded. It's brutal but this full contact challenge for our recruits is the only real way for them to see where they need to improve.

I peek over at Aphrodite whenever something particularly violent happens. Her grimace makes me want to engulf her in my arms, sheltering her from the brutality I've grown accustomed to.

"Ares!" My mother beams. "I hate to admit this, but your idea has worked brilliantly. I've never seen the villagers this excited about an Olympian event."

I look around the arena to see the villagers in various stages of enjoyment. Each of them cheer on the current trainees battling each other. A lightness fills my chest. I may do many things wrong in my life, but being a good leader is not one of them. I didn't like my orders to stay here at first, but seeing the joy on the villagers faces slowly chips away at that. "It's nice of you to admit it, mother. Besides, if all goes to plan, we'll have a waitlist for recruits by the end of the day. Our people just want to know they're worth something more to us than just subjects."

Hera pats my shoulder. "You sound like a true ruler. I knew you'd settle into your role well. All we had to do was get you here long enough."

Aphrodite's laugh draws my attention to her. She's talking to Dionysus and Eileithyia. Hephaestus is off talking with Poseidon. My molars grind when I think about the way he grabbed her when they made the announcement about the baby.

I see my mother follow my gaze out of the corner of my eye. She turns to me, lifting her chin. "Ares, I have a woman I'd like you to meet. She—"

"I'll pass."

"Ares," she sighs. "I may have said you're settling into your role well, but getting married would only strengthen that. Besides, I think you'll like this woman. She won't lead you astray like others here."

I suddenly feel very hot. My eyes narrow as I turn back to my mother. "I haven't done anything you or father haven't done before. I think you should—"

"Hera, just the person I wanted to see," Athena saunters in, grabbing hold of my mothers arm. "I have someone I want you to meet."

Athena leads my mother away but her eyes never leave mine. I nod, giving her my silent thanks for saving me. I almost made a scene. But that still doesn't make my ichor cool any more. All I see is red and only one thing can make it go away. *Her.*

I'm entering the small circle Dionysus, Eileithyia, and Aphrodite have formed in a matter of seconds. I lean to Aphrodite's ear but I never stop walking. "Follow me." I don't look back to see if she's following me to avoid suspicion. But the truth is, I know she is.

I wait until I approach what is going to be my office at the arena in an abandoned corridor. When she passes the threshold, I snatch her by the waist into the deserted room. She yelps, but I absorb the noise by sealing my lips to hers.

Aphrodite relaxes into my kiss and matches my fever. Her hands rake through my hair and down my back. I break our sealed lips to kiss her neck, licking and sucking on the skin. She gasps, "Ares, what are you doing? The entire city is on the other side of this door."

"I don't give a damn. I need you."

I kiss her again and she doesn't fight me on it. Gripping her thigh, I slide the fabric of her gown closer to her waist. My cock grows painfully hard. She moans into my mouth when I squeeze her ass. It all gets too much. I need every part of her.

I dip my fingers beneath her gown and almost come on the spot when they come back soaked. I smirk, bringing my fingers between us. "Do you like the idea of me fucking you in here while everyone we know is just a few feet away?"

Her eyes go molten when I lick my fingers. "Mhmmm it sure tastes like you do."

When she doesn't answer, I dip my fingers back into her dress. I ghost them over her slick slit. She arches into my touch when I feel the swollen bud of her clit on my finger tip. "Answer me, seductress."

I dip the tip of my middle finger into her cunt. A moan falls from her lips. "Yes."

"Good girl." I dip my middle finger into her, feeling her slick cunt stretch around me. She gasps, gripping my shoulder. I use my thumb to circle her already swollen clit. "Already so eager for me."

I kiss her once, then trace the outline of her jaw. My lips press against the flesh under her ear. I insert another finger, gripping her hips as she arches into me. "Tell me what you want, seductress."

She wines when I curl my fingers, rubbing that soft spot inside of her. "You. I want all of you. I want everything."

I don't waste another second before stealing her breath with a feverish kiss. I speed my work with my fingers. She starts to grow limp and squirmy beneath me.

I continue working her with my fingers, letting my lips explore her skin. I feel her cunt pulsing around me, getting closer and closer to its release. When she's finally on the cusp of coming, I remove my fingers completely. She whines at the loss of contact, but I can't take another second of my cock not being inside of her.

I waste no time removing my cock from my clothes before running it along her slit. "Ares, do not tease me."

I smirk, pleased with how eager she is for me to fuck her. I push into her, slowly at first until I'm fully seated. We both moan when my hips meet hers. My head falls against hers. "Gods, Aphrodite."

I retreat then thrust forward with more force this time. I can feel her stretching around me. Aphrodite clings to me, using her leg to push my hips deeper. Something about her eagerness brings back my urgency. I quicken my thrusts, gripping her thigh for dear life. I use my right hand to brace me against the wall I have Aphrodite pinned against.

She wines when I use my left hand to reposition her hips, taking her deeper. I close the distance between our faces, letting my lips ghost hers as I say, "Shhh seductress. You have to stay quiet no matter how good you're taking my cock."

Something about the downright provocative look in her eyes makes me lose all abandon. I nail her again and again against the wall. "Do you know how wild you drove me, letting him touch you? I wanted to kill him for even standing next to you."

Aphrodite finally breaks her silence. "But he can't fuck me the way you do."

I nearly combust right then and there. I hold nothing back, letting us get caught up in our own passions for each other. I can't get enough of this girl. She is the air that I breathe.

Her back arches from the wall, pushing her breasts into me. Her pussy suffocates my cock as she comes with my name on her lips. I only get a few more pumps before I sag against her, whispering, "Aphrodite. Aphrodite. Aphrodite."

We stand like that for a while, enjoying our quiet corner of the world where it's just us. I kiss her forehead, then lift her chin. "I love you, Aphrodite."

She smiles with swollen lips and a face that looks freshly fucked. "I love you, Ares."

"Now—" I smack her ass after we've fixed our clothes and her hair. My chest feels lighter. "Go out there and act like a lady that isn't dripping my cum."

CHAPTER 32

ARES

No one tells men how sexy it is to see the woman you love carrying your baby. Aphrodite is nearly three months pregnant now, and her belly has only started to swell, but seeing it start to bulge as she examines herself in the mirror is a new level of sensual.

Aphrodite's delicate fingers smooth over her pale belly. "I can't believe we can already see our baby."

She closes her peplos, letting the loose fabric fall against her body. Aphrodite's gown settles against her skin, her brows pull and she frowns. "Since the baby has yet to be announced to the villagers, I suppose they'll think I've indulged in too much bread. My belly isn't round enough for an unkeen eye to know a baby is causing it."

Something dark burrows deep within me at the self-deprecating side of Aphrodite. I stand from the bed and stalk over to her like a hunter homing in on its prey. "I will escort anyone who turns their nose up at you to Tartarus myself."

She rolls her eyes as she turns toward me. "Ares, I'm serious."

"So am I," I say, turning her to face the mirror as I hug her from behind. I kiss her neck and grin when I feel her shiver. I trail my lips down her arm, sneaking around her side until I'm facing her. "You are by far the most beautiful, kind, and exquisite woman I've ever met."

She smiles, and something in my chest warms at the sight. I feel like a wimp, but I don't care. I rip Aphrodite's peplos open and she gasps. "Ares."

"Shhh." I kiss her, then bend to my knees before her. I told myself a long time ago that I'd never kneel to anyone, and here I am doing it willingly for her. I settle my hands on her ever-growing belly and press my lips to the center of it.

"Aphrodite, you are carrying my child. You may not like the changes it is bringing, but I am quite pleased every time I look at you. I see the evidence of my baby inside of you. You are the mother of my child."

I kiss her feverishly, and she melts. Aphrodite gasps against my lips, and I swallow it with my tongue.

It was hard pulling myself away from Aphrodite. But the look on Hebe's face when she said Mother and Father wanted to see me was enough to draw me from my estate.

"What are you doing here?" I sneer at my brother in the throne room.

Disgust that mimics mine lines my brother's face when he sees me. "I could ask you the same thing."

"Now, now, boys, enough of your little sword fight," My mother calls from behind us. I offer her a greeting that immediately drops when my father enters.

"Why did you need to see both of us?" Hephaestus asks, and I roll my eyes at the emphasis he puts on both.

"You aren't the only two coming. Your sisters should be here—" My father stops when the door opens and Hebe and Eileithyia enter. I swear I see his eyes soften at his daughters' appearance. Seeing compassion in my father's eyes is an anomaly. I wonder if that's how others will see me when the baby is born.

Something tightens around my heart, and I swear I sputter a breath when I remember Aphrodite and my baby will never be mine in the eyes of everyone else.

"Why was I summoned? I told you I am not to be included in any more business for the Olympians." Eileithyia crosses her arms.

My mother's eyes harden. "Yes, you've made that clear. We've started preparing for the arrival of Artemis as your replacement and Apollo since they refuse to be separated."

"So why are we here?" I ask, frustrated at how they are beating around the bush.

My mother sighs when my father gives her an encouraging nod. I know whatever information she's about to deliver is going to make at least one of us mad. My father has a knack for making my mother deliver the bad news to her children.

"With Eileithyia leaving, we have a new opening for a senior position in the Olympians. In other words, if your father and I are both away at the same time, this member would serve as acting leader."

"So how do we come into play?" my brother asks.

"We are appointing Ares," Zeus announces when my mother remains silent.

My muscles tense. "What?"

"You have got to be kidding me. Why? I'm the one who's been here through it all. Meanwhile, he was gallivanting around the mortal realm doing gods know what," Hephaestus rambles.

My father's eyes darken like storm clouds. "That's enough. Your mother and I agreed. Ares has the authority to handle it. You do not."

"This institution is a joke. As is this family." My brother glares at each of us before storming out of the room.

I wait until the door clicks shut before turning back to my parents. My sisters stand behind them, looking nervous. "You should have told me this in private. I may not like the bastard, but you didn't have to rub his loss in his face."

"Ares—" My mother reaches for me, but I rip my arm away before she has a chance to hold it.

"I accept the position, but you should have done this a different way." I leave them without another word. While beating my brother usually makes me happy, I worry for Aphrodite. He's proven he's unstable when it comes to me. I don't want Aphrodite anywhere near him right now—or ever if I can help it.

CHAPTER 33

APHRODITE

Dear Journal,
They say to be seen is to be loved. The truth
is he makes me feel seen, loved, heard, and
everything in between. Returning to the waters of
Cyprus was the one thing I needed to be
reminded of who I am at my core. This time,
I'm never going to let myself forget it.

Alexandra and I are enjoying a peaceful afternoon with tea on the balcony. "I've been thinking about the baby's room. Blue and White seem fitting do they not?"

Alexandra smiles. She knows I chose them because of my room at Ares's estate. "I think it—"

"I'm going on a trip to the mortal realm. I'm not sure

when I will be back," Hephaestus announces he walks onto the balcony. He's been on a rampage since his meeting with Hera and Zeus. It's been a month since Ares was anointed a senior member of the Olympians, and yet Hephaestus still sulks like it was yesterday. I've been sneaking in and out of our estate the entire month just so he doesn't get curious as to where I'm staying.

Past me would have loved Hephaestus to say. Yet all I see now is the married life we could have had if he had tried a little harder. It also makes me wonder what would have happened if Ares had come back to Olympus a little sooner. Perhaps he would be my husband and not his brother. Our baby wouldn't grow up not knowing their true father.

I feel sad that Hephaestus was passed up on the position, but at the same time, I can't feel much for a man that nearly killed me. "I shall see you when you return."

He bids me a goodbye and leaves as easily as he came. I turn to Alexandra. "Where were we?"

She sips her tea, then exchanges it for a raspberry tart from Kyra's. "I believe we were deciding how you would like to set up the baby's room. You have a few months, but I know you like everything to be perfect."

I look down at my belly, fighting back tears. "I'm afraid nothing is perfect in my life. It never has been and never will be."

"Whatever do you mean?" Alexandra asks, her brows knitting. She places her hand on mine and it forces me to meet her eyes.

"My child will grow up without knowing the love of their father. Instead, they will get the man I have to walk on eggshells with." I wipe a stray tear from my cheek. "Maybe this is my punishment for finding love. Perhaps, I was never meant for true love. I'm a fraud."

Her delicate and slightly rough hand squeezes mine. "You were forced into this marriage, Aphrodite. No one can blame you for finding someone to love you after you and Hephaestus called your marriage quits."

"That does not change the way my baby has to be raised." The tears take over. Damn pregnancy hysterics.

She shrugs. "Maybe not. But the sincerity with which Ares loves you, and you love your baby is proof enough that you are not a fraud. You never were."

* * *

I've been rifling through fabric samples for the baby's room for what feels like hours. Alexandra said she'd be back, but I've yet to see her again. I'd rather not be alone for dinner, but alas, it appears that will be the case.

The front doors bursts open, and I jump. Ares waltzes in, scoops me in his arms, and hauls me over his shoulder.

"Ares! What are you doing? This can't be safe for the baby!"

"You're right, seductress." he smacks my ass, then contorts me until he's holding me like a bride.

I latch my arms around his neck, looking at him with wide eyes. "What do you think you're doing?"

All he does is smirk before saying, "We're going on an adventure."

He sets me down when we get to the edge of the village.

He doesn't say another word as we weave our way through the villagers and I follow him—eager to find out what tricks he has up his sleeve.

"Ares, where are you taking me?" I ask as he leads us toward his stables. The anticipation eats at every nerve in my body.

"Relax, darling. You will see when we get there." Suddenly, he's on me and rips a strip of fabric from the bottom of my peplos.

"Ares! You ripped my gown." My mouth is a gaping hole as I inspect one of my favorite dresses.

He takes the shred of fabric, covers my eyes, and cinches it to my head. "I will fix it when we get back."

I decide against asking why he's covered my eyes. I know he won't tell me, and I also know Ares would never do anything to put me in harm's way. "Since when does the god of war know how to sew?"

His breath warms my neck, and he lifts me into what I gather is his chariot before settling against my back. "After having your clothes continually sliced on battlefields, you pick up mending skills."

The horses huff, and I rest on Ares's chest as the chariot starts racing out of the stables. The warm air and humidity stick to my skin. The gentle crash of waves tickles my eardrums. Excitement fills me at the sound.

Ares guides me off the chariot when it comes to a halt, turning his horses loose like he always does before he's back on me. His lips press against my neck, and I shiver. "Are you ready, seductress?"

"Yes," I say in a much breathier voice than I expected.

I squint as I adjust to the light. A lump forms in my throat. The aquamarine waters are darker, like cobalt, and they stretch toward the setting pink and orange sun. Waves thrash against giant rocks on either side of the beach.

Cyprus.

"I seem to recall a promise I made before we became us." He hugs me from behind. "I told you I was going to take you to Cyprus. Though, when I did, we were so worried about Eileithyia, we barely got to experience it."

I take a deep breath of the salty air. The warmth spreads through my veins. I step out of Ares's arms and into waves. As I walk into the water, I realize how lost I've been since I moved to Olympus. I think I forgot how to be happy.

I forgot who I was.

I lost myself.

I lean back into the warm water and allow my salty tears to meet the ocean—my little contribution to the thing that made me who I am. The waves hold me as they come and go. With each rise, the darkness that has inhabited me for so long washes away.

I don't know how long I let the ocean guide me. When I open my eyes, I feel like the person I've been estranged from since my departure from the place that built me. Ares stands in waist deep water.

He smiles when I start swimming toward him.

"There's the woman I love."

A blush creeps up my cheeks. I jump into his arms when I finally get close enough. "Thank you."

I realize how right Alexandra was. I am not a fraud. I am loved the way I've coaxed mortals to love.

Ares puts me down and settles his hand on my belly before kissing me deeply. I'm breathless when he releases me. "I love you, Aphrodite. This may not be my baby in the eyes of Olympus. But our love is intertwined in every way as long as our baby breathes. Our love, however quiet, shall have a physical remembrance that will walk the earth and every universe above."

"I love you, Ares."

CHAPTER 34

APHRODITE

Dear Journal,
It's weird how quickly your day can go from good to awful. Like the toss of a coin. I knew Hephaestus would make my relationship and their father's relationship to this child hard, but I didn't expect it to be quite so hard. Now I can only hope that love will prevail.

"Is the baby okay? I've felt a strange fluttering in my stomach the last few days. Is that normal?" I ask. My anxiety seizes every bit of my nerves like a fire in a field of dry grass. Eileithyia's smile is a drizzle of rain over my nerves.

"Everything is perfectly fine with your baby, Aphrodite. Based on the growth rate of the baby, I'd say you're following the gestation pattern of mortals. All is well so far. Those flutters are the baby moving."

My anxiety is replaced with comfort. "Really?"

"Yes." Eileithyia nods, then turns to Artemis who's been standing in the corner. She's been following Eileithyia the past few weeks to smooth the transition between them. "Would you like to feel the baby's position?"

Artemis is timid. Her pale fingers settle on either side of my belly. She presses until she settles on the baby. Her silver-blonde hair—similar to Zeus's—falls into her face. She tucks it behind her ear before looking back at Eileithyia. "I feel the baby."

"Good. This is what a baby should feel like when the mother is drawing near twenty weeks. Now that you've got to feel the baby at this stage, we must visit another expecting mother in the village. Her baby is going on thirty-nine weeks, so she will deliver any day."

Eileithyia waves goodbye and I do the same.

When the door clicks shut, I walk to the mirror to admire how much my belly has grown now that I'm halfway through my pregnancy. The love I have for my baby flows between us like a golden thread that strengthens every day. I've felt it from other mothers with their children, but never quite this strong.

I depart my estate with an extra giddiness to my step. Dionysus is waiting for me at the edge of the property when I get there. I latch my arm on his before saying, "Fancy seeing you here."

* * *

THE HOUSE IS dark when I enter except for the flicker of candle light peeking through the dining room door. Hephaestus is probably scratching the furniture with the weapons he's inspecting.

His apprentice's voice stops me a few steps from the entrance. I'm hidden from view, but I hear their voices as if I'm in the room with them. "What are you going to do with this one? It doesn't look like anything Ares or Athena asked for."

Hephaestus lets out a chuckle and I can almost imagine his expression when he says, "That blade is for Ares. But not one he will wield…"

"Meaning?"

"I've been working on this iron blade since my brother returned. He's been testing me. He thought I'd forget about him telling my wife about my affair or fighting me in the mortal realm, but little does he know, I'm about to have this blade curse for him. One slice of this blade and his soul will be ripped to shreds. Even Hades won't be able to save him."

Bile charges up my throat. I clutch my mouth and rush from the estate as quickly and quietly as I can. The second my feet hit the grass, I spill the contents of my stomach over and over again. I am clammy and shaky by the time my mouth tastes like nothing but the lining of my stomach. I doubt Hephaestus will be able to find anyone strong enough to curse such a blade. But for some reason, I can't shake this feeling that something really bad is going to happen.

CHAPTER 35

APHRODITE

Dear Journal,
Being an Olympian has tested my morals more than being the goddess of love ever has. I think I started losing myself when I was sworn in. It makes me sometimes wonder whether I'd find my old self if I left it all. But he reminds me who I am regardless.

The air in the throne room is stifling today. Between the extra bright sunshine peaking through the pillars and my baby's foot in my lung, everything just feels wrong. Not to mention, I'm being forced to sit next to Hephaestus all day.

Zeus called for an emergency meeting for the Olympians as soon as day broke this morning. Turns out, the meeting he so desperately needed was actually a trial. Now we've been sitting here for the past hour, or at least what feels like it, listening to Zeus give us all of the information about the man that stands in chains in front of us.

"Now—" Zeus claps his hands "the real reason why we're here. Augustus is being charged with high treason."

Dionysus rolls his eyes in his chair across from me. "Oh please, you love to throw that term around. We all know you just want to kill him because he was one of the Titan's warriors. You've killed all of them except the few that are smart enough to stay hidden."

Zeus glares at Dionysus.

Augustus smirks in the middle of the room. "Finally one of you Olympians prove yourselves intelligent."

"That's enough from you," Hera spits at him. She turns to her husband, "Continue dearest."

"As I was saying, Augustus here is being charged with high treason. Several citizens of Olympus have come forward saying that he was passing out these," Zeus waves a stack of papers in the air before passing them to each of us down the line, "at the gladiator event. I think you'll see why I've come up with these charges without jumping to conclusions."

Dionysus narrows his eyes at Zeus's jab. My eyes grow wide when I read the thin, worn paper.

Death to the Olympians. Nothing but blood pours from their dirty hands. It's time their blood spills like the ones before them.

"What are the proposed punishments?" Ares asks, tossing the paper into the middle with something dark looming in his eyes. Even from across the room, he oozes death. Maybe it's something twisted in me or the hormones from his baby, but I have to clench my thighs because I'm so turned on.

Zeus takes on some sort of sinister smirk similar to his son. "Execution, immediately."

Augustus scoffs, his long blonde hair falling over his shoulder with the movement. "Of course. I always knew my days were numbered in Olympus. It was just a matter of time before one of you caught on to who I was."

"That's enough out of you," Zeus spits.

"What? You can be the only one to exchange sharp wits?" Augusta looks at each of us individually. When his green eyes lock on mine, my hand instinctively shoots out to my belly. Almost as if my baby has the same instinct as me, their foot or some other limb meets the hand that covers them as a shield. "Each and everyone of you are a joke. The citizens of Olympus talk, you know? Each of you are either a drunk, a slut, or a rapist. So what does that say about the citizens you rule?"

"Enough!" Ares shouts, slapping the arms of his limestone chair. "You have said enough."

"Agreed," Athena says with pulled brows.

"You're only making your grave ever so looming," Apollo says from his chair next to Ares. He surprises me. Apollo and Artemis have appeared nothing but timid to me. Being that this trial is their first official Olympian ordeal, I'm surprised he has the courage to speak up. Does he think he was something to prove to Hera? If so, he's right.

"I know how he feels," Hephaestus whispers next to me. It's barely loud enough for me to hear but I hear it nonetheless. My hand tightens on my belly. Is he going to side with a man that wants us all dead?

"What other evidence do you have, Zeus?" I ask, trying to soothe myself by rubbing my belly. It's weird. Before I got pregnant, I used alcohol as my crutch. Now that I get sick on it, I connect with my baby. I wonder what it will be after I deliver.

"Do you need much more?" Zeus asks. There's a bite to his tone. I know it's deep-rooted in his failed inquisition of me. But I say nothing.

"It was a fair question. You've presented enough. So has the accused," Poseidon points out. I release a breath, relieved that I'm no longer in the line of question.

Zeus nods, stroking his beard. "I do have other evidence. But do we need much more? The accused has already admitted to his crimes."

We all remain silent for a moment, each locking eyes with another. We have a man's life in our hands. Despite what the man has claimed, we know the weight of our decision.

"All those in favor of a guilty charge," Zeus says, standing as he does so.

One by one nearly every one of us stands. First it's Hera, then Ares, and so on. Even Dionysus stands. I'm hesitant at first but the dark look in Augustus's eye when he met mine was enough to make me shiver. He has the power to make each of us fall. I wouldn't be much of a mother if I didn't use this to protect myself and my child.

I stand, clutching my swollen belly as I do. Hephaestus catches my back as I stand, helping to steady myself. I look at him with a gracious smile because what else is a wife supposed to do with her husband?

Every Olympian is standing.

"I hereby convict Augustus guilty of high treason against the Twelve Olympians," Zeus announces in a booming voice.

The executioner burst through the door with their long sword gripped tightly. His face is covered in an ominous mask. Athena thought it wise to switch the executioner with each Olympian trial to protect their identity, which I suppose gives the recruits another layer of trust towards us.

The two guards that flank him take one step ahead of him, gripping each arm of Augustus. The guards pull each of his arms taut, leaving his head and neck exposed. They bend him forward so that his head is free. The executioner lines his sword up with Augustus's neck. He pulls the blade back, ramming it down in one fell swoop.

I flinch when Augustus's head is severed from his body. His blood sprays on the limestone floor. I stand from my chair, exiting the room as quickly as I can before I vomit on the floor. Despite how dangerous Augustus might have been to us, I can't stomach that I was part of his death.

CHAPTER 36

ARES

"I want all of you to be on your best behavior while Artemis and Apollo settle into their new roles. Once their estates are finished, we will host their official welcome ball." My mother glides across the floor with her arms crossed behind her back. It reminds me of the pre-war talks I give my men. I suppose this is my mother's form of that.

I groan internally. "Mother, we just held the gladiator event at the training arena. Why do we need so many flashy events so close together?"

"You will address me as Hera when we are discussing official Olympian business." Hera spits and turns on me with a glare. My sister fights a smirk or some sort of laugh, and I try not to roll my eyes. "To answer your question, Eileithyia's departure will have the villagers questioning our capability to rule unitedly. By hosting a welcome ball for our newest members, we will draw their attention away from our loss and toward Artemis and Apollo. It is imperative we do not do anything else to rock the boat before this event. Are we clear?"

"Crystal," I grunt.

My mother's flare turns soft. "Good. You all may go."

Artemis and Apollo scamper out quickly with Hermes following behind. Their young ichor is nowhere near ready to deal with this family and establishment. I'm sure my mother will ensure their transition into our organization goes as un-smoothly as she can without the villagers finding out.

My father heads toward his quarters in the Acropolis, talking with Poseidon about who knows what. Everyone else makes their way out, except Hephaestus, Aphrodite, and Eileithyia.

"Can you believe mother is already treating my departure as an inconvenience rather than admitting that it's her fault?" Eileithyia asks, shaking her head with disapproval.

"Have you met our mother?" I laugh, but Aphrodite and Hephaestus are having what seems like a tense conversation and it catches my eye. Towering over my sister makes it easy to watch their conversation unfold.

Hephaestus's jaw clenches while he glares at Aphrodite. Her eyes show nothing. She doesn't look sad or angry or mad. She looks tired. He leaves her with the same glare before he turns it on me, and I return the favor.

"Be careful around him." Eileithyia pulls my attention

away from my swine of a brother. "To you he may still be the same Hephaestus that whines and has the personality of a doorknob. But he's been around our parents long enough to become cunning when he wants to be."

"I appreciate the concern, Sister. However, I think I can manage." I offer before making my way over to Aphrodite. She rubs her swollen belly absentmindedly and seeing it round with our child makes her even more attractive. I didn't think it was possible for Aphrodite to get hotter but seeing her like that does something to me. It makes me want to get her pregnant again.

"What did he say?" I ask, feeling a streak of jealousy and protectiveness wash over me.

Aphrodite rubs her belly again. She swallows, avoiding my eyes when she says, "He said he's going to the mortal realm. He's not sure when he'll be back because what he's trying to find is extremely rare."

I'm confused why she seems so torn up about Hephaestus's departure. "That's a good thing, isn't it? You don't have to live in a constant state of fear at your estate. You can stay with me again."

Something is still amiss. "It's wonderful. Let's go home."

* * *

I TOLD Aphrodite to go grab her belongings from Hephaestus's before coming to ours. We could have gone together, but after the way Hephaestus reacted when he thought about us being together, I don't want to risk anything—especially with the baby. It also gives me time to put some finishing touches on a surprise I have for her.

"Ares? I'm home," Aphrodite calls.

I catch myself smiling at the way she calls this place home, and I start to wonder when I became such a softie. I hope my enemies never catch wind of it. I greet her with a kiss before saying, "Hello, seductress. I have a surprise for you."

Her eyes light up and I smile even more. Gods, she is adorable. I lead her to the back of the house and out to the patio on the ground level.

"I'm going to need you to close your eyes for me." I cover her eyes with my hands and hers clasp around my wrist.

"What if I fall? That won't be good for the baby."

"I won't let you fall. I've got both of you." I lead us into the small gardens and stop us in the center. I kiss the top of Aphrodite's hair. "Are you ready?"

She nods.

"One. Two. Three." I remove my hands from her eyes and watch her as she takes in the gardens I've built for her.

"Ares, is this—"

"A rose and peony garden built for you. I thought that during our secret visits with the baby, we could come here." I'd spent weeks finding the perfect flowers that wouldn't take much effort for me to upkeep. I don't have a green toe or whatever the fuck it's called. "You once said roses were your favorite, but I haven't seen you look or touch one since you found out about Hephaestus's affair.."

"Oh, Ares." She rubs her chest as she turns to me. Tears fill her eyes, and my stomach hollows.

"Is something wrong? Did I get the flowers wrong?"

She shakes her head and cries more. "No, everything's perfect."

My brows pull taut. "Then what is it?"

"Roses symbolize love and beauty. After that night, I had never felt more like a fraud. As though I lacked everything I represent." She wipes a tear, and all I can do is pull her into my arms.

I tighten my arms around her, nuzzling into her neck. "We may go somewhere else if you'd like. We do not have to stay in the garden if it upsets you."

She shakes her head, pulling back in my arms to look up at me. Her wet, sea glass eyes meet mine. "The garden is perfect. I'm crying because no one has ever done anything like this for me. They've never cared enough. No one has ever loved me enough."

I take her cheeks in each of my hands and lean down until I'm eye level with her. "I love you, Aphrodite. If I could kill every person who has ever wronged you, I would.

"Unfortunately, that would be half of the Olympians so I'm not sure that would go over very well." She giggles through her tears, and I continue, "Either way, your days of feeling overlooked and underappreciated are over. Gods, I would have settled for stolen glances from you for eternity if I had to. But I was lucky enough to get more of you. You are the air that I breathe. You're everything."

Aphrodite's eyes lighten and her wet cheeks pull tight with the smile that spreads on her lips. "I love you, Ares."

She kisses me tenderly, and I pull her against me as best I can with her belly. My tongue traces the outline of her lips, and she lets me in. My fingers run through her hair and tug roughly. Aphrodite pushes away from me, her eyes large.

"Did I hurt you?"

She shakes her head, and her hand falls to her belly. "The baby is moving."

Aphrodite takes my hand, placing it low on the right side. We wait, still as trees for only a second before I feel—a kick. It's like the smallest of taps against my hands. Our baby. A lady-bug lands on our hands. I start to remove it but she stops me, letting it crawl on our inter-locked hands.

We meet each other's eyes with the same wonder-filled expression before I kiss her again. Hard.

APHRODITE

Dear Journal,

It's been easy these past few weeks with Hephaestus's revenge plan to forget how great it feels when I help people. Watching the mortals find fulfillment, and Hebe blossom because of my aid is more rewarding than I remember. I suppose it's the small victories I need to cling too in these coming weeks. The love I have for my soldier has only blossomed with the growing of our baby. I can't wait to see him become a father.

I've spent the past week at the Acropolis on the Mount from sun up to sun down. Cyprus has been holding a festival in my honor. While the mortals are honoring me, I feel like I should be honoring whatever god listened to my pleads. For the first time since I moved to Olympus, everything feels right. Ever since I found out I was pregnant, I've forced myself to look at what is right in my life. Turns out, I had a lot going for me once I stopped dwelling on what was wrong.

Hera has been so pleased with my uptick in mortal approval that I'm being given a study in the Acropolis like other senior members of the Olympians. I'm finally being accepted by her. I'm sure the grandchild I carry for her also had something to do with it, but I don't care.

I circle the basin beneath my chair in the throne room one final time for the evening. The enchanted water reveals a sculptor I've seen a lot of this past week. His love flows from him like a river looking for the sea. It's enchanting. His prayers have not fallen on deaf ears.

He kneels at the foot of the sculpture he'd named Galatea. I remember the day he finished the work. My powers sparked. To him, the white-marble stone is nothing but perfect. Galatea is the only woman in his eyes. His devotion to the work is admirable, something some mortals don't even have for their human partners.

"Aphrodite, Aphrodite, please. I will do anything. Show me a woman as perfect as Galatea. I shall be forever indebted to you. I will craft great statues in your honor." Pygmalion prays over and over, rocking back and forth on his knees in front of the sculpture.

My hand starts to warm just as it has hundreds of times before. I circle the enchanted water with my fingers letting it ripple against my flesh. I take a deep breath, closing my eyes as I do while my powers seep from my skin and into the mortal scene. When I re-open my eyes, the statue of Galatea begins to glow, taking on a bright, milky-white glow. The light continues to get brighter and brighter until Pygmalion is forced to shield his eyes.

The light is extinguished and a voice fills the otherwise silent studio Pygmalion was praying to me in. "Pygmalion?"

His eyes grow large and he falls onto his rear. "Galatea?"

What was once a white-marble statue, now stands a beautiful woman with milk-white skin and bright red hair. She examines her hands, stretching her fingers like it's a foreign concept—and to her it is.

Pygmalion stands, placing a hand on Galatea's cheek so soft you'd think he was going to shatter her. When his hand finds warm skin in place of the cold stone he'd fallen in love with, his love explodes. It seeps through the water basin, hugging me tight. "My gods, it's you."

Galatea melts into his touch before he seizes her lips in one searing kiss.

I swirl the water once more, letting the scene fade. I've done all I needed to. They will find their happiness without my aid now as I've already blessed them with a happy life.

The power of their love keeps me warm all the way home. I find Hebe lounging on the drawing room couch. "Oh, hello, Hebe. I'm afraid your brother will be at the training arena all evening. The success of the gladiator event has him and Athena scrambling to find room for everyone interested in training."

"That's okay." She sits up, straightening her gown as she does so. "I came to see you."

"Me?" I turn, quite surprised. Don't get me wrong, I enjoy Hebe's company. But we've never sought each other out. I wonder if that would be different if I had married Ares instead of Hephaestus.

She nods, suddenly looking a little nervous. She runs her hands over her knees. I turn to pour her a glass of what was my favorite wine before I got pregnant. "Here, drink this. It will help with the nerves."

She accepts it with a timid smile. "Thank you."

As the wine seeps into her body, I can see her nerves dwindle. I take a seat next to her, hoping that some of my powers will comfort her. "What is it that's pestering you?"

"I want to leave Olympus. Well, I am leaving Olympus." She looks over her shoulder and I find it hard to mask my shock when we lock eyes.

"Why? You are the last of your parent's children that I would have expected to leave. You always seemed to love it here." I run my hand over my belly while the baby moves. I still have close to ten weeks left according to Eiliethyia, and yet I'm shocked at how much I can feel the baby's movements. It makes me worry about how uncomfortable I'm going to be right before I deliver.

Hebe shifts on the couch so that we can face each other. "You helped me realize that I didn't love this city at all. In fact I was void of love entirely."

The golden tether I feel between me and my baby masks itself for a moment. In its absence, I'm finally able to feel how strong Hebe's has grown. In place of that golden tether is an impenetrable chain. "Cassander."

She nods with a blush. Her light brown hair falls into her face. She tucks it behind her ear before saying, "So you understand?"

I take her hand, giving it a reassuring squeeze. "Of course I do. I felt the connection between the two of you the moment you locked eyes. I didn't even have to aid you in finding him."

Her eyes go soft, sparkling in the dimly lit room now that the sun has sunk. "I really do love him. You were right in Cyprus. I can't decide how it ends before it's even begun."

My heart warms. That golden chain between her and Cassander just grew even stronger. "I'm glad you decided to take my advice."

She shrugs, taking a sip of her wine. "The mortals worship you for advice like that. All I had to do was go on a walk with you. I figured the least I could do is listen to it."

We both giggle at that.

"How are you going to tell your parents?"

"I told them this morning. They weren't happy about it but I'm not an Olympian so there's nothing they can do about it. They threatened to bring me back every time I left until I promised them I'd use my influence to encourage the mortals to worship them."

"And did that work?"

Hebe nods before finishing the wine I'd given her. "My mother seemed pleased with it. My father seemed sad but I am his favorite so I'm not surprised."

I'd be lying if I said a piece of my heart hadn't just broken.

They let Hebe leave—something I'd prayed for every night until Ares and I met again. I blink away my tears and swallow the lump in my throat. "I'm happy for you."

"Thank you." She smiles.

"Have you told your brother yet?"

Hebe shakes her head. "I wanted to tell you first. After all, you are the one I have to thank for convincing me to take this step."

"I'm sure he will be saddened by your absence."

"He'll be okay. He has a love of his own now after all." She waves me off.

I smile at that, looking down at my swollen belly. The crack in my heart is filled just as quick as it appeared. "When will you leave?"

"Right after I tell Ares and Eileithyia. I have an arrangement with Hermes to take me." She takes my hand, giving it a squeeze. "Can I ask one thing of you in my absence?"

"What is it?"

"Protect my brother's heart. He's the strongest man I know, and you've promised him the world. You and this baby *are* his world now. Don't let anything or anyone rip those away from him"

My eyes start to sting again for an entirely different reason. "I promise."

"Good." She smiles, pulling me into her embrace. "I'm going to miss you, dear sister."

CHAPTER 38

APHRODITE

I never knew picking a wooden cradle would be so hard. The

shop in town has one made with almost every type of wood there is and in every color finish imaginable.

"I think I'll take the light Cyprus cedar." I point to the first one that caught my eyes. I should have known that would be the one when I read where it was from.

"Good choice. The Cyprus cedar is also my wife's favorite. She says it's the best for the babies." The craftsman grins. "When is a good time to deliver the cradle? We make them all by hand so it may take some time, but I can rush it for you, Goddess."

"Whenever you finish making it is fine. There is no rush required. I still have about three months." I still can't believe I will have a baby of my own in just a few months. Our bond grows stronger and stronger every day, and it reminds me of how lost I felt before Ares and our child. They have helped me learn who I am, and they don't even know it.

"Nonsense, making a cradle for an Olympian is an honor." The craftsman's eyes light up. "My wife will be ecstatic when I tell her I'm making a cradle for the goddess of love."

"I can assure you I am not that different from the two of you. I need no preferential treatment, Mister—"

"Georgio," he finishes. "And as you wish, ma'am."

"Thank you." I finish the order form for the cradle, and I pay Georgio a little more than he asked. He was a good man who was practically bursting at the seams with love for his wife, and he deserves a little help with his business.

* * *

THE SMELL of spilled wine and spirits makes my nostrils burn and stomach roll. A man nods his head with a greeting grin as he passes me. I almost laugh at how naturally he walks around naked but then I remember where I am. A woman passes me next with her peplos untied, barely covering her bare chest. She does some sort of curtsey before saying, "Goddess."

I offer her a smile because that's all I can muster without laughing, and I don't want to be unnecessarily rude. I finally find Dionysus in his drawing room. "Seems I missed quite the party."

"A party indeed." Dionysus smirks, and it's nothing short of feline. "It's a pity you're in the family way now. I expect you'll be quite boring once that baby arrives."

I fight the rage that washes over me. I know Dionysus is kidding, but something about the dismissal of my baby has me seeing red.

"Calm down, Aphrodite. There was no inkling of truth behind that. If anything, you'll be off with its father even more. You may even be pregnant again before it's three months old." He laughs.

"Are you done?" He did nothing to dissipate my anger. My fingernails dig into the palms of my hand at how tightly I clench them.

The scent of wine seeps from his skin, and it makes me gag but I mask it. He hands me a chalice. "I'm being an asshole because I've missed my friend. Here, drink."

I'm hesitant about taking the cup, but he reassures me before I can say anything. "It's okay. It's juice. Last time we talked, you said wine made you sick."

The fire inside settles into a warm, fuzzy blanket wrapped around me. "Thank you."

"I've seen Hephaestus around. How has that been?" Dionysus sips his wine.

I take a nervous sip of my juice, and it makes me realize how much I relied on alcohol before I got pregnant. My skin crawls.

"It makes seeing Ares extremely difficult. After I told Hephaestus I was with child, he insisted he would take a more active role here rather than staying with his mistress."

Without missing a beat he asks, "Does he know it's not his?"

I freeze, chalice halfway to my mouth before meeting him with wide eyes. "That's not true."

Dionysus levels me with an expression that looks like I called him stupid. "Aphrodite, you may be able to convince everyone in Olympus that your baby is Hephaestus's, but I am not one of them. Nor do I need to be. I'm the one who told you to fuck Ares."

"Either way, Hephaestus can never know it is not his child. He especially can't know it is Ares's baby." I rub my belly when our baby kicks it particularly hard.

"Do you really think Hephaestus will care? He spent your entire marriage and engagement sleeping with another woman."

I swallow thickly, my hands growing clammy. "Hephaestus almost killed me when he even *thought* I was sleeping with Ares. If he finds out about this baby it'd be a death sentence for both of us."

Dionysus goes cold, and his eyes go almost black. "He what?"

Most of the villagers and mortals may not realize that the Olympians have a dark side. I may have tapped into Dionysus's, and I would hate to be on the receiving end of it. "Don't worry, Di. Ares took care of it the night it happened. You don't need to do anything."

"That bastard deserves *everything* that comes to him. Next time I see him I'm going to—"

"Enough!" I snap. I'm tired of being made helpless. I'm an Olympian dammit. I can hold my own. "Change the subject. Please."

I watch as the darkness slowly dies to the light I usually see in Dionysus's eyes. He chugs the rest of his wine and sets it down with a clamber. "Do you plan on having slutty party sex with Ares at Apollo and Artemis's welcome ball?"

We both laugh and it feels good. I needed my friend.

CHAPTER 39

APHRODITE

Dear Journal,

It's strange, that feeling you get when you know you'll always be protected, but something is still lurking in the darkness, waiting to strike the moment you're weak. I got that feeling today. The only thing I felt in response was a wave of protectiveness for my baby. They say you become stronger when you become a mother. You're willing to do anything to protect your child. I haven't had my baby yet, but I will let this world burn before anyone touches them, or my soldier.

"Ares, what is with all of these surprises? You gave me a garden two months ago. I don't think I need to be spoiled this much." I say as Ares guides me through the estate with covered eyes.

"You deserve everything. I'd give you the world if I could. But this will have to do for now."

Ares uncovers my eyes to the sunlit blue and white room I decorated many months ago. But it's different.

Rather than the large bed I had centered on the wall, there is a wooden cradle stained with the lightest stain. The small cot inside is lined with the same soft fabrics the bed once had. Across the dressing cabinet sits a smaller version of it with a cushion pad. Cloth diapers lay next to it in a neatly folded stack.

"You built a nursery?"

He presses his lips against my neck. "Of course. I may not be able to see you as often as I want, but our baby will need somewhere to sleep when you both get to visit. Besides, I may not be able to give you the world, but I have a feeling this baby will feel like it."

I intertwine our hands and lean into his touch. "I don't deserve you."

He kisses my neck again then my cheek. "You deserve so much more."

* * *

I ENTER my estate in a love-drunk haze. Hanging my himation on the hook by the door, I fight the smile that's wanted to fill my cheeks. Nothing could ruin this day. Ares and I had the most splendid morning, and now we have to attend Apollo and Artemis' welcome ball.

My stomach drops and I swear I feel the baby drop with it when I see Hephaestus standing in the foyer. "What are you doing here?"

"My mother had Hermes hunt me down to remind me about the ball. I figured it wouldn't hurt to accompany my wife." His eyes are suspiciously light. It makes bile creep up higher.

I have to take several deep breaths to keep from throwing up all over our marble floor. "Did you find the material you were looking for?"

He shakes his head, but the light never leaves his eyes." No, but I did get a good tip from a mortal before I left. I was looking for it in Greece. They told me I have to go to the Baltic Sea to get it. It'll take about six weeks to get that deep in the mountains. I'll leave after the ball."

He places a foreign kiss on the top of my head. "How's the baby?"

I take another deep breath, swallowing the bile that escaped my stomach. I plaster the best fake smile I can on my face. "So far so good. Eileithyia says it's growing steadily. I have about eight weeks before they make their arrival."

"Wonderful. I'll have extra time to get everything settled here before our child makes their debut." His smile has a hint of madness in it. He squeezes my hand before walking away, but not before he says, "Get ready for the ball. I'll be here for you when you're ready."

Alexandra is waiting for me when I get to my bedchamber. She has my party dress laid neatly on the bed and my jewels on the dresser. "Would you like to bathe before the party? If we start now, you should have enough time."

A wave of pain starts at the top of my stomach and rolls down. I exhale, not wanting to raise concerns from Alexandra. The pain subsides shortly after. "A bath would be lovely."

She helps me in and out of the warm, eucalyptus scented water. After the bath, we waste no time. She pulls some of the front strands of my hair back and ties them into braids before stuffing miniature gold flowers throughout. Once I get into my white peplos, we fasten it with both gold and silver jewelry to signify my support of the new Olympians as their colors are gold and silver.

As we're putting the last of my jewelry on, my stomach tightens again. My hand covers my belly. It feels rock hard. The pain takes my breath away for a moment.

"Are you alright?" Alexandra walks around with worried-filled eyes. She scans me and alarm overtakes her when she sees me grabbing my belly. The pain subsides and I release it.

"I'm fine. The baby kicked me really hard."

It's a lie, but I can't afford to miss this party. If I did, I'm afraid Hera would hunt me down, baby or not. Besides, Eileithyia will be there if anything is wrong.

Alexandra gives me a look that I know means she doesn't believe me, but she says nothing. "Very well. You're ready."

"Thank you." I bid her a good night before going downstairs to find my husband waiting for me.

"You look nice." Hephaestus grins and it still feels foreign to see him being nice after so long of being ignored and abused by him.

"Thank you," I say before we climb into our chariot and

head toward the Acropolis. Hera was worried that hosting the party in either Artemis's or Apollo's estates would show favoritism, so she deemed the Acropolis neutral enough. Although I don't think either of them particularly care about favoritism, especially from the woman that tried to kill them before they were born.

Dozens of high-profile villagers are already filing into the Acropolis when Hephaestus and I stop in front. Hephaestus climbs out first, then offers his hand to help me down.

My skin crawls when I make contact with him. I miss a step coming down when my stomach contracts again. Hephaestus grabs me by my shoulders and steadies me before he asks, "Are you alright? You almost took a spill. We wouldn't want that."

The tightness subsides, and I take a few steadying breaths to regain my composure. I square my shoulders, lift my chin, and slip into the role of happy wife to the man at my side. I say, "Never better. Let's go."

The throne room is set up like it was for Ares's welcome party nearly a year ago. Both Artemis's and Apollo's chairs are decorated to signify it's their party. A band sits in a crescent beneath Zeus's and Hera's thrones, playing a melody for the party patrons to dance to.

Hephaestus leans into my ear so I can hear him over the music and crowd. "Shall we dance so my mother doesn't complain about us not fulfilling our roles as Olympians? I suspect everyone will only expect one dance from you since you're so close to giving birth." My heart beats a little faster at his closeness and not in the same way it does with Ares.

I take his hand at the conclusion of the current song.

Thankfully, the next one is slower, so I don't have to move as much. As we dance, I look everywhere but at Hephaestus. Somewhere in the middle of the songs, I find Hera looking very pleased at the edge of the dance floor. She raises her glass to me and smiles that calculated smile of hers.

We turn, and as if on instinct, I find Ares like a moth to the flame. I'm already dancing in the middle of the fire, waiting for everything to burn up around me until it engulfs me. His eyes lock on mine, and I see the primal madness shining in them. Hephaestus and I turn again, and based on the way his hands tighten, he must see Ares too.

My stomach cramps worse than it ever has and I lurch forward. I grip Hephaestus's arm like my life depends on it. Lucky for me, the song ended just as the cramp began so everyone was too busy getting ready for the next song to notice my outburst.

"Aphrodite, what's wrong?" Ares is behind me before I even look back. I could *feel* him.

"She's fine. Why don't you go back to whatever whore you were trying to seduce." Hephaestus looks at him with a scowl, and I finally see the man I've come to know as my husband.

Ares takes a step closer, jaw and fists clenched. "She's clearly not okay. She can't even stand up straight."

"She's fine. She's not your wife." Hephaestus leans over me to get closer to Ares.

"No, she's yours. But you better believe that if she were mine, she'd be worshipped instead of discarded and beaten. She needs a real man, not a coward like you."

My belly contracts again, and I keel over more. Ares

catches me, and now I'm stuck between my husband and the man who treats me the way a wife should be treated.

"What is wrong with her?" Eileithyia rushes over and kneels to meet me at eye level.

"According to her husband nothing," Ares grumbles.

"Why don't you go in the corner and play with your swords." Hephaestus matches his brother's sneer.

"Eileithyia, I—" My sentence is cut short by the gasp that overtakes me at another cramp.

"Gods, you're having contractions." Eileithyia's eyes grow wide, and it causes me to panic.

"Is the baby okay? Eiliethyia, please tell me it's okay. It's too early to deliver." I'm supposed to have another eight weeks left. Tears well in my eyes, but I try to keep them from falling so we don't create more of a scene.

"It will be okay if I can get you out of here and somewhere calm enough to stop your contractions." Eileithyia comes to a stand above me. "We need to get her somewhere quiet. The noise and chaos will do nothing but make her contractions progress. We can go to my old study."

"I'll take her," Hephaestus says.

"No, I will take her. I'm stronger," Ares challenges.

"I'm her husband."

"Stop!" Eileithyia scolds them. "Your feud is only making it worse. Ares, help me take her to my study. It's on the second floor in the east corridor."

"But—"

Eileithyia holds up her and stops her brother before he can say anything else. "No. I don't care if you're her husband in name. A husband would never nearly kill his wife and unborn baby. You've done enough."

Hephaestus glares at his siblings, then looks down at me and says, "I'll see you in a few weeks. I have to get that special material from the Baltic Sea."

We barely make it a step out of the throne room when Hera marches towards us. "Ares, what did you do to your brother?"

"I didn't do anything, Mother. I can't help that he's a whiny coward." He guides me another step and my belly relaxes slowly.

"Do not speak of him that way. He is your brother!" Her voice raises to almost a shriek.

"Eileithyia," I mutter when the tightness starts again.

"Ares." She helps me stand up straight. "She needs to get away from this party."

Ares looks at his mother, then at me, then at his mother again. "Eileithyia, are you able to get her there while I handle this? I will meet you when I'm finished."

She nods, and we leave on without him. The cramps go through cycles of tightening and loosening the entire way to Eileithyia's study.

"Eileithyia, Hephaestus can't leave. Someone needs to stop him," I whine as she helps me onto the cushioned couch in the center of the room.

"Why would anyone want to do that? He almost killed you a few months ago," she says and presses on my belly in several spots.

"He's going to try to kill Ares. He's going to the Baltic Sea to have an iron blade cursed to rip Ares soul to shreds." My belly tightens again, and this time, it hurts so much it draws tears to my eyes.

Eileithyia's hand stills. "What? How long have you known?"

"I never thought he'd manage to find someone with enough power to do it, so I didn't say anything. But he's on his way to do that very thing. Ares can't die." The pain intensifies

"Aphrodite, calm down. Based on the speed and consistency of your contractions, if I can't get them to stop, you will have to deliver this baby. I need you to breathe so I can help you." Eileithyia grabs my hand and squeezes. She brushes my hair back and her hand settles against my cheek.

I take several deep breaths with her and the contractions ease but don't stop with each breath. "He can't die."

"He's not going to," she assures me and guides me through another long breathing exercise. I continue breathing while she gets up to grab a bottle of oil from the shelves against the far wall of her study. She rubs her hands in the oil before settling back on my belly. Her eyes close. Eileithyia's hands begin to warm against my skin. My contractions ease and I feel my baby move higher up in my womb. It's slow and uncomfortable, but the higher it moves, the more my pain subsides.

In this light, I'm able to see how much she looks like her mother. Gods that must pain her with all the things that woman has done to her. I hope she finds peace in knowing that her character sets her miles apart from her mother.

Eileithyia continues to hold my belly, and my contractions turn to mild cramps. It isn't until they stop altogether that she asks, "Have you told Ares?"

"Told me what?" Ares's voice meets my ears from what I assume is the threshold of the study. He crouches next to me, taking my hand. He places a kiss on the top of it. "Is she okay? Is the baby okay?"

Eileithyia nods while examining my belly before she says, "She's fine. She and the baby have both settled. I was able to move the baby away from the cervix to stop the labor. However, I am ordering you to house rest. You may not participate in any Olympian business until after this baby comes."

"I don't think Hera will like that very much," I say and rub my belly now that the baby has decided to stay there.

"Leave that to me. There is much that the two of you need to discuss, so I will leave you to it."

Ares waits until the door snicks shut before kissing my hand again. "What is it you wanted to tell me?"

The last thing I want to do is get the baby worked up again. "Hephaestus is plotting an assassination attempt against you."

He stills the hand that was rubbing my belly. "What?"

"I overheard him a few weeks ago talking about getting an iron blade cursed by a witch so it wouldn't only kill you but rip your soul to shreds too. I didn't say anything because I never expected him to find someone that had that much power, but he has and now he's on his way to the Baltic Sea to do it. I'm sorry I didn't tell you."

Ares is silent for a while, and it makes me nervous. When he resumes circling my belly, I release half of a breath. The absence of anger in his eyes allows my nerves to settle. "Aphrodite, you don't need to be sorry. You made the right decision. Although I would have preferred it not get you so worked up that you nearly deliver our baby two months early."

"So you aren't mad?" I ask as he kisses my forehead.

Ares positions us so I'm lying between his legs and against his chest on the couch. The rubs my arms languidly. My left arm reaches back to hold his. "No, I'm not because you forgot the biggest part of this plot he's cooked up."

"What's that?"

"If he wants to kill me, he's going to have to outfight me."

CHAPTER 40

"**W**hy didn't you want to take Eileithyia's study in the Acropolis?" Athena asks as she enters my makeshift study in the training arena. It's not much yet but it will be.

"If my parents want me to step into my role as their second in command, then I need a study that aligns with my duties. Having my study here allows me to oversee the troops more closely and therefore make a stronger Olympus." I answer but my attention is focused on the fabric samples Aphrodite sent earlier.

I don't know if she knows, but she could pick the ugliest color in existence, and I'd still love it because she picked it. Settling on the deep crimson and gold patterns, I look at

Athena. "Besides, I want that study to remain empty to remind them that they drove their daughter from Olympus."

"Ah, passive vengeance. I like it." Athena takes a seat across from me.

"Did you need something?"

"You've been distracted since Artemis and Apollo's welcome party. I'm trying to figure out why. Did you meet a girl?" She leans forward, elbows on her knees.

I try to look bored with the conversation.

"You did. What's she like?" Athena's smirk turns into amusement. "Women around Olympus have been dying to know what Ares's type is."

I roll my eyes. I'm thankful Athena bought my silence as admittance because the further I lead people away from Aphrodite, the better for the baby. "Why do you care?"

"I don't." Her face smooths into the stoicism I see her use with the recruits. "In fact, I'd rather not discuss our love lives, but if it is going to cloud your judgement in the arena, then it needs to be handled."

I drop the papers I was holding and lean over my desk with annoyance clawing and overtaking my veins. "My love life will never interfere with my work. I know how to keep them separate. There is no handling that needs to be done. Clear?"

Athena stares for several seconds. "You looked like our father."

Whatever pride I felt is extinguished, and my cheeks burn. "I thought you didn't want to be referred to as his daughter."

She giggles, and it annoys me. "I don't but that was a marvelous reaction on your part."

"If you're done patronizing me, I have better things to do."

"I'm done if you're not willing to share what's bothering you." She starts to stand, but I stop her. "Do you know if it's possible to curse a blade to rip someone's soul apart?"

Athena turns on her heel with a furrowed brow. "I don't think I've ever heard of such a thing. Although, it would be an amazing weapon. Could you imagine the order we'd have with the threat of a weapon like that?" Athena makes my determination to get this weapon from my brother even stronger. "Why do you ask?"

I shake my head. "No reason. I'm brainstorming to improve our ranks."

Her skepticism doesn't leave her as she starts for the door. "As long as you're focused on the arena."

APHRODITE IS in the garden when I get back home. The second I see her my cock swells. She's lying on a blanket in the middle of the garden I built for her with her peplos unfastened and beneath her. Her smooth legs glisten in the sun and they lead into her swollen belly and breasts that I didn't think could get any better before I got her pregnant. "Seductress."

She uses her hand to shield her eyes from the sun. "Hi, soldier."

"What's all this?" I ask as I saunter over to her.

"Eileithyia says the sun can be a good way to help the baby and I remain at ease. I figured if I'm going to be lying out here, I might as well allow my whole body to feel its effects. She shrugs and unshades her face again.

"I see," I say.

I stand over her and unfasten the string that holds my chiton together. Aphrodite turns as my chiton slips from my skin and pools at my feet. My cock is already so hard it almost hurts.

"What are you doing?" Her voice is a whisper as I kneel on the ground and force her legs open.

I push through her legs, kissing her neck. "Enjoying the sun."

She gasps when I take her sensitive nipple in my mouth and flick it with my tongue before biting it lightly. I switch nipples, palming her free breast in my hand while my mouth works the other.

I work her nipples with my mouth while my fingers trail down her belly only to find her pussy soaked. I groan against her nipple, coating my fingers in the slickness between her tights. Circling her clit, she arches into my touch. "Ares."

"Do you like it when I use my fingers to fuck you?" I say against her throat, then suck the pale skin there as I push my middle finger into her. She pants while I work the finger in and out. I add a second finger and she gasps. "I asked you a question, seductress. Do you like it when I finger fuck you?"

"Yes," Aphrodite whines, and I curve my fingers up, rubbing the spot that makes her melt beneath me. "Oh gods. Don't stop."

I do what she doesn't want, and I remove my fingers. She protests. "Ares."

"Shhh. Let me take care of you, seductress." I throw her legs over my shoulders, bending down until I'm able to lick a strip up the side of her pussy. She shivers, and I do it again to the other side then blow a cold breath against it. Goose bumps erupt on her skin.

Without hesitation, I delve my tongue in and out of her. I take turns tongue fucking her pussy and sucking her clit. It doesn't take long for her thighs to start choking my neck. It only turns me on even more.

I don't let up until Aphrodite is a shaking, moaning mess beneath me. Her eyes are shiny with passion when I finally come up for air. I kiss her, making her taste herself against my tongue, and she welcomes me.

She smiles against my lips. "Eileithyia was right, the sun is quite good."

I kiss her one last time. "Indeed."

CHAPTER 41

APHRODITE

"Aphrodite, how good it is to see you. It feels like ages since I've seen you." Orion says from behind the bar. "Can I get you a drink?"

I shake my head. I'm not sure how much more I can grow and still be able to walk. Everything is swollen, my pelvis hurts, my ankles scream at me after walking far distances—hence why Eileithyia told me to stay home as much as possible. I don't know how I'm supposed to carry this baby another month.

"I'm afraid not. The baby doesn't like wine the same way I did. Although as soon as they're born, you'll be the first person I see."

"I'll hold you to that." He chuckles while polishing a glass as he does so. "What can I do for you?"

"I'd like to buy a bottle of wine for Eileithyia. She's helped me so much with this pregnancy. I'd like to give her a going away gift."

"It's a shame she's leaving. She's probably the main reason the transition for the Eleven, or Twelve Olympians as you are now, went so smoothly. She's the one that cared about us commoners. Anyway, her favorite wine is the sweet red muscadine. I'll grab one for you."

I rub the right side of my belly while the baby moves, hoping I soothe them back to a resting state. Orion comes back with the bottle he promised, and I smile. "Thank you. How much do I owe you?"

"It's on me. Tell Eileithyia I said goodbye."

"Thank you, Orion."

As I turn to leave, Hephaestus's apprentices enter the bar. "Oh Aphrodite, you heard the good news already."

"Good news?" I ask.

"Hephaestus found what he was looking for. He's on his way back now. Nico just came back with the message," he points to the other apprentice at his side.

"I thought he said it was going to take six weeks. It's only been four." My heart quickens in my chest and my mouth feels dry.

"I guess he was able to navigate the terrain better than he expected." His apprentice shrugs. "He'll be back in a few days."

I have to remind myself how to walk to get out of The Muses. By the time I make it back outside, I feel like I can't breathe. I try to walk as fast as I can with how pregnant I am.

Hephaestus is coming back. With the sword. To kill Ares.

A stabbing sensation fills my womb and I cling to the wall next to me for stability. The wine bottle shatters on the ground with a loud crash. "Shit."

"Aphrodite? Are you okay?" Dionysus finds me leaning against the wall.

The pain intensifies, and I press my hand to my belly to try to find relief. I groan and tears almost prick my eyes. "I need Eileithyia. Now."

"Let's get you home." Dionysus wraps his arm around my back and hooks his hand under my armpit to help me walk.

The contraction goes away as we walk, and I try to do the breathing exercises Eileithyia showed me last time. We make it halfway through the village before another contraction has me doubling over again. "I can't do it."

"Dionysus, what's going on?" Alexandra walks out of a shop she'd been in. She kneels in front of me and her face smooths in understanding. "I'll get Eileithyia."

"Get Ares. I can take her to Eileithyia," Dionysus commands.

Alexandra nods and she's gone as quick as she came, and Dionysus hauls forward again. "We're almost there, Aphrodite. Just a little bit further."

"I can't." I shake my head, tears brimming. I try to breathe but a contraction in my back keeps me from doing it properly.

Dionysis is silently looking around us before he settles me. I lean against him, letting my head drop as I take several deep breaths through my contraction. He sighs, "Fuck it."

He scoops me up in his arms, his right arm beneath my knees and his left supporting my back. With surprising strength, he walks us through the streets with ease toward the outskirts of the village.

"It's too risky to take me to Ares's estate. There are too many people that could see us." I try to argue, but I know it's no use. I need a safe place to rest, and Dionysus knows.

"Eileithyia's estate is in this direction too." We make it to Eileithyia's estate in record time but by the time we get there, my contractions have me in tears. "Eileithyia!"

"What the hell are you doin— Aphrodite?" Eileithyia's eyes are wide when they find me.

"She's in labor. I found her in the street hunched over in pain." Dionysus starts to set me down, but Eileithyia stops him.

"Help me take her to my guest room." She guides Dionysus through her estate. "Does Ares know?"

"Alexandra is trying to find him. Eileithyia," he stops, waiting for me to safely make it into the bed. Eileithyia turns to him, and Dionysus continues. "Take care of her."

Eileithyia nods. "Thank you for bringing her."

Dionysus departs as another contraction rips through me. "I thought I told you to rest?"

I don't even care about the jab "Eileithyia, I can't deliver my baby today. It's too early. They're supposed to have a few more weeks."

"Sometimes babies want to come early, especially if the mother is in distress," Eileithyia answers, sitting between my legs to check.

Ares bursts through the door, eyes mad until they find me. "Aphrodite."

He's at my side in an instant. He takes my hand, kissing it before looking at his sister. "How's she doing?"

"Give me a moment," is all she offers.

"Ares, I can't deliver this baby today. I'm a failure. I can't even carry our baby to term."

He brushes a hand over my hair, kissing my forehead and grabbing my hand as she says, "You are the furthest thing from a failure. My ambitious genes are to blame for our baby wanting an early debut."

Another contraction rips through me. I arch off the bed, and cry at the pain. I attempt to breathe through Eileithyia's check of my cervix, but it doesn't do much when paired with a contraction.

"Gods, you're nearly ready to deliver. You were fine this morning. What the hell happened?"

"I ran into Hephaestus's apprentices. He found what he needed." The room stills. "He's coming back for Ares."

Another contraction barrels through me like one of Ares's horses on the battlefield. "Aphrodite, I need you to try not to worry. Your cervix is dilating too quickly. If you keep it up, you could die from ichor loss. Our immortality grants us a lot of things but surviving after losing a large percentage of ichor is not one of them."

"Look at me." Ares grabs my cheeks, forcing me to meet his brown eyes. "Breathe with me."

I follow his lead. I breathe in for five seconds, hold it for four, then breathe out for five. We repeat that process several times and he rubs my cheeks each time.

"I am going to be okay. Hephaestus will not kill me. I've increased the number of guards patrolling my estate, and I have an arsenal in every room of my estate. You will not lose me. Understood?"

I nod and a tear trickles down my cheek. He kisses them off. "Promise me I won't lose you too."

"I promise."

He coaches me through each contraction and while I want to scream at every one of them, he lets me grip his arm as tight as I need.

"How's she doing?" Ares asks, but his hand never leaves mine.

Eileithyia does another cervix check. I will be glad when I'm done with those for good. "I believe her labor slowed in time to avoid death. But she is still at risk considering how fast she dilated."

"What?" I try to sit up but they both encourage me to lie back down.

"You don't need to worry. I have saved countless mothers from the same issue. I will make sure you both live." Eileithyia squeezes my leg. "You are fully dilated through, so you'll need to start pushing during the next contractions. I'm going to have you scoot to the very edge of the bed with your feet on the ground. Ares, support her from behind. This will be the least painful position for you and baby."

I scoot into position, cradling my swollen belly for the last time as I move. I place my feet on the ground and immediately feel the pressure on my pelvis lessen. Ares gets into position, encompassing me with his arms as he flushes his chest against my back. His fingers link with mine, and he kisses the back of my head.

"Aphrodite, on the next contraction, I want you to start pushing. Not too hard to start, okay?" Eileithyia sits on the floor, placing a pillow between my feet and a blanket on top of it.

"I'm scared."

Ares squeezes my hand three times. "Do it scared."

I look back at him, returning the gesture. "Do it scared."

We settle back into position, and I listen to Eileithyia's breathing drills as a contraction begins. "You're doing great, Aphrodite. A little harder. Good girl."

The contraction ends, and I fall into Ares's back, panting with slick skin. I can feel the baby, and I can't say I enjoy the sensation.

"On the next one, push the same way you did in the second half of that last one. The more you do it like that, the smoother and faster we get the baby here."

I do as she says as the next contraction comes. A yell pulls from my lips as I feel everything stretch around the baby's body. Ares tries to soothe me, and he says, "You're doing so good."

The amount of sweat on my skin is absurd by the end of the contraction, but Eileithyia makes it all feel worth it when she does another check. "You did amazing. On the next push we should have the baby's head. We can take a break after that if you need it. These next few are usually the most painful while you deliver the head and shoulders."

I shake my head, leaning forward a little more. "I just want my baby here and safe."

With the next contraction, I pull whatever strength I have locked away and push. A scream erupts from my throat this time because Eiliethyia was right, the head and shoulders feel like someone has taken a hot knife and cut me.

"Good girl. A little bit more and the hardest parts are over," she urges me. At the end of the contraction, I collapse against Ares, panting for dear life. "Ares, she might give you a run for your money on strength. She delivered baby's head and one shoulder in that single contraction."

"Thats's my girl," he says and kisses the side of my head.

"The next contractions, you should be able to do small ones. The baby is far enough out that your birth canal will work with you and ease the rest of its body to us." Eileithyia meets my eyes, encouraging me for this last bit. "Are you ready to meet your baby?"

An exhausted smile touches my lips. We wait for the next contraction which stalls a little longer than the others. I don't complain though because it allows me to catch my breath. The next one spreads through my hips and I follow Eilei-thyia's guidance. I feel an immediate release of pressure and our baby's cry fills the room.

All the love I felt growing from the tiny baby inside me blossoms and engulfs me, more than ever before. Eileithyia tends to the baby, wiping it off with the blanket between my feet.

Ares wraps his arms around me and leans forward to kiss me. "You did it, my love. We have a baby."

"I did it." I smile through my tears.

"You have a daughter," Eileithyia says with a smile. Our tiny baby is wrapped in a bundle in her arms. "Ares, would you like to hold her? Baby girl's home for the past months is ready to come out as well."

I encourage Ares to hold her, so he moves from behind me, taking our daughter in his arms. The sight of our tiny girl in his giant arms is enough to make my heart burst. Our family.

Eileithyia coaches me through the final pulsing pushes to deliver the afterbirth before she helps me back into the bed. "You did amazing. You'll have some discomfort for a little while, but I have a feeling this little girl will make up for it."

Eileithyia brings my daughter over to me, and my tears run like a river. My fingers trace her delicate face and button nose. "Hi, sweet girl. I'm your mom."

Her finger latches onto mine, and my heart grows three sizes. We sit happily secluded from the rest of the world. "When will you leave Olympus?"

"Tomorrow now that my niece has been delivered safely. Artemis is trained enough to carry out your postpartum check-ins." Eileithyia sits not far from the bed with her elbows propped on her knees. "What would you like to call her? I shall like to know since I won't be here for her naming ceremony."

I kiss her soft, tiny head, and she moves into my touch. "Elena. It means shining light, and she is the shining light that gave my life meaning again."

"It's beautiful."

Ares grabs my shoulder and places a gentle kiss on the crown of my head. "Just like her mother."

"Would you like to hold her? You won't get many opportunities after you leave," I ask Eileithyia.

"I would love to."

Ares scoops her from my arms, smiling as our baby coos. He rocks her as he circles the bed. He only makes it halfway to Eileithyia before our expressions turn worried. "Why is she glowing?" My stomach fills with lead and I swallow thickly.

Eileithyia pales, and her eyes grow wide. "I—"

Elena's skin had taken on a soft, pale glow in Ares's arms —like a piece of gold in the sun.

Ares's jaw clenches, and his eyes are a mix of worry and anger. "What's wrong with our baby? Eileithyia! Why is she glowing?"

Eiliethyia meets Ares at the end of the bed. I try to crawl to them, but it hurts too much. She examines our daughter, and her worry turns into something more uneasy.

"I've only ever seen this a few times. It's quite rare..." she rambles, but Ares stops her.

"Why is our daughter glowing?"

"She is the daughter of two full-ichord Olympians. When a child is created out of love, the sharing of the parent's powers, combined with their commitment manifests in their children. It only happens when their godly parents hold them. It can sometimes happen with demi-gods, but that's even more rare."

"Why didn't you tell us this before?" I feel like I'm going to vomit. "Are you sure it's only when we hold her?"

Eileithyia nods, taking Elena in her arms. "I'm positive. It can sometimes take a while to manifest, but once it does, it can last for the first year of their life."

Sure enough, Elena's glow pales as Eileithyia walks her over to me. I take my daughter from her and the lead feeling in my stomach weighs me down more when her skin starts to glow.

"Why didn't you tell us this sooner?" Ares's lip curls.

"I told you it was rare. It only happens when the parents are genuinely in love," Eileithyia argues.

"I told you we loved each other countless times." Ares's eyes go slightly mad.

Eileithyia sighs. "You know how rare it is for people to fall in love, especially members of the Olympians. How was I to know what you said was true? Love declarations are a lot easier to make than they are to feel."

"You could have warned us!" Ares challenges. Elena latches on to my finger, and I start to cry because I know what I must do, and I know I'll never be the same. "I could have made a plan. What are we going to do with a baby that glows in our arms and a man that wants to kill me for even thinking I want his wife."

I kiss Elena's head, letting my tears flow like the Olympus river that feeds into the sea. "Elena will live with Ares."

"What?" Ares and Eileithyia ask snapping their heads toward me with equally wide eyes.

I sniffle, trying to soak up these moments with my daughter. If I could burn them into my memory I would.

"You said it yourself, Hephaestus wants to kill you for even thinking about being with me. What do you think he'll do when he notices our daughter glows in my arms?"

"Aphrodite." Ares's eyes soften, but he sits on the bed next to me. Eileithyia remains silent.

"No," I croak. "He will kill me and our daughter if he ever finds out. I'm not willing to chance it."

"Darling, we will find a way around it. We could—"

"No!" I shake my head. My heart feels like it's splitting in two. "I would rather die than risk something happening to her. Ares, you must take her and protect her. Promise me you will care for our daughter. He can't take her. She's a piece of you and me. As long as she lives, Hephaestus cannot take that piece away from me. You must protect her."

He doesn't argue. Instead, he leans forward with his own glassy eyes and kisses me. When he pulls back, he rests his forehead against mine and a tear wets my cheek. "I will take her."

"You may stay here for the night. I will check you in the morning before clearing you to return home." Eileithyia offers her goodbye, and we're left in silence.

Elena yawns in my arm, and my heart gushes. I trace her tiny face, realizing I won't be able to see her sweet face all the time. "I will visit when I can. Until then, I will send Alexandra to help you. She's looked after me since I moved here. She is the one person I trust to care for Elena when you're at war."

"Are you sure this is what you want?" Ares cradles Elena's head and his other arm wraps around me.

It feels like someone has stabbed me in the heart. "This is

the only way I can protect her. Even if it nearly kills me to do it."

"I will not let any harm come to her."

I smile, but it's broken. "I expect nothing less. After all, you did the same for me."

We sit in silence, admiring our baby while the weight of our new reality strangles us. "We shall need a story of how I came to have a baby and you without one."

I swallow, and it physically pains me. Baby-less—that's how the people of Olympus will view me. "We'll say she came from a love affair you had with a mortal woman. We'll tell them she didn't survive childbirth and had no family to care for Elena. No one will question it. As for me, we'll say the baby couldn't survive the early delivery. It wasn't in the right position for delivery."

"Aphrodite—" He tries to soothe me by rubbing my back.

I move away from his touch. "This is what needs to be done. It's getting dark, and Eileithyia has left us. I suspect there will be a few stragglers hanging around the estate to get news of the new baby. You should take her out the back way. I will have Alexandra bring you a few extra blankets and clothes since I won't need them at my estate."

"We can stay awhile longer."

I shake my head. The tether between Elena and I strengthens by the second. I'm afraid if Ares does not take her from me soon, I will never be able to let her go. "I need you to take her before she consumes every part of me. I'm afraid she might already have."

I give Elena one last, long kiss on the crown of her head before Ares scoops her out of my arms. I take the chance to remove the opal necklace he gave me many months ago. "Give this to her when one day she reminds you of me, and she shows the promise of loving something the way I love the two of you."

Ares forces me to look at him through my tear-stricken eyes. His are wet and leaking. "This does not change my love for you. The second I find a way to stop Hephaestus, I will plead for us to be a family."

"I know." I nod, closing my eyes and kissing him one last time. "I love you, Ares."

"I love you, Aphrodite."

My tears rush like the waves of the sea, and my heart breaks into a million pieces as they walk out of that door. My entire world, gone in an instant, leaving nothing but a hollow void in its place.

CHAPTER 42

APHRODITE

The story of Elena's arrival spread through Olympus like wildfire. It seemed everyone bought the story of Ares's affair as I thought they would. We let it slip that the child I lost was a son to lead them further away from the truth. Since Artemis was away, helping a mortal woman with a difficult labor, Eileithyia was able to feed Artemis the lie.

I haven't been out of my estate since coming back from Eileithyia's estate, but I assume the villagers would look at me with pity that would only make it worse. Ares left with my heart that day. I did the right thing, but I didn't expect it to hurt so damn much.

I sent Eileithyia with my journal detailing mine and Ares's great love affair. The last page included a letter I wrote to Elena, but the chances of her finding it with Eileithyia in the Underworld are slim. Nonetheless, it let me immortalize my pain on paper.

I spent the day in what would have been Elena's room, folding up all of the clothes and blankets.

"Aphrodite." Hephaestus's soft voice brings fresh tears to my eyes. I'm surprised I have any left in my body.

"Yes?" I wipe my cheek, folding the last baby blanket we had.

"What are you doing?"

"I'm giving all of the things we had for the baby to Ares. He doesn't have anything for his daughter since he never expected to take her. And since we don't—" I can't finish my sentence.

Hephaestus takes me into his arms and I sob. I've felt so out of touch with everything since Ares took Elena two days ago, Hephaestus's touch doesn't even bother me. "I'm sorry I wasn't here for you. I was so blinded by my hatred for my brother that I let it ruin our marriage. I became someone I'm not, and I took it out on you. I was ready to kill him."

"What?" I feign ignorance, but it only makes my hurt worse. He's the reason I don't have my baby.

"I was hunting for a special blade to kill him once and for all. I still want to use it on him because he still somehow bested me and has a baby while we have nothing."

"But you aren't going to use it?" I hold my breath, waiting for him to decide if everything I did—sacrifcing my role in my child's life—was for nothing.

"No. I gave it to my mother and father. My mother caught wind of it and scolded me. Then she told me how much you needed me. We lost sight of ourselves because of him. We've lost too much."

I release my breath, letting my husband hold me in his arms. He may be wrong about losing myself, because the truth is I feel more lost than ever without Ares. But I can breathe now because my entire world is safe, tucked away in their little corner of the world together. They're safe.